I0735217

MADE FOR THE MARQUESS

Second Sons of London
Book Four

Alexa Aston

© Copyright 2022 by Alexa Aston
Text by Alexa Aston

Dragonblade Publishing, Inc. is an imprint of Kathryn Le Veque Novels, Inc.
P.O. Box 23
Moreno Valley, CA 92556
ceo@dragonbladepublishing.com

Produced in the United States of America

First Edition June 2022
Trade Paperback Edition

Reproduction of any kind except where it pertains to short quotes in relation to advertising or promotion is strictly prohibited.

All Rights Reserved.

The characters and events portrayed in this book are fictitious. Any similarity to real persons, living or dead, is purely coincidental and not intended by the author.

ARE YOU SIGNED UP FOR DRAGONBLADE'S BLOG?

You'll get the latest news and information on exclusive giveaways, exclusive excerpts, coming releases, sales, free books, cover reveals and more.

Check out our complete list of authors, too!

No spam, no junk. That's a promise!

Sign Up Here

www.dragonbladepublishing.com

Dearest Reader;

Thank you for your support of a small press. At Dragonblade Publishing, we strive to bring you the highest quality Historical Romance from some of the best authors in the business. Without your support, there is no 'us', so we sincerely hope you adore these stories and find some new favorite authors along the way.

Happy Reading!

CEO, Dragonblade Publishing

Additional Dragonblade books by Author Alexa Aston

Second Sons of London Series
Educated By The Earl
Debating With The Duke
Empowered By The Earl
Made for the Marquess

Dukes Done Wrong Series
Discouraging the Duke
Deflecting the Duke
Disrupting the Duke
Delighting the Duke
Destiny with a Duke

Dukes of Distinction Series
Duke of Renown
Duke of Charm
Duke of Disrepute
Duke of Arrogance
Duke of Honor

The St. Clairs Series
Devoted to the Duke
Midnight with the Marquess
Embracing the Earl
Defending the Duke
Suddenly a St. Clair
Starlight Night

Soldiers & Soulmates Series
To Heal an Earl
To Tame a Rogue

To Trust a Duke
To Save a Love
To Win a Widow

The Lyon's Den Connected World
The Lyon's Lady Love

King's Cousins Series
The Pawn
The Heir
The Bastard

Medieval Runaway Wives
Song of the Heart
A Promise of Tomorrow
Destined for Love

Knights of Honor Series
Word of Honor
Marked by Honor
Code of Honor
Journey to Honor
Heart of Honor
Bold in Honor
Love and Honor
Gift of Honor
Path to Honor
Return to Honor

Pirates of Britannia Series
God of the Seas

De Wolfe Pack: The Series
Rise of de Wolfe

The de Wolfes of Esterley Castle
Diana
Derek
Thea

PROLOGUE

Waterloo, Netherlands—June 1815

L IEUTENANT-COLONEL PERCIVAL PERRY halted in his tracks, exhausted.

This day would be one for the history books. Years from now, military strategists would study this battle, one Percy hoped would be the final one in this endless, bloody conflict with Bonaparte. It wasn't good enough that the Coalition had defeated the Little General last year and exiled him to Elba. No, Bonaparte had escaped and formed a new army, which had been soundly defeated today.

The heavy rains of last night had left the battlefield as mush. Fighting hadn't commenced until almost noon—and had been fierce throughout the afternoon. As dusk descended, all three French columns had failed, with their artillery and supplies falling into the hands of Anglo-allied and Prussian armies.

It was close to ten o'clock now and he didn't think he could make it back to camp. Every place on his body ached. While his sword was sheathed, he almost dragged his rifle and bayonet. His temples pounded, a headache pressing against them and the back of his head.

But he was alive, by God. Only a few scratches. A minor miracle considering how many men had fallen today on both sides.

As he trudged back toward camp and Wellington's command post, Percy forced himself to look straight ahead. Because what lay all about him was a horror almost too great to conceive.

Bodies lay scattered across the land, the tinny scent of blood thick in the summer night's air. The wounded, many missing limbs, were mixed among the dead as they cried out. For help. For water. For their mothers, wives, and sweethearts. The various languages swirled about him. Perry hardened his heart and kept moving forward. He knew the medical tents would be filled to the brim with wounded men. He himself had assigned various soldiers under his command to look among those injured—and only transport those that had a true chance of survival. These that were left lying in the blood and mud would be the ones the town of Waterloo dug thousands of graves for.

He arrived back at camp, scanning for Win as he went. He had not seen his cousin since mid-afternoon and prayed Win lived.

As he drew closer to Wellington's tent, he saw officers he knew heading away from it. Approaching more quickly now, Percy greeted the sentry on duty, who saluted him.

"What word is there?" he asked, his voice hoarse from shouting commands over today's gun and cannon fire.

"The last report we received was that Wellington and Blucher were meeting at Genappe at nine this evening, Lieutenant-Colonel."

"Any casualty notices reported for the day?"

The soldier looked grim as he said, "His Majesty's army lost around fifteen thousand men. That's both dead and wounded. The Prussians, last we heard, totaled around seven thousand."

"And Bonaparte's forces?"

"They're saying prisoners of war might be as many as eight thousand, with another twenty-five thousand killed or hurt."

"Any standing orders?" he asked, astounded at the figures the sentry had revealed.

"I'd get some sleep, Lieutenant-Colonel," the soldier recommended. "From what I gather, Wellington's army will be on the march tomorrow, headed toward Paris."

"Then Bonaparte has yet to be captured."

"I believe that is correct."

"Goodnight," Percy murmured, turning away from the sentry and making the long walk back to the tent he shared with Win.

When he arrived, he found himself alone. Cold sweat broke out across his brow. Win had to be alive. Percy couldn't lose him. His cousin was as close as a brother to him. They had gone to school and university together and served alongside one another during the past seven years of war. He had always depended upon Win, never more so than when their trio of good friends from Cambridge left the military one by one, returning to England to claim titles. The five had called themselves the Second Sons because they were all the second males born into their families, destined for military service. Through odd circumstances and fate, Spence, Ev, and, finally, Owen had all become peers of the land, selling their military commissions and returning to England. All three had wed, with Spence and Ev already becoming fathers and Owen about to be one in two months' time.

Percy collapsed on his cot, too tired to remove any of his clothing. As he lay there, he thought how much he had begun to hate his life. How jealous he was that his friends had escaped this bloody war. How that bloody bastard Bonaparte's escape had extended this lengthy war. If only today marked the beginning of the end for the Corsican dictator.

He hoped it signaled the end of fighting for him. Percy felt as if he were about to lose his soul, thanks to all these years of conflict. He needed to escape. To have a quiet, uneventful life. To find the man he once was before war invaded his body and soul.

The tent flap moved and he quickly sat up in anticipation.

Win walked through, a broad smile on his handsome face.

He leaped to his feet and wrapped his arms tightly about his cousin. They pounded one another on the back, grinned at each other, and pounded some more.

Win was the first to break free. He reached under his cot and withdrew a bottle of French brandy. Opening it, he took a swig and handed it to Percy, who sat on his cot and did the same, returning the bottle. They passed it back and forth several times before he shook his head and Win retained custody of the bottle.

"They haven't found Bonaparte yet," Percy began. "I hear we're clearing out tomorrow morning for Paris."

His cousin nodded. "I have heard the same." A shadow crossed his face. "I stopped by the hospital tents. That was a mistake."

"We will be leaving many men behind," Percy agreed. Hesitating a moment, he admitted, "I wish I were one of them."

Win's startled look had him quickly amending his words. "No, I don't wish to be dead or severely injured. But I am so very tired, Win. Tired to my bones. To my soul."

"We all are."

He shook his head. "This is different. I feel as if I am being swallowed up," he shared. "That if I don't get out, nothing will be left of me."

Perplexed, Win asked, "What would you do if you sold out, Percy? We are second sons. We are meant for a lifetime in the army. Once this conflict finally ends—and it will because we have the Little General on the run and have decimated his troops—we will be sent other places. A few months ago, before the treaty was signed at Ghent, it might have been the Americas. We could still be shipped overseas to Canada to help in its defense. In case those pesky Americans get a wild idea to try and invade again."

His cousin leaned over and placed a hand on Win's knee. "But we will be together."

"You don't know that," he said woodenly. "You could receive orders to report to Canada. I could be sent to India. Or back to England. The Caribbean. There is no guarantee we will fight side-by-side for the rest of our lives, Win. We could be assigned posts thousands of miles away and never see one another again."

Win leaned back, his brow furrowed. "You have always been a gentle soul, Percy. That is a compliment. You see with your heart, as well as your mind. I understand how war has ravaged your soul. But what choice do you have? Do *we* have?"

"In Rupert's last letter, he told me his estate manager was thinking of retirement. I want to go home, Win. To Kingwood. I wasn't raised to be the marquess. I won't be jealous of my brother. I just need the peace and quiet of the country. Of home. I have missed Essex and dream of it. If Rupert has already hired a new steward, perhaps I could be his game warden. Anything but a man who kills for a living."

Win studied him a long moment and then said, "Then go home, Percy. Rupert will make a place for you. Do it now—before it is too late."

"Oh, I will wait until we see this thing with Bonaparte through. I owe it to king and country."

A wave of exhaustion hit him. Mixed with the brandy, it made him sleepy.

"We will talk more of this, Win. But for now, I must close my eyes."

He did—and blackness enveloped him.

PERCY AWOKE, HIS mouth dry from the brandy he had consumed the previous night. He glanced over and saw Win beginning to stir.

He wondered if it had been wise to share with his cousin what had lain so heavy on his heart for so long. In truth, Percy had never wanted to go to war. As a second son, however, his only option had been the military. He had understood at a young age, thanks to the simple explanation from his father, what his role in the family would be. That he would be the son given over to the military and if war came, he would lead men into battle. It was ironic because he hated the sight and smell of blood. Skinning his knee as a child not only pained him but looking at the scrape would throw him into a frenzy.

For that reason, he had campaigned to go into the navy. Unfortunately, most noblemen who turned their sons over to that branch of the military did so at a very young age. He would have had to leave home at twelve—thirteen at the latest—in order to move up through the ranks. His mother had put her foot down regarding that plan, saying she would not turn over her child to men. Even his father had agreed, sharing two stories with Percy that came secondhand from friends. Both instances his father recalled made Percy's hair almost stand up on end. Papa had said the navy was known for its cruelty and harsh punishments. He preferred Percy follow his cousin, Winston, into the army once the pair had completed university.

That had settled matters and Percy had been glad he had not only Win but the other Second Sons accompanying him to war. His years at Cambridge had been ones of learning and great fun, thanks to Owen, Ev, and Spence. The latter two were more reserved as Percy was but Owen and Win were outgoing and charming and did everything in their power to bring the other three Second Sons out of their shells.

He had been able to tolerate the war when it was the five of them standing together. As his friends left, however, it seemed as if the world were closing in on Percy. He was glad he had shared his feelings with Win and yet hated how his cousin and closest friend had encouraged him to sell out.

Because it would leave Win alone in the world. Wherever he was sent by his commanding officers, Win would be separated from the solid friendships of the Second Sons.

Percy swung his legs from the cot and Win did the same. Both men set about readying themselves for the day, knowing they would have troops to rally and prepare for the long march toward Paris.

The tent flap stirred and he looked up, seeing a private with a bundle of letters.

"For Lieutenant-Colonel Percival Perry," the soldier said, looking barely old enough to shave.

"I am Perry," he said, reaching out and collecting the two. He glanced to Win, who shrugged.

"You thought Terrance would write to me?" His cousin snorted.

Terrance was eight years older than Win and Percy and had never had anything to do with either boy. He had been wild from birth and Percy assumed since the years they had left England that Terrance had become one of the biggest rakes and gamblers of Polite Society. The only letter Win had received from his brother was when Terrance wrote four years ago of the Duke of Woodmont's death. Terrance hadn't even told Win what his father had died from.

And hadn't answered a single letter Win sent after that.

Eventually, Win stopped writing them and never spoke of home.

Percy turned to the letters in his hand. The top one came from Rupert. He sat on his cot and eagerly tore it open, always happy to hear from his brother, who was three years Percy's senior and had always looked out for Percy and Win while they were at school. No boys had dared to bully them because Rupert Perry would have made mincemeat of them if they had.

The letter was typical Rupert, giving Percy the local gossip in the neighborhood and then sharing that he was off to London for the Season, hoping something might come of it this year. Glancing at the date, Percy saw it was dated over two months ago. He wondered if Rupert meant this might be the year he took a bride. His brother was two and thirty now and had mentioned in his last correspondence that he was seriously considering finding his marchioness. Percy hoped his brother would. No one was kinder or would be a better husband and father than Rupert.

"Any news from Rupert?"

"The usual. Talk of spring planting and gossip about his tenants and acquaintances in the neighborhood. It sounds as if he also might offer for someone this Season."

Win pulled on his boot. "He should. It's about time he settled down and got an heir."

Percy refolded the letter and set it on the cot beside him. Picking up the other letter, he broke the seal, not recognizing it or the handwriting on the front. His eyes looked first at the date, which was three weeks ago, then fell to the bottom of the page. He frowned, not being acquainted with a B. Harris. His eyes returned to the top.

26 May 1815

Dear Lieutenant-Colonel Perry,

It is with deep sorrow that I must inform you of the passing of your brother, the Marquess of Kingston. Lord Kingston was in London for the Season and had gone sailing with friends on Saturday last. Unfortunately, the weather grew rough, with high winds, and the sailboat was overcome. Your brother and two others drowned. A fourth made it to shore but died shortly afterward.

I am sorry to break this news to you through a letter but traveling to see you in the Netherlands was impossible. I pray that this letter finds you well and that the Coalition will find Bonaparte and end this evil from the face of Europe.

It goes without saying that you must resign your commission and return to England to take up your title and duties as Marquess of Kingston. Once you have left the military, please come to my offices in London (address below). I will be able to give you a clearer picture of your state of affairs since I served as your father's solicitor for several years and then your brother's, as well.

My deepest sympathies to you, my lord.

Your humble servant,
B. Harris

The page fluttered to the floor as a numbness filled Percy.

Rupert. Dead. It seemed impossible. Yet this Harris must be telling the truth.

Win was saying something to him but he couldn't seem to make out the words. His cousin reached for the letter and scanned it quickly.

"My God, Percy. You are Lord Kingston."

This was not how he wanted to leave the army. He never would have wished for his brother's death. He didn't even want the bloody title. But he had no choice. Lieutenant-Colonel Percival Perry had ceased to exist.

In his place stood the Marquess of Kingston.

CHAPTER ONE

Ontario, Canada—August 1815

MINTA NICHOLLS STOOD on the wharf, her father to her left and her twin sister on her right. Sera took Minta's hand and squeezed it in anticipation.

Looking out, she saw the long-awaited ship now sailing into the harbor. They had every indication that Mama would be onboard. Mama had stayed behind in England when Papa had been appointed as an assistant to the Administrator of Upper Canada four years earlier. While Papa had taken his daughters to Ontario with him, Mama had remained in England to nurse her father in the last few weeks of his life. They had expected her to follow shortly.

Then the war with the Americans broke out and Mama was stuck in England. Minta thought it bad enough England was already at war with Bonaparte and resented the brash Americans for trying to take advantage of England's attention being elsewhere and attempting to annex parts of Canada to their new United States.

What was supposed to have been a year in Ontario had turned into four. Minta and Sera had missed making their come-outs in Polite Society. Their aunt, Lady Westlake, had always promised a Season for the twins. Now, however, they had missed it and the two Seasons beyond that. If they returned by next spring, they would be two and twenty, already considered on the shelf by many of the *ton*. Minta already worried about finding a husband.

Not Sera. She had lost her Canadian sweetheart in the Battle of Lundy's Lane and still mourned for him, despite the fact there had been no formal arrangement between them. Minta hoped returning to England and taking part in next spring's Season would bring Sera out of the sadness that clung to her.

"I think I see Mama!" cried Sera. "Look, to the right."

"It is Mama," she agreed, squeezing her twin's hand.

While Minta had missed her mother terribly, she knew it had been far worse for Sera. Sera and Mama were so like one other, reserved in nature. Minta took after her father, Sir Radford Nicholls. He was a larger-than-life figure and enthused about everything. In a way, Minta felt a bit guilty that because of her vivacity, she was always noticed well before Sera. Because of that, she had grown quite protective of her twin over the years, never more so than during their sojourn in Canada.

"I hope your mother will like the house," Papa commented. "Of course, you girls have put nice touches on it."

She wondered how her father felt about seeing his wife after such a long time. She knew theirs had been that rare love match, and the thought they had been apart for so long tugged at her heart. She couldn't imagine how lonely her father had been.

Anticipation rippled through her as the ship drew near and Mama caught sight of them on the docks. She began waving wildly, which was very much out of character for her. It let Minta know just how eagerly Mama looked forward to the reunion with her husband and daughters.

By the time the ship docked, they had moved close to the ramp and watched as Mama was the first down the gangplank. Sera started to break free from Minta to rush to their mother, but Minta held her fast, predicting Papa would want to be the first to greet Mama. Sure enough, he moved swiftly toward the gangplank, his gaze focused on his wife. Mama lifted her skirts and ran the rest of the way, throwing herself into his arms. In an uncharacteristic display of public affection, Papa briefly kissed Mama and then grinned at her.

"Come see the girls," Minta heard him say and Mama briskly moved the rest of the way down the gangplank and reached them.

Minta released her hold on Sera's hand and her sister flung herself into Mama's arms. By now, both women were crying and Minta herself blinked back tears. Mama and Sera embraced for a long moment and then Mama pulled back and cradled Sera's cheek.

"My Seraphina, how you have grown into such a beauty."

Her twin blushed profusely, as she did whenever she received any compliment.

Mama turned and smiled broadly. "Araminta, my darling. Come here."

She moved to her mother and warmly embraced her, the familiar smell of roses clinging to Mama. Suddenly, tears poured down Minta's cheeks and she realized how much she had also missed Mama.

Holding her at arm's length, Mama said, "You, too, Araminta, have grown into a beauty just as your sister. Oh, how I regret these years apart from you girls."

While Papa saw to Mama's luggage, the three women linked arms and returned to the waiting carriage.

Sera insisted on sitting by their mother, lacing her fingers through Mama's as she asked, "But how are you, Mama? The three of us have had each other these past few years. I am so sorry about Grandpapa's death."

As usual, her mother looked stoic and briefly told them about the last few days of her own father's life. Letters had been sparse during the war and so they began filling in the blanks as to what had happened during their long separation.

Papa joined them in the carriage, sitting next to Minta, smiling across at his wife.

"I cannot tell you how good it is to see you here," he proclaimed. "We have missed you so very much, my love."

With watery eyes, Mama echoed the same sentiments.

Twenty minutes later, they arrived at what had been their assigned home in Ontario. While Papa had been the chief civilian aide to Major General Isaac Brock when they'd first arrived in Upper Canada, he had taken over a large part of duties as the Administrator of UC, the title held by Brock, since the major general was already so involved in the military affairs of Upper Canada. When Brock was killed in battle the following October, the crown had assigned a new Administrator for Upper Canada. With the war continuing, however, the subsequent military commanders focused more on battles and were frequently gone, leaving Papa, a civilian, in charge of the day-to-day duties.

Minta wondered just how long her father would remain in this post. Now that the war with the Americans had ended, thanks to the Treaty of Ghent, she assumed a permanent administrator would be named. She did not know whether Papa would feel obligated to remain or if he would ask to be reassigned and come home to England.

Whatever his plans might be, however, Minta would be returning to London as soon as possible. She hoped her aunt's offer of providing a Season still held. She would ask Mama about it, but wanted to give her a little time before broaching the subject.

Papa allowed the twins to show Mama around the house, a spacious three-story home which had been bare when they'd arrived. Furnishing and decorating it had been an arduous task but one Minta and Sera enjoyed very much. It had given them both confidence for the time they would be managing their own households. Minta wondered if she would marry a man with a title as her aunt had done. She hoped so. She knew despite what a wonderful man Papa was, that Mama's parents had not liked the fact their daughter had fallen in love with a mere baron. They had favored her aunt, who had wed the Earl of Westlake.

After they had shown Mama the house from top to bottom, her mother's praise was effusive for their efforts.

"I am simply astounded that you could take a blank canvas and create such a lovely home," Mama praised.

"We did it together," she said. "It will probably be my favorite project I ever work on."

"Until you have a household of your own, Araminta," Mama said. "Come, let us call for tea. We can have a nice chat then. For now, I am going to freshen up."

"I will see to tea," Sera said and left them.

Minta went to their parlor, her father absent since he had duties to see to. He had told them he would return in time for dinner.

A quarter-hour later, the three gathered in the intimate parlor.

"This will be your space, Mama," Sera said. "There is a larger room we have used for limited entertaining, though not much of that has gone on during the war."

"I only received a handful of letters from you girls," their mother said. "I wrote you and your father once a week but I was told that very few of those letters would get through with all the naval battles disrupting the post. Because of that, I seem to need to get to know both of you all over again."

Mama gazed from Sera to Minta and added, "When you left me, you were on the cusp of womanhood. You are both now matured and so lovely."

Mama looked to Sera and said, "I do know that you have a man you are interested in. Captain Marsh. Tell me about him."

Immediately, Sera's eyes filled with tears. Even Minta's throat grew thick with emotion, hurting for her twin.

"I must excuse myself," Sera said abruptly. "I have something in my eye." She fled the room.

"What did I say wrong?" Mama asked. "Has the young man broken it off with her?"

"Captain Marsh died in battle last July, Mama," Minta explained gently. "Although no formal betrothal existed between them, Edward had promised to court and marry Sera when he returned from the war."

Her mother's cheeks flushed. "Oh, dear. I have put my foot in my mouth, reminding my dear Seraphina of something so painful to her." She hesitated and then asked, "Did your sister love this man? You would know better than anyone."

She shrugged. "They were quite fond of one another, Mama, but I cannot say Sera loved Edward. They had only known each other for a short while before he left to go to the front. I think that is why he wanted no betrothal announced between them. In case he did not return. He would not have wanted Sera to grieve."

"And yet Seraphina still does," Mama said wisely.

"She does. She has spoken very little about Edward's death, even to me." Minta paused a moment and then decided to plunge ahead.

"I know you have just arrived in Ontario, Mama, and I have yet to learn from Papa what his plans are. I believe it would be in Sera's best interest, however, to return to England and attend the Season next April if Aunt Phyllis still wishes to sponsor us. We have only had one letter from her during the entire war. You stayed with her and Uncle West. What are your thoughts?"

"Of course, Phyllis still wants you," Mama insisted. "The both of you. We spoke many times about that very thing. If your father wishes to remain here in Canada, then I will stay with him. I would want you girls to go to Westfield. I think you are right. Seraphina must get over this loss. The sooner, the better. The Season—and finding a husband—would be the perfect solution."

"Then you wouldn't be upset with us leaving? We have been apart so long and that would mean another long separation if you and Papa remain here."

Mama took Minta's hand and squeezed it reassuringly. "I have always wanted what was best for you girls. I think this time with your papa has been good for you but you need the company of Polite Society. Oh, I so hope that you both will find a love match as I did."

Minta wasn't especially interested in a love match. She knew they were uncommon among members of the *ton*. She was independent from birth, the first exiting her mother's womb, and always had a mind of her own. She did not see herself misty-eyed, catering to a husband's every whim. She wanted the thrill of society and all the many activities it provided. She also wanted the assurance of a husband and his name. She looked forward to providing an heir for her husband but she assumed they would go their own ways and pursue their own interests, just as her aunt and uncle and most other couples of the *ton* did.

She figured Sera would have a very different opinion, however. She did not think Sera had been in love with Edward Marsh, only the idea of being in love with him. It would do Sera a world of good to get away from Ontario, particularly since they seemed to run into Edward's parents far too often for Sera's emotional wounds to heal.

"We will enjoy some time together," her mother promised, "and then I will suggest that the two of you return to London. Crossing the Atlantic in the harsh winter months is difficult. I would not want you to wait until spring because there would be no time to outfit you with a new wardrobe, which Phyllis has promised for you and Seraphina."

"When do you think we should return then, Mama?" Minta asked with enthusiasm.

"I believe early September would be best. By then, I would know your father's plans and if we were to accompany you or if I needed to find a chaperone for the two of you."

Minta did not point out that she and Sera were already one and twenty years old and of legal age. She hoped her parents would return with them but if that proved not to be the case, she prayed an appropriate chaperone could be found because she did not see Mama letting them leave otherwise.

"Shall we keep our conversation between us?" Mama asked. "We will talk again in a couple of weeks and begin making plans."

"Whatever you say, Mama," Minta said, eager now to know what her future held.

And by this time next year, she would have completed her first Season, hopefully with a fiancé in hand.

CHAPTER TWO

Kingwood, Essex—February 1816

PERCY AWOKE WITH a start and immediately flipped to his side, grabbing hold of the pillow and burying his face into it as the scream tore from his mouth. His quick action allowed the unholy noise to be muffled so that only a small sound escaped. Slowly, he released the pillow and turned onto his back, feeling the sweat that drenched him.

He still had trouble sleeping after all these months away from the front and when he did, nightmares of the war came to him as if he had never left. He saw the charges. Smelled the blood. Heard the cries of the barely living. The scenes haunted him.

He wondered if he would ever escape the horrible memories.

Rising, he washed and padded naked to the chair sitting by the window. Though the room was chilly, he sat there, bare, hoping to cool his body before dressing and going to breakfast. He was in a routine now, for the most part, since his return to England almost seven months ago. He rose early and breakfasted. Met with Smith, his steward, though the man was on the verge of retiring. Percy had even gone for brief visits to the other two estates he had inherited, along with Kingwood, which was the country seat of the Marquess of Kingston. He had hoped one of those two stewards might transition to Kingwood and take

Smith's place. Instead, he found each of them fairly new to his position and not capable of handling the affairs of a larger estate.

He supposed once Smith retired that he would have to find someone to replace the man. For now, he asked that Smith stay on for a full year from Rupert's death. That would give Percy time to glean as much information as possible from Smith, as well as look for an adequate replacement.

He'd had plenty of advice, thanks to the Second Sons who now resided in England, just one county south of him in Kent. Percy had visited each of his friends, meeting their wives and children. Spence, Owen, and Ev had all come to Kingwood, as well, riding the property with him and dispensing advice when asked. Having the trio only a few hours away by carriage brought relief to Percy.

Yet, at the same time, the three men he knew were very different. Oh, Spence and Ev were still a bit reserved and Owen was someone who had never met a stranger. Percy still felt comfortable in their company. Subtle differences had occurred, however. In part, he knew it was because of the titles the three men now held. They had gone from the duties they had fulfilled as officers in His Majesty's army to taking on the responsibilities of their titles and all that entailed.

Moreover, all three men had wed and had children. In their visits together, he had come to know and appreciate the ladies he called the Three Cousins, who were now wed to his friends. They were remarkable women—and they had influenced their husbands in broad and subtle ways. Percy understood just how close all three men were to their spouses and how taken they were with not only their wives but their children.

He had never given children an ounce of thought. Nor marriage, for that matter. Yet he understood now that he was a marquess, it was his duty to find a wife and sire an heir to continue the Perry line for another generation to come. That fact had come out during each of his visits to his friends' estates. Adalyn, in particular, told Percy she had a knack for placing couples of the *ton* together and would be happy to help him find a bride.

That thought terrified him.

He might look in control on the outside, but inside he swirled with turmoil. The war had affected him in ways both small and large. What woman would want to be in his bed, only to be awakened by his screams and shouts? It also felt as if something were missing inside him. Never one to express his emotions, Percy felt dead inside. He didn't seem to experience joy or happiness. It wouldn't be fair to claim a wife and have her tied to life to a man who felt nothing. Yet he wanted to feel again. Live again. Perhaps, even love, as his friends did.

Of the three, Owen had been the one to pull Percy aside and tell him when he did seek a bride, to make sure he loved her. Owen admitted he had never truly believed in love, even seeing how besotted Spence and Ev were with Tessa and Adalyn. Once he had found it with Louisa, however, he understood what his friends had. Owen said he wanted that for Percy, too.

He thought he should ring for Huston and dress for the day. Owen and Louisa were staying at Kingwood for a few days, along with Margaret, their infant daughter. The three were early risers and would most likely be at breakfast soon. He and Owen were going to meet with the manager of Percy's mill today and then Owen and his family would return to Danfield for a couple of weeks before making their way to town for the upcoming Season.

Percy dreaded the thought of the Season. Endless parties. Standing about talking with strangers he had nothing in common with. Dancing with young misses who would be dazzled not by him but his lofty title. Tessa had warned him about that, something Percy never would have considered. He didn't even know how to dance. He supposed he had better learn by April, when the Season would begin.

The thought depressed him to no end. He had never been comfortable around others and froze up when meeting strangers. Socializing—and finding a bride—would be even worse than going to war.

He rang for Huston and the valet shaved and then dressed Percy for the day. He liked the servant simply because Huston said so little, merely performed his required duties. Huston had been with Rupert for many years, ever since his brother had left Cambridge. It had been Huston who had accompanied Rupert's body back to Kingwood for burial. Huston who had dressed his master and sat beside the coffin. Upon visiting Rupert's grave when he'd first arrived, Percy had found a bouquet of fresh flowers upon it, later discovering Huston placed an arrangement upon the grave weekly.

Percy left his bedchamber and went downstairs to meet his friends for breakfast. As he had guessed, Owen and Louisa were already present in the breakfast room, little Margaret cradled in the crook of Owen's arm.

It had surprised Percy how involved his three friends were with their children. His own father had been kind but distant to his two sons and his mother paid him and Rupert very little attention. Sometimes, it surprised him how loving and open Rupert had turned out. Once again, he wished that his brother would have wed and provided an heir so that Percy wouldn't be in the position of being the Marquess of Kingston and having to do so. Yet his brother's death had allowed Percy to leave the army. For that, he was grateful, though he felt at times he barely clung to his sanity as it was.

"Good morning, Percy," Louisa said, giving him a gracious smile.

"Good morning," he replied, liking Louisa a great deal. She had tamed Owen and Percy felt that his friend would live up to all the potential within him, thanks to his sweet wife.

He looked to Owen, who was doing everything one-handed since he held Margaret in the crook of his arm. She was six months old now and beginning to learn she had a voice. Suddenly, she squealed and then smiled in delight at the noise she'd made.

Owen finished buttering a toast point and held it up to his daughter.

"Why don't you gum this, my little love?" he asked.

"You know she only has three teeth, Owen," Louisa pointed out. "She is going to gnaw on it at best."

Owen smiled at his wife. "Then let her gnaw away."

By now, Percy had gone through the buffet and put a few items on his plate, returning to the table. A footman seated him and another brought him a hot cup of tea. While most of his friends favored coffee in the morning, Percy still preferred tea. He wasn't fond of the bitter taste of coffee, no matter how much sugar and milk he put in it. What passed for coffee on the battlefront was like drinking sludge. No, give him a cup of strong tea anytime. Even multiple times a day. It was one of the reasons he was grateful to be home again.

"What do you two have planned today since it is our last day at Kingwood?" Louisa asked.

"We are going to the mill," Percy told her and launched into a brief explanation of their day.

The entire time he spoke, he watched as Owen played with Margaret, a huge grin on his face.

For a moment, Percy experienced a yearning, one so powerful because it struck him from nowhere. Though he knew nothing about children, he realized the same had been true for his friends and saw how comfortable they'd grown with them. Perhaps it was in the cards for him to find a bride and have a family, after all.

Bailey entered the breakfast room with a single letter upon a silver tray.

"My lord, a message has arrived from Westfield. A reply is expected."

Percy took the message from the tray and broke the seal. Scanning it, he frowned.

"Is something wrong?" Louisa asked.

"No, it is simply a neighbor asking me to dinner again."

"I didn't know you had been socializing with any of your neighbors," Owen remarked, shifting Margaret to his other arm. "Who is it and how many times have you dined with them?"

"It comes from Lord and Lady Westlake," he revealed. "And no, I have yet to dine with them or anyone else."

Owen eyed him with a steely glance. "You said 'again', Percy. Have they invited you previously?"

"They have several times but I have not been able to go."

The thought of spending an evening with strangers and enduring meaningless conversation held no appeal to him.

"I will decline this time since you are here."

"Nonsense," Owen said. "You will go—with or without us. I know Lord Westlake. He is an interesting man and Lady Westlake is very kind."

"You could tell them yes," Louisa said, "and go without us. Or you could point out that you have guests and I know they would extend the invitation to us, as well."

"I would rather spend your last night at Kingwood with just the three of us," he said flatly.

This time, it was Louisa who gave him a stern look. "You will accept this invitation, Percy, and not use us as an excuse to decline it. You want to become involved in the neighborhood and meet your peers. As a child, you probably didn't meet most of these people but it is time you should since you now hold the title."

"As a child, my parents were rarely at Kingwood," he revealed. "Rupert and I were always away at school or it was us here at Kingwood during our summer breaks. Papa and Mama did not come to the country often, much less entertain here."

"All the more reason for you to do the opposite," Louisa declared. "You are going to want to wed and have children, Percy. You need to be a leader and not someone who isolates himself from his community."

"Accept the invitation, Percy," Owen urged. "Either with or without us, but you are going this evening."

Disgruntled, he decided it wasn't worth arguing with his friends, especially on their last day at Kingwood.

Rising, he said, "Then I will excuse myself to reply and meet you in the stables in half an hour," he told Owen.

"Very well," his friend replied, turning his attention back to Margaret and cooing to her softly.

Percy went to his study and placed a fresh piece of parchment on his desk. He had been an excellent student, with perfect penmanship, so dashing off a response to Lady Westlake shouldn't be difficult. He had rejected her three previous invitations with no problem.

Accepting, however, was another matter. He thought how to word his reply and finally began writing, mentioning his visiting friends and how it was their last evening at Kingwood. He let the countess know that they would be open to joining the Westlakes for dinner or he asked if that were not convenient, that their dinner be put off to another time. Reading it over twice, he was satisfied with what he had written and sealed it, ringing for Bailey.

"Here is my answer to Lady Westlake," he told the butler. "She will most likely send a response to it. I will be with Lord Danbury out on the estate so please give it to Lady Danbury. She may read it and reply if a further response is required."

"Very good, my lord," Bailey said, taking the message and leaving the room.

A knock sounded at the door and he bid whoever it was to enter. Surprisingly, Louisa stepped inside.

"May we speak a moment, Percy?" she asked.

"Of course. Have a seat." He indicated one of the chairs in front of his desk.

"No, that won't do," she said. "I won't have some barrier between us."

Instead, she ventured to the window, where a pair of chairs looked out over the lawn, and took a seat in one of them. He followed, curious as to what this was about.

Louisa took his hand in hers. "We don't know one another

well, Percy, but you are like a brother to Owen, Spencer, and Everett. Since I married Owen, I have gotten to know his friends quite well, especially since they are wed to my cousins. Already, I look upon you as my brother, as I do those two men."

She hesitated and said, "I am a bit worried about you, Percy. There are times you look off into the distance, as if you are no longer present, but still on those battlefields guiding your men through the turmoil of war."

Her insight frightened him.

"It is a bit hard to put the war behind me. I spent my entire adult life as a soldier."

Louisa squeezed his hand gently. "Not just a soldier, Percy, but an officer. A lieutenant-colonel. You rose through the ranks for a reason. You had tremendous responsibilities placed upon your shoulders. The same is true now that you are a marquess. I know the Second Sons have done their best helping you understand the workings of your estate and business matters. Political ones, too, as you will soon take your place in the House of Lords.

"But there is an adjustment to civilian life," she continued. "I believe it must be harder for some than others." Her gaze penetrated to his soul. "If you ever need someone to talk to— someone who would not judge you—then I am here. I would be happy to merely listen and not dispense advice." She smiled. "That is a man's way. He thinks he listens and readily advises his friends, when sometimes he should simply listen to what is being said and be there for them."

Percy swallowed. "You truly understand things, Louisa. Thank you. I may take you up on your offer."

She squeezed his hand a final time and released it. "My advice from breakfast, however, stands. I do think as Marquess of Kingston, you are the ranking peer in your neighborhood. Others will look to you as a leader. Become involved. Get to know your neighbors and those in the closest village."

Louisa sighed. "And I do think you should wed sooner than

later. Spencer and Everett thought to wed out of duty and quickly produce an heir. Owen balked at the very idea of marriage and planned to sow his wild oats for several years before settling into the role of husband and then father. All three of them were bruised in different ways from the war. Even from their childhoods and how being a second son led them to being overlooked and neglected. Having a woman they love by their sides, one who can be a partner and helpmate, has helped all three of them put their experiences in the war behind them.

"I think marriage could do the same for you, Percy."

"But . . . all of them found love," he protested. "I will be frank, Louisa. I just don't see that for myself. While Spence and Ev are reserved, I am more withdrawn than either of them. I can be distant with others. Taciturn. I truly am only comfortable in the company of the Second Sons. And now their wives. The three of you have been most welcoming to me."

He stood and began pacing. "But the thought of finding a wife—of perusing the Marriage Mart—frightens me more than leading a charge against the enemy."

Percy halted, raking his hands through his hair.

"I am not filled with the easy charm of Owen. I have difficult speaking with others I do not know. The thought of having to move among the *ton* and talk night after night with my peers, let alone dozens of women, terrifies me."

He turned away, looking out the window, not able to look at her as he added, "I feel I am damaged, Louisa. That no woman would ever want me. That I will fail miserably as a husband and father."

She rose and came to him, placing a hand on his forearm. "You will have the six of us by your side, Percy. The Second Sons and the Three Cousins. We can help smooth the way for you. Slowly introduce you to agreeable people in society. Help you navigate the Marriage Mart."

Louisa wrapped her arms about him, hugging him tightly. "You are a good, kind man, Percival Perry. Remember who you are at your core. Yes, you are the Marquess of Kingston—but you are also Percy. You have much to offer a woman beyond your title and wealth. You are intelligent. Generous. Kindhearted. You will make for a wonderful husband and father. Look to your friends if you doubt that. None of them were meant to have a title. Yet they have adapted to their new roles in life. None of them thought they would find love and yet all three did. Not a one of them knew a thing about babies and now all three have taken to the role of father like a duck to water."

She released him. "Put your best foot forward this Season, Percy, but don't change who you are for others. The right woman will be drawn to you."

He swallowed. "I hope you are right, Louisa."

She looked at him sagely. "Adalyn, Tessa, and I will get to know any woman you find interesting. We may even put a few in your path that we think will suit with you. Just be open to the idea of marriage—and love."

"All right," he agreed. "Thank you. For looking out for me. For being the perfect woman for Owen."

Louisa kissed his cheek. "I am always here when you need me, Percy."

She left the study and he took a moment to collect himself. A bit of relief rippled through him, knowing he would have his friends—and their amazing wives—looking out for him when the Season began.

CHAPTER THREE

Westfield, Essex

MINTA EXCUSED HERSELF from breakfast and went to a small parlor that Aunt Phyllis had designated for Minta's use. It had a piano in the corner and so she practiced singing and playing every day. She also used the room to read and write letters. It felt wonderful to have a bit of privacy, especially because there were always so many servants around.

She had visited her aunt and uncle with her parents and sister before but living with them let her see how very different this world was from the one she had grown up in. Papa had an adequate salary from the government and they had a couple of servants in Ontario. A cook and maid lived in while a washer-woman had collected their laundry twice a week.

Westfield, however, had too many servants for her to count. The household teemed with footmen and maids, supervised by a butler and housekeeper. The stables also had several servants. On the estate itself, there was everything from a blacksmith to a farrier to the many tenant farmers. That didn't even include the London servants. Minta had arrived in London back in October and remained in town with Aunt Phyllis and Uncle West until just before Christmas, when they had come to Westfield. Uncle West preferred town life and so the childless couple remained in town for most of the year. They returned to the country estate and usually stayed from late December until early March, when Aunt Phyllis was eager to return and start replenishing her wardrobe for the new Season.

Thanks to her uncle's generosity, Minta already had several new gowns, which had been made up while they were in town. The dressmaker had created those gowns for Minta and promised a slew of others once she returned in the spring. It felt wonderful wearing such pretty clothes and she looked forward to the ballgowns that would await her.

It did make her sad, though, to be experiencing all of this without Sera. The twins had never been separated until Minta stepped onto the deck of the ship that brought her across the Atlantic from Canada back to England. She wished with all her heart that her sister could be with her as they conquered the Season together.

She understood, however, that Sera needed time to heal from losing Edward, as well as spending time with Mama. While Minta adored being around people, as did her father, Sera and Mama were shy and liked a quieter life. She only hoped that her twin would return by next Season. Minta would be an old hand at it by then.

And perhaps even a married woman.

The possibility of marriage had her as excited as the idea of all the many social affairs she would attend. The only troubling thing would be not having Sera by her side to talk about everything she experienced. How was she to know which gentleman she should wed if her sister hadn't even met him? To go from sharing a bed and most of her day with Sera to being separated by thousands of miles was troubling. Sera was so levelheaded and always steered the more quick-acting Minta in the correct direction. Without Sera's advice and guidance, Minta worried she would make the wrong decision and accept an offer from a man her sister wouldn't like.

Sitting at the writing desk, she decided her first letter this morning would be to Sera. She wrote to her twin every week and her parents every other week, hoping her letters were getting through in a more timely manner now that the war was over. She had already received three letters from Sera, who seemed content to remain in Canada and was introducing their mother to the small society there.

Minta had just begun her letter when a knock sounded on the door, followed by her aunt flying into the room, holding a page in her hand.

"Oh, Minta, I am thrilled!"

"What is it, Aunt Phyllis?"

She rose and went to the settee where her aunt took a seat.

"The marquess is coming to dinner tonight. And he is bringing Lord and Lady Danbury with him."

Having no idea who these people were or why the prospect of them coming to Westfield for dinner had her aunt so worked up, Minta sat expectantly, knowing Aunt Phyllis would quickly clue her in.

"The Marquess of Kingston, my dear," her aunt explained. "He is one of our neighbors. I have not seen him since he was a boy. He was recently at war, you know. His brother died in a tragic accident last year and the title passed to the second son. I have asked him to dine with us several times but he has always been engaged. Until now," Aunt Phyllis said, her enthusiasm bubbling over.

"Lord and Lady Danbury are great friends of his and visiting Kingwood now. Since they are leaving tomorrow, he asked if he could bring them along or he would come to Westfield at another date. Naturally, I wrote to him immediately and told him they were more than welcome. Lady Danbury is very sweet and kind, while Lord Danbury is quite dashing."

"You are excited to reacquaint yourself with the marquess now that he is an adult?" Minta asked.

Aunt Phyllis pursed her lips and then said, "It is always good to know a marquess, my dear. Especially when he is a neighbor."

She smiled. "I especially want him to meet *you*."

Her aunt's knowing look let Minta know where this conversation was heading.

"You think to introduce us before the Season even begins."

"Exactly." Aunt Phyllis smiled triumphantly. "The previous Marquess of Kingston was a lovely man but dying childless caused the title to pass to his younger brother. He will be conscious of that fact and most likely wish to wed sooner rather than later in order for the title to remain in the Perry family and not pass to another branch or even revert to the crown."

Taking Minta's hand, her aunt squeezed it. "This is a perfect opportunity to get you in front of the marquess before he peruses the Marriage Mart. You are such a lovely young woman, Minta. I hope this will give you an advantage over the other girls of this Season."

"There is always the chance that he won't like me, Aunt," she reminded. "Mama always worried about our hair being red. She was afraid we would stand out—and not in a favorable way."

Aunt Phyllis waved away that thought with her hand. "Nonsense. Both you and Sera are beautiful and charming. And if Lord Kingston proves to be not interested in you, it is his own fault. At least meeting him will give you a bit of practice with society before you even make your debut."

Rising, her aunt concluded with, "Wear the azure gown this evening, Minta. It will bring out your eyes."

She smiled. "It is one of my favorites. I will be happy to do so."

Aunt Phyllis left and Minta sat several minutes, pondering over what tonight would be like. She had worried slightly that she would feel a bit out of place entering Polite Society at her advanced age. The same might be true for Lord Kingston. Obviously, he was not raised to be the marquess and only found himself one after his brother's death. He, too, might feel a bit out of sorts. It would be lovely if they could enjoy one another's company here in the country. It would give them both a familiar face to see once the Season began.

Minta began her letter to Sera and then found she couldn't concentrate on it. Putting it aside, she decided to come back to it—after tonight.

Hopefully, she would have something interesting to write about come tomorrow.

⇶⇷

HUSTON DRESSED PERCY for the dinner at Lord and Lady Westlake's estate, fussing over his cravat.

"That's enough, Huston. I am certain that I am quite presentable."

"Of course, my lord."

He glanced into the mirror, hardly recognizing himself outside his military uniform. He had worn nothing else ever since he'd left Cambridge and reported for duty. Fortunately, the Second Sons had taken him in hand and a day trip to London had been planned soon after his arrival. The trio had taken him to their tailor, shirtmaker, and bootmaker. He had been fitted and left London with a few items. More had arrived at Kingwood after two weeks and Percy would be fitted and accept his final wardrobe once he returned to town. He knew Adalyn had already spoken to the tailor about what would be needed.

It was just one of many ways the Second Sons had been helpful. They—and their wives—had helped him with learning about his responsibilities regarding his estate and his duties in the House of Lords. Since he didn't know how to dance, the Three Cousins had promised to teach him once they were all in London together. Adalyn also told Percy she would help him learn how to flirt.

He had grown hot and red in the face at that remark.

In truth, he had very little experience with women and none in flirting. Oh, Win had seen to them both losing their virginity during their Cambridge days and helped suggest women for Percy to couple with in the years before they graduated. His innate shyness seemed to put off most women, however. Oftentimes, when he told Win and his other friends he was off for a night of adventure with a willing woman, Percy had merely walked the streets of Cambridge, visiting book shops or stopping for a meal, then sitting on a park bench until coming home in the wee hours.

The years at war had not been amenable for conducting any kind of love affair. While Win and Owen seemed to always manage to discover pretty widows—or even willing wives whose husbands were away at war—in the villages they were stationed near, that had not been a practice Percy was willing to partake in. He also avoided the camp trollops, those who followed the legions of soldiers as they made their way across the land. He worried about the diseases the women carried and chose not to become involved with any of them.

As a result, it had been years since he had been with a woman. Already shy in nature, his lack of experience around the opposite sex had him worried—no, frightened, if truth be told—about what the upcoming Season might be like. The only good thing would be that so many of the unattached females would be fresh from the schoolroom and not know how awkward he truly was.

At least, that is what he hoped.

Thank goodness tonight would only involve Lord and Lady Westlake. Percy remembered they were childless. The couple had come to Kingwood once or twice during his childhood. He remembered Lord Westlake being quite imposing and Lady Westlake rather chatty.

"Anything else, my lord?" asked Huston.

"No, thank you. I am all set."

Percy left his bedchamber, passing the door to the bedchamber of his future marchioness, again wondering why Rupert hadn't bothered to wed and provide an heir.

In the foyer downstairs, he waited for Owen and Louisa to appear. Soon, they came down the staircase.

"Had to kiss Margaret before we left," Owen said matter-of-factly.

He could only shake his head at the change in his friend from rake to doting husband and father. Owen and the other Second Sons proudly discussed their children's teething as if it were as important as world politics. Perhaps it was. His friends had chosen to center their lives around their families. If only he could find a decent woman and do the same.

They went out to the waiting carriage and headed east.

"Didn't you say Win's family lives nearby?" Owen asked.

"Yes, twelve miles to the west of Kingwood," he replied. "Terrance, Win's older brother, is now the Duke of Woodmont. Where Rupert and I were always close, Terrance never gave a fig about Win."

"Have you seen Woodmont since you returned to England?" asked Louisa.

"Neither hide nor hair," Percy admitted. "Terrance spends a majority of his year in London and only visits Woodbridge upon occasion. He is as wild as they come and according to my solicitor, did not bother to attend Rupert's funeral."

"What a shame," she said. "It seems that Win would make for a better duke than his brother. Is he married?"

"Not that I know of." He thought a moment. "Terrance must be a couple of years shy of forty. He should think about marriage and an heir. Then again, Terrance has always thought of no one but himself."

"Where is Westfield?" Owen asked.

"Bailey told me it is about six miles from Kingwood. We will pass through Kingsbury, the local village which lies three miles away, then it will be another three miles to Westfield."

"I think you will like Lord Westlake," Owen said. "He is as quick as a whip and always has a ready story."

"Lady Westlake is kind but a bit of a featherbrain," Louisa

added.

"From what I gather, they only come to their country estate for a short time each year," Percy said. "Bailey seemed to think they usually arrive for Christmas and return a good month or more before the Season begins."

"Lady Westlake will most likely be acquiring a new wardrobe during those weeks," Louisa said. "She has quite a regal bearing and is known for her keen sense of fashion." She smiled at Percy. "I am glad you decided to accept their invitation. It will be good to meet your neighbors. And now that I hear that they and your cousin aren't in the area all that often, it is vital for you to come to know not only your other neighbors but others in the village. As I mentioned, they will look to you for leadership."

"It is a good thing Woodmont isn't in the area often," Owen said. "I have met him and the only thing he could lead anyone to is a gaming table or a phaeton. I had not remembered he was Win's brother when we did meet. Poor Win."

"Terrance is Win's only sibling," Percy said. "That is why we were always good friends. We were so close in age. We went away to school together. Rupert looked after the both of us."

They arrived at Westfield and he took in the estate with new eyes, now owning one himself. Where in the past he might merely glance at the fields, he now studied everything, looking to see what others might do so that he could help his tenants be profitable and happy.

The carriage came to a halt and they descended, being admitted by the butler and led up to the drawing room.

When they entered, Lord and Lady Westfield came to their feet, along with a young woman of great beauty. His eyes were drawn to her rich, abundant hair, a blend of red and bronze which he had never seen before. He hadn't known anyone else would be present tonight and suddenly found himself tongue-tied as he and his friends went to greet their hosts, the beauty watching him with animated blue eyes.

Adalyn had schooled him on manners of the *ton* and so Percy knew it was up to him to begin the introductions since he was the ranking peer. He swallowed hard, trying to find his voice, and finally forced himself to speak.

"Lord and Lady Westfield, how kind of you to invite us to dinner this evening." He turned, indicting Owen and Louisa. "May I present to you Lord and Lady Danbury?"

Pleasantries were exchanged as he felt his heart pounding rapidly, causing his mouth to grow dry.

"Thank you for coming tonight, Lord Kingston," Lady Westlake said. "And we would like to introduce you to our niece, Miss Araminta Nicholls, daughter of my sister, Lady Nicholls, and Sir Radford Nicholls."

Miss Nicholls stepped forward, her skin glowing luminously. She was a few inches above five feet and possessed a curvy figure.

"I am most happy to meet you, Lord Kingston," she said, her voice low and throaty, sending a chill along his spine as she offered him her hand.

Taking it, Percy brushed a kiss upon her gloveless fingers, warmth filling him. He released it and quickly turned to his companions.

But no words came out.

Smoothly, Owen stepped forward. "Ah, Miss Nicholls, what a pleasure." Owen also kissed the woman's hand and presented her to Louisa.

"I am sorry we have not met before, Miss Nicholls," Louisa said.

"We would not have had that opportunity, Lady Danbury," Miss Nicholls said. "I left England five years ago when my father was named as the assistant to the Administrator of Upper Canada. My twin sister and I were only going to stay a year and then return to make our come-outs together. Unfortunately, we were forced to stay in Canada when war broke out, as it was too dangerous to try crossing the Atlantic with so many sea battles occurring."

Lady Westlake slipped an arm about her niece's waist. "It was terrible for my sister. She had remained behind to nurse our father during his last illness, expecting she would join her family in Ontario after a few months. Instead, they were separated for years."

"That is dreadful," Louisa agreed. "When did your mother arrive in Canada?"

"She came last summer," Miss Nicholls told them. "It was wonderful to see her again after so long a time. Papa was going to stay on in Canada for a bit. The post of administrator has turned over several times since it is held by a military man and the war was not kind. Still, Mama encouraged me to return to England and come and stay with my aunt and uncle so that I might finally make my come-out, albeit a bit late."

"What of your twin?" Owen asked.

"Sera decided to stay in Ontario. She is extremely close to Mama and she also lost a sweetheart in the war. I am hoping she will join me in England by next Season."

Percy finally found his voice and said, "It must be hard being separated from her."

Miss Nicholls turned her full attention on him and his heart skipped several beats. "Oh, it is, my lord. Sera and I have shared our entire lives. We had never been separated for a single night. It made for a hard decision to leave her behind and move forward with my life."

"Do you seek to wed, Miss Nicholls?" Louisa sagely asked.

The young woman nodded. "I would like that very much, my lady. I know because of my advanced age that I am already at a disadvantage, with so many young ladies set to make their come-outs. Still, I will hope for the best," she said, positivity brimming from her. "I would also hope to help Sera find a husband once she returns to England, as well."

"My cousins and I would be happy to help you in this endeavor," Louisa said. "They are Lady Middlefield and Her Grace, the Duchess of Camden. Before her own marriage, the duchess was known for being a bit of a matchmaker."

Miss Nicholls' eyes lit up. "Oh, do you think she would be willing to help me?"

"I know so," Louisa confirmed. "All three of us will." Turning to Lady Westlake, she asked, "When do you return to town, my lady?"

The three women began making plans to get together once they all were in London again, while Lord Westlake and Owen began talking about their estates. Percy remained silent, taken by Miss Nicholls, glancing casually toward her now and then.

"I remember you as a boy, my lord," the earl said. "Lady Westlake and I came to visit with your parents a few times years ago."

"Yes, my lord," he said, remembering how imposing Lord Westlake had been and how now he merely seemed like an ordinary, middle-aged man.

The butler arrived. "Dinner is served, my lord."

They paired up and Percy found Miss Nicholls on his arm, the tantalizing scent of vanilla coming from her. He wished he could lean in and inhale it. He wished he could taste her.

The thought shocked him. He had never been so attracted to a woman in his life. He recalled some of the things Owen used to brag about after his romantic encounters.

And suddenly, Percy wanted to do some of those very things to Miss Nicholls.

He glanced away from her, feeling the heat fill his face. They had no conversation before arriving in the dining room, where he seated her and took his own seat opposite her.

Dinner went by swiftly. Percy would be hard-pressed to name a single dish he consumed though he did spend a good deal of time staring down at his plate. He listened to the conversation but contributed nothing, feeling ill at ease. Especially with the beautiful Miss Nicholls in his direct line of sight.

Once the meal concluded, Owen took the reins and said, "Thank you for a lovely evening and for extending your dinner invitation to my wife and me. We are leaving early in the morning, however, and should probably return to Kingwood to make certain our daughter is fine and that everything is ready for our departure tomorrow morning."

"Perhaps we can dine again when we are all in London," Lord Westlake suggested. "Would that be amenable to you, my lord?"

Percy realized the earl spoke to him. "Certainly," he said brusquely and hoped he didn't sound rude.

The Westlakes walked them out to their carriage, with Louisa and Miss Nicholls making plans to have tea with Tessa and Adalyn.

"I will write to my cousins when we return to Danfield to-morrow," Louisa promised. "It was so good to meet you, Miss Nicholls, and delightful to see you again, Lord and Lady Westlake."

"We look forward to seeing you in town," Owen added, glancing to Percy.

"Thank you for having us to dinner," he said as they entered the carriage.

Once inside, he sat against the cushions, closing his eyes.

The Westlakes probably thought him dull since he had contributed next to nothing to the conversation.

What was worse was that Araminta Nicholls would never consider giving him a chance. She was vivacious and interesting. The last thing she might want is to be saddled with a boring marquess.

"Bloody hell," he murmured under his breath.

CHAPTER FOUR

"WELL, THAT WAS certainly disappointing," Aunt Phyllis declared the moment the footman closed the door.

Uncle West winked at Minta and said, "I believe I will go to the library and read for a bit in order to allow you two to discuss the evening. Goodnight, Minta dear."

Her uncle departed and her aunt said, "Shall we retire to the drawing room?"

Minta knew Aunt Phyllis wanted to gossip about their guests in private and so she agreed to accompany her aunt upstairs again.

Once they were settled in the drawing room, Aunt Phyllis said, "I am so very displeased," she began.

"What is wrong?" Minta asked, already having a good idea what her aunt would complain about.

"First of all, the evening ended so early."

"Well, Lord and Lady Danbury did mention their departure early tomorrow morning. I am certain they wished to be well-rested before they set out for home. I thought they were lovely," she added.

"Oh, I did like them both very much. I had met Lady Danbury previously and she has such a sweet disposition. And that Lord Danbury," her aunt said, her eyes gleaming. "What a charmer that one is. Lady Danbury has her hands full with that rascal, I daresay."

"They seem very devoted to one another," she commented, dreading what they would speak of next.

She didn't have long to wait because her aunt then said, "The marquess was a sore disappointment. While quite nice-looking, he barely said two words the entire evening." Aunt Phyllis looked at Minta sympathetically. "I had hoped you meeting him before the Season began would give you an advantage over the others seeking a husband. Now, however, I can't see how he would be the one for you. You are full of life, Niece. I found the Marquess of Kingston to be most dull. Most likely, he is arrogant and thinks he is above others."

"I think you are mistaken about him, Aunt," she said quickly, springing to his defense. "True, he was very quiet but he was in the presence of strangers to him."

"He could have made more of an effort," her aunt insisted. "Of course, he will not have any trouble finding a bride if he does plan to look for one on the Marriage Mart. After all, he is a marquess. His title and looks alone will stir interest in him among the *ton*."

His looks had certainly stirred Minta. Though she usually found darker-haired men more attractive, the blond marquess had her heart aflutter from the moment he'd arrived. He was just over six feet and possessed an athletic frame, with broad shoulders and long legs. His warm, brown eyes were quite observant, taking in everything about him. If a Greek statue had come to life, she believed it would appear exactly like the Marquess of Kingston.

She also believed he was uncomfortable in their company for a few reasons. Sera could be incredibly shy around those she had never met and Minta thought Lord Kingston might be the same. Once her sister got to know someone, she opened up and was relaxed in his or her company. Perhaps the same could be said of Lord Kingston. Lord and Lady Danbury appeared to be extremely close to the marquess and she didn't think the couple would suffer fools gladly.

Another thought had come to her during dinner when the marquess ate silently. He had recently inherited his title, a title which had belonged to his brother. That meant he had not been raised to be a peer of the realm and had never been in many social situations. Second sons almost always committed to the military and from what Lord Danbury had said, both he and Lord Kingston had not only attended university together but also served in His Majesty's army side-by-side for a good many years. With the previous marquess' death so recent, it meant that Lord Kingston had not held the title for long and was still in mourning for his brother. She knew from her visit here to Westfield just how busy her uncle was with the estate and his various responsibilities. Lord Kingston had left the world of the military behind and now joined ranks with those members of Polite Society. It was possible tonight's dinner had been his first foray into it. If he was truly shy, as she suspected, he had probably remained silent out of fear that he would make some mistake.

"I think, given time, Lord Kingston will settle into his title," Minta proclaimed.

"Even if he is a marquess, I think you can do better," Aunt Phyllis declared.

"Better?" she chuckled. "Better would mean a duke, Aunt. I don't see any duke—or any marquess, for that matter—wanting to wed the daughter of a lowly assistant to the Upper Canadian Administrator."

Aunt Phyllis took Minta's hand and squeezed it. "Oh, I want so much for you and your sister. I was fortunate enough to wed an earl and have led a life of luxury. My parents were so disappointed when your mother married Radford. No, don't get your hackles up, Minta. I like your father a great deal and I know how much my sister loves him. It has been a more difficult life for her, though. She has had things to worry about that I am never troubled by. She is a wonderful mother and I must admit I am a tad jealous for her having two such wonderful girls as you and

Sera. Westlake and I are in a position to help you and your twin and that is what we will do. Do not sell yourself short, Minta. You are a natural beauty and so friendly and kind. I believe you will attract a gentleman with a title."

"He would have to be incredibly wealthy, Aunt. You know I have a piddling dowry."

"Not anymore," her aunt revealed. "Westlake and I talked it over and he is going to add five thousand pounds to the amount your father has set aside. He will do the same for Sera once she returns and makes her come-out."

Shock rippled through Minta, hearing the large sum. Her current dowry was two hundred pounds, which she believed would not have attracted anyone but the wealthiest of suitors who had no need of it.

"That is extremely generous of you and Uncle West," she said in awe. "I don't know how to thank you."

"It will be thanks enough to see you have a successful Season and wed at the end of it. Are you open to that idea since your parents and Sera are still in Canada?"

"We talked of that very thing," she said. "Both Papa and Mama urged me to live my own life. Papa said if I received an offer and wished to accept it, I should marry as soon as possible and not wait for a time when they might return to England. He said Uncle West could act on his behalf as far as negotiating the marriage contracts. I believe he was to write Uncle and share all of this. Perhaps he already has."

"That is good to know, Minta dear."

"I don't know if I will ever be able to convey my gratitude, Aunt Phyllis. You and Uncle West have already provided me with a wardrobe for my Season and now this dowry."

Her aunt cradled Minta's cheek and then kissed it. "You two girls are the closest we will ever have to having children. I hope we will remain close for many years and that you will have a household of children of your own for us to spoil."

Giving Minta a fond smile, she added, "I suppose we should

turn in for the night."

Once in her bedchamber, Minta rang for her maid, who prepared Minta for bed, taking down her hair and brushing it out before plaiting it.

"Anything else, Miss Nicholls?" asked Bertha.

"No, that will be all. Goodnight," she told the servant.

Climbing into bed, she found sleep hard to come. Usually, she dropped off with ease but tonight was different.

Because her head was filled with thoughts of the handsome, taciturn Lord Kingston.

***

TWO DAYS LATER, Minta was at breakfast with her aunt. Her uncle had already finished eating and gone down to the stables to check on one of his horses which had a cough.

The butler entered the breakfast room with a smile on his face, bringing a silver tray directly to Minta.

"Miss Nicholls, the post has arrived from town and everything in it is for you."

Tears sprang to her eyes as she thanked him, taking the bundle of letters sitting on the tray and holding them close to her heart.

"May I be excused?" she asked.

"Of course, my dear. I know how eager you have been to receive word from your loved ones."

She left the breakfast room and went to her small sitting room, where she spread out the letters on the writing desk. Two were in Mama's hand, one in Papa's, and four had been written by Sera. Before Minta left for England, Mama had said they would direct all of their correspondence to the Westlake townhouse since her sister and brother-in-law spent a majority of their year there. Only two letters had arrived before they departed for the country, which had disappointed Minta tremendously. Apparently, these had accumulated and had now been sent down to Westfield. She hadn't realized how much she had needed to hear from her family as she broke the seal on every letter and then arranged them by date.

She read the single letter from her father first, his image coming to mind. In it, he told her what he had been up to since her ship departed from Ontario. Minta had always enjoyed hearing about the details of the administrator's office and she could hear her father's voice as she read the letter. He closed it on a personal note, telling her how much he missed not only seeing but talking with her.

Know that you are missed and loved and I look forward to the day I can see you again, my darling, darling daughter.

Tears sprang to her eyes at her father's words. She blinked them away and set the letter aside and took up the first of Mama's. Her mother talked about settling into her role in her new home in her first letter, mentioning various neighbors she had met and the routine of her days. In the other one, however, Mama grew personal and told Minta that while she had cherished this time with Sera, she wished Minta could have stayed. Mama emphasized that Minta had done the right thing, however, and should enjoy her time at Westfield and the upcoming Season.

My hopes for you, my dear girl, are that you enjoy the society you find yourself in and that you will find a gentleman to love. I know it is not usually the way of the ton *but I do hope you can find a love as great as the one I have held for your father all these years. Don't let your head rule your heart, Minta. Too many young ladies in Polite Society do so, marrying a title rather than a man. Choose a husband wisely, for you will spend decades with him and you want one who will love you—and make you laugh.*

She wiped her eyes with a handkerchief she pulled from her

sleeve, touched by her mother's words. It surprised her when an image of Lord Kingston came to mind. She did not consider the marquess good husband material, at least for her, and figured the only reason she thought of him was because he was the only gentleman close to her age she had met. Although her aunt and uncle had introduced her to a few people while they were in town, none of those were near her in age, much less any of the men being single. Minta did know that, oftentimes, a woman her age wed a man twice that but she had hoped she would marry someone closer to her own age.

She set Mama's letters aside and now gathered Sera's, checking once more to make certain they were in the order in which Sera had written them. Minta settled into her chair and took up the first one, a smile on her lips as she began reading. She easily heard her sister's voice in the words on the page. In the letters, Sera wrote of daily activities and how happy she was to have the time with Mama. The first three letters were breezy in tone but the final one had a much different one to it.

Dearest Minta,

I wonder how many of these letters are getting through to you. I know how many we wrote to Mama during the war and how few of those she actually received. I know I am addressing these to Uncle West's London townhouse but that you may have already left there for the country. Or who knows? You may have already turned to town by the time you receive this.

Minta, I think I made a mistake staying in Canada. Although I enjoy the quiet life here, even more so now that the war has ended, I miss you dreadfully. In a way, I almost feel selfish. I have had Mama and Papa all to myself and have tried to soak up every minute of that, especially with Mama. You know how alike the two of us are. Being reunited with her has made a difference, especially in my grief.

Yes, I seem to continually run into Edward's parents. His mother, in particular, always clings to me as if I am the last link to her dead son. Just when I feel that I am moving past

Edward's death, I see her again—and the pain is fresh once more. I believe in order to move past this tragic event that it would be best if I left Ontario altogether.

There is a possibility that Papa will be reassigned and come back to England within the next year. Minta, I do not want to wait that long. I have missed you dreadfully and long to be together again with you.

Because of this, I am going to tell Mama and Papa that I wish to return to England. The ships are booking up quickly with so many others wanting to go home, as well, so it may take me a while before I can secure my passage. I actually went to the shipping offices yesterday and inquired, finding out the next available berths for passengers would be at the end of April. I asked the shipping clerk when that would put me in London. He said with good weather most likely mid-June. If the weather turns out to be a bit stormy and rougher, then it would be the end of June.

I am determined to be on that ship, Sister. I know I will have missed the majority of the Season and so I won't bother trying to attend events this year, but I simply must be with you again. I want to hear about all the new friends you have made and the many suitors who are calling upon you. I fear if I don't return soon that you will wed and move off far away. If you do receive an offer and the gentleman's country estate is a great distance from Westfield, then that would give me at least a few weeks to spend with you before your wedding and departure if I book the late-April passage.

I am posting this now and will work up my courage to tell our parents that their second daughter is also leaving them. Though I am certain it will sadden Mama, she will understand. Papa has already encouraged me to go, seeing how down I have been with you gone.

I do hope this letter reaches you, Minta, my wonderful twin, and that you are enjoying being with Aunt Phyllis and Uncle West. Have a wonderful time at all those balls and other events and pray that I have a safe journey to you.

All my love,
Sera

Minta placed the final page on the desk and burst into tears. She sobbed in relief, knowing that before the Season ended, her twin and she would be together again. If she did receive an offer of marriage, that meant Sera would stand by her side as Minta made her vows. Nothing could have pleased her more than this. She dried her tears and then read through each letter again slowly, savoring every line written by her family. She then took the letters upstairs and placed them under her pillow for safekeeping.

Returning downstairs, the housekeeper told her that her aunt wished to speak with her and Minta went to Aunt Phyllis' sitting room.

As she entered, Aunt Phyllis beamed at her. "We have received an invitation to dinner this evening, Minta. We are to dine with the Marquess of Kingston."

"So soon?" she asked. "I wonder why."

"Perhaps Lord Kingston realized he had made a poor first impression upon us and wishes to correct that assumption. At any rate, we are to sup with him tonight."

The idea of seeing the handsome marquess again intrigued Minta. She wondered if she was correct in assuming he was shy. Wouldn't it be wonderful if she could get him to open up? Why, it might even allow them to become more than acquaintances and on the road to a friendship.

Or more . . .

Her aunt told her when they would leave and the two of them went upstairs to choose the gown Minta should wear. She didn't think anything would come of this dinner with Lord Kingston, but she wanted to look her best all the same. They went through the limited number of gowns suitable for dinner because much of her wardrobe which had been completed consisted of morning gowns, which were not suitable for an evening meal with a marquess. They finally settled upon a teal gown and then Aunt Phyllis rang for Bertha. Her aunt had the maid arrange Minta's hair in several different styles before they all agreed upon one which seemed the most flattering.

As Bertha styled Minta's hair, Minta shared with Aunt Phyllis that Sera would be arriving sometime in June. Her aunt was delighted by the news and despite Sera wanting to refrain from attending any events, Aunt Phyllis was determined to talk her into coming to several.

The rest of the day passed quickly and then it was time to prepare for their engagement. Minta only had to change gowns since they had decided to leave the final hairstyle in place. Once she was dressed, she headed downstairs, anticipation filling her. She hoped they would get to know a little more about Lord Kingston this evening. She hoped since they had already met him that his initial shyness might have died away and they could enjoy their meal, along with decent conversation.

Her head must have been in the clouds, thinking of all of this, because somehow she missed a step and tumbled the remaining few stairs to the bottom of the staircase.

Uncle West, who was waiting in the foyer, quickly ran to her and righted her, placing her on the last stair.

"Are you all right, Minta?" he asked, concern on his face.

She rotated her ankle and winced. "No, Uncle. I think I might have sprained my ankle."

"Minta!" her aunt cried, rushing down the stairs.

The butler and a footman also hovered nearby as her uncle checked her ankle, rotating it gently.

"I do believe your diagnosis is correct and that it is a sprain, Minta. We should send for the doctor at once. I'll also sent a footman to Kingwood to let Lord Kingston know we won't be coming, after all."

"No, don't do either, Uncle West," she protested. "I sprained my ankle once before, years ago, and know exactly how to care for it. My little accident shouldn't keep you and Aunt Phyllis from dining with his lordship."

They argued about it for a few minutes but Minta prevailed. She allowed her uncle and a footman to carry her back up the stairs to her bedchamber and then rang for Bertha to undress her and help her into her night rail and dressing gown.

Aunt Phyllis appeared. "Are you certain you wish for us to go without you, Minta? I don't believe the marquess is interested in our company. I think he was looking forward to seeing you, my dear."

"Please, Aunt, go without me and give my apologies to Lord Kingston. I should only be indisposed for a day or two. We can host Lord Kingston for tea in a few days if you truly think he is so eager to see me."

"Very well." Aunt Phyllis placed a kiss upon Minta's brow. "I will look in on you when we return." She sighed. "Hopefully, this evening will not be as dull as I now expect it to turn out."

"I will see you later."

After her aunt left, Minta wondered if Lord Kingston would truly miss her presence at the table this evening.

Because she would certainly miss seeing him.

CHAPTER FIVE

S HE HADN'T COME.

Percy had hidden his disappointment when Lord and Lady Westlake entered the drawing room without Miss Nicholls. The only reason he had extended the invitation to the earl and countess to sup with him was in order to see their niece again. And she hadn't accompanied the Westlakes to Kingwood.

Lord Westlake had explained how his niece had taken a tumble down the stairs, spraining her ankle. Percy had not known whether to believe the earl or not, wondering if this was merely an excuse for Miss Nicholls not to come to dinner.

Ever since he had first laid eyes upon her, she had never been far from his thoughts. It was odd to go from never giving a woman a single thought to having a majority of his thoughts centered around one.

He knew he had made a poor impression upon her and Lord and Lady Westlake. He had tried. Really tried. But his usual reticence had enveloped him, almost swallowing him whole. He never understood why his throat constricted and nerves rushed through him whenever he met new people. Even after being acquainted with others, he only truly had ever relaxed in his brother's company and that of the Second Sons, who were as brothers to him.

Being a soldier had been different. He had cared deeply for his men and yet, outwardly, looked at them dispassionately. Somehow, leadership in the military—and especially in a time of war—had come to him easily. He supposed it was only in social situations that he seemed to freeze up.

Today, he was going to learn whether or not Miss Nicholls had feigned her injury in order to avoid his company. Percy knew he must take a bride and she would make for an excellent marchioness. He hoped he could get to know her before the Season began, else he doubted he would ever have a chance with her. Already, the thought of being in the glittering ballrooms of the *ton*, surrounded by dozens—no, hundreds—of people, made his belly grow sour. He couldn't imagine having to introduce himself over and over, not only to his peers but to young ladies that he would then have to court, competing with other bachelors for that privilege. He had hoped establishing a connection with Miss Nicholls before the Season started might give him an advantage in wooing her.

Although he had no experience in pursuing a woman, he did know that women enjoyed flowers. Percy now went out to the gardens and saw few blooms. Knowing it was February, he should have realized this. Then he thought of the conservatory and how there must be some flowers blossoming there. He had not visited it since his return to Kingwood and quickly made his way to it.

Stepping inside, he felt the warmth envelop him as he began to browse through the various plants and flowers. He found exactly what he was looking for and went and located where the gardening tools were stored, claiming a pair of shears and cutting with care so as not to bruise the flowers. Returning the gardening shears to where he'd found them, he took tissue and wrapped the bouquet in it.

He was ready now. Armed with what he hoped was considered a suitable gift for an invalid. Or at least someone claiming to have a sprained ankle.

Summoning Bailey, he asked that his carriage be brought

around as he intended to visit Lord and Lady Westlake. Within a quarter-hour, the carriage arrived and Percy climbed inside, bouquet in hand. He rested it in his lap, hoping his small token would be accepted with pleasure.

Half an hour later, he arrived at Westfield, studying it in the light of day. His previous visit, along with Owen and Louisa, had occurred as dusk was setting and so he had not been able to have a good idea what the property looked like. All the lessons he had taken to heart from the Second Sons regarding estates stayed with him and Percy keenly observed what Westfield looked like and if it thrived or not. From what he had gathered, Lord and Lady Westlake only spent a fraction of the year in Essex at their country estate. Westfield looked to be in good order, however, and Percy assumed their steward to be an excellent one.

The carriage pulled up in front of the main house and he climbed from it, bouquet in hand. A butler greeted his knock and Percy said, "I am here to call upon Miss Nicholls and see how her ankle fares."

The butler ushered him inside and said, "Poor Miss Nicholls did take a bit of a fall last night, my lord. I saw it myself and was worried for her. She is in good spirits, however, and I am sure she would be delighted to have your company."

The butler indicated a parlor to the left and added, "If you will wait here, my lord, I will let Miss Nicholls and Lady Westlake know that you have come to call."

Percy waited but a few minutes before the servant returned. "If you will follow me, my lord."

They went up the staircase and instead of the drawing room, which he was familiar with, they went to a sitting room awash in sunlight.

As Percy entered, Lady Westlake rose and he greeted her, seeing Miss Nicholls' legs propped upon a settee.

"We are so grateful for your visit this afternoon, my lord," Lady Westlake said, eyeing him with curiosity.

"I was concerned about Miss Nicholls' health," he stated,

turning to her and stepping toward the settee.

She lifted her hand and he took it in his gloved one, wishing he could touch her without wearing them. Bending slightly, he kissed the back of her hand and reluctantly released it.

"It was quite thoughtful of you to call on us and check on me, my lord," she said, her blue eyes sparkling, drawing him in.

Once again, Percy found himself tongue-tied in her presence. He thrust the bouquet at her and she took it.

"I suppose these are for me," she said, a twinkle in her eyes.

"Yes," he said stiffly. "I hope you will enjoy them. They are from my conservatory."

He watched her sniff the flowers. She looked to her aunt and said, "Would you ring for a maid, Aunt Phyllis? I would like to get these into water as soon as possible so that they will stay fresh."

"Of course, my dear." Lady Westlake rang for the servant and then said to Percy, "Won't you have a seat, my lord?" She indicated a chair.

He took it and an awkward silence followed. Nothing was said until the maid arrived. Miss Nicholls told the servant to put the flowers in water, even indicating which vase she would like to be used.

"And bring them back here if you would, Hetty," she added. "I want to enjoy them as soon as I can."

"Yes, Miss Nicholls," the maid said, exiting the room with the flowers.

Percy swallowed, not able to think of a single thing to say. Then he recalled the weather was always a safe topic and said, "It is a nice day for February. Cold but quite sunny."

"I am sorry to hear that," Miss Nicholls said, surprising him. "I enjoy a brisk walk every day and regret that I am missing the sunshine out there today."

"Perhaps I could take you for a ride in my carriage," he offered, and then glanced at her outstretched legs. "I suppose that sounds foolish since you need to keep your ankle elevated."

"No, not at all," Lady Westlake insisted. "I think it would do

Minta a world of good getting out in the fresh sunshine." The countess frowned. "Of course, she cannot walk to the coach."

"Then I will carry her to it," he said assertively, taking charge of the situation as if he were going into battle.

He glanced to Miss Nicholls and saw a blush staining her cheeks. "Is that agreeable with you?" he asked.

"It would be lovely to leave the house," she agreed. "You do not need to carry me, however, my lord. I can have a footman do so."

"Nonsense," he declared as he rose from his seat.

Stepping toward her, he asked, "Will you allow me to lift you, Miss Nicholls?"

Her blush deepened but she nodded. "That would be acceptable, my lord," she told him. "Although I should send for my pelisse since you mentioned it is chilly outside."

"I have robes in my carriage," he told her. "We can wrap you snuggly in one of those."

"It is so kind of you to offer a ride to my niece," the countess said. "Perhaps after your little outing, you would care to stay for tea, my lord."

"If it would not inconvenience you, my lady, I would be happy to do so." He glanced to Miss Nicholls. "Unless Miss Nicholls tires of my company, that is."

"Feeding you tea will be your reward for putting up with me," the young woman declared. "I am ready if you are, my lord."

Percy stepped to her and lifted her from the settee, walking steadily so as not to jar her ankle.

"Aunt Phyllis, would you hand me that cushion?"

The countess picked it up as Percy halted and handed the cushion to her niece. "A good idea, Minta. You can use this in the carriage to elevate your ankle."

As they left the room and he headed down the corridor, Percy inhaled the scent of warm vanilla wafting from her skin.

"You smell divine," he blurted out, seeing a pleased look

appear upon her face.

"I always wear vanilla," she told him. "Sera, my sister, prefers jasmine."

They didn't speak again until they arrived outside. Percy called up to the driver to take them through the local countryside for an hour. A footman opened the coach door and Percy moved up the stairs, setting Miss Nicholls upon the leather seat. She stretched out her legs and he slipped the cushion she held underneath her ankle. Reaching for one of the two folded robes sitting in the corner of the opposite seat, he draped it across her lap and legs and then took the seat opposite her. Using his cane, he rapped on the roof and the carriage started out.

Miss Nicholls turned to him and said, "Thank you for getting me out of the house today, my lord. Although I enjoy sedentary activities to an extent, I much prefer being out and about."

Realizing the movement of the carriage was bouncing her ankle, he asked, "Might I come sit with you, Miss Nicholls? I am afraid the movement of the coach is jarring your ankle about. I would not want to injure it further."

A radiant smile lit her face. "That would be helpful, my lord. I was afraid I would have to twist toward you during the entire ride. If you are sitting at my feet, I will be able to see you much better—and have my ankle secure."

He set his walking cane aside and moved to the opposite bench, where he gingerly lifted her legs and the pillow and sat. Placing the cushion in his lap, he lowered her legs to it, interesting tingles rippling through him.

Percy placed a hand atop her trim ankle and said, "I am trying to anchor it from movement. I don't want to hold it too firmly though. Is this pressure too much?"

"No, it is fine," she told him.

He tried to think of something to say, something casual yet witty, yet nothing came.

"You do not have to try so hard, my lord," she said. "Conversation should occur naturally between others. Sometimes, no conversation at all is needed." She smiled at him, causing a glow to fill him.

Her words emboldened him and he said, "You seem to have insight into me, Miss Nicholls."

"I realize that you are uncomfortable around those you do not know," she said astutely. "I most certainly understand that because my twin, Sera, is quite shy around those she meets. All our lives, I have been the one more outgoing, while Sera is a bit shy. When she gets to know someone, though, she can be as lively and entertaining as anyone."

Miss Nicholls paused, looking at him steadily. "I see the same in you, Lord Kingston. You probably are most comfortable around your family and close friends but being around strangers can be difficult for you."

"You are beautiful as well as insightful," he observed. "You have also hit the nail upon the proverbial head. I do have trouble opening up around those I do not know. My nature has always been extremely reserved. I was very close to my brother, Rupert, who held the title before I did."

"Was he your only sibling?" she asked. "Or do you have younger ones, as well?"

"No, just an heir and a spare. My parents were barely interested in the two of us, much less in having other children."

"It is quite the opposite for me," she revealed. "Both Sera and I are quite close to our parents. They were a love match and are open in their affection, both to each other and us. While I am more like Papa and a bit closer to him, Mama and Sera are peas in a pod. I wish I could have had more siblings but Mama almost died giving birth to twins and the doctor warned her never to attempt to have more children."

"It is wonderful you are so close but you mentioned they are still in Canada. Why are they there—and you here?"

She bit her bottom lip and a flush of heat filled Percy. It took everything in his power not to lean over and kiss her.

"I think I mentioned that Papa was named as the assistant to the Administrator of Upper Canada several years ago. Sera and I went to Ontario, only intending to remain a year before returning to England to make our come-outs."

"And those pesky Americans foiled your plans, didn't they?" he asked. "You mentioned the other evening how the war prevented you from returning home."

Miss Nicholls nodded. "Civilian travel across the Atlantic ceased. Only troops and needed supplies were transferred to and fro. Sera and I remained in limbo for those years." She sighed. "Now, I am considered to be on the shelf at two and twenty. Other girls my age have already wed and many have started their families."

His thumb stroked her ankle. "You certainly are not on the shelf, Miss Nicholls. If anything, your maturity will separate you from the giggling girls making their come-outs. Your beauty will draw men to you." He swallowed hard. "Are you looking for a husband?"

"I think most every woman is, my lord," she said softly. "Women are maternal by nature. They want to have children and titled peers certainly need their heirs."

He wanted more than anything to ask if he could be among her suitors come the Season but paralysis set in. He could not speak, as if some witch had enchanted him and cast a spell that kept him from saying what was in his heart.

The silence between them stretched on and Percy saw the moment slipping away. Miss Nicholls' gaze turned from him, settling upon her lap.

They kept their thoughts to themselves the remainder of the ride. When the carriage returned to Westfield, he decided she'd had enough of him and he'd made a fool of himself, thinking this spirited, vivacious woman would ever consider a future with him.

"Let me see you inside, Miss Nicholls," he said politely, gathering her in his arms, enjoying the feel of her curves against him and that enticing scent of vanilla invading his senses.

"Thank you, my lord."

Percy carried her inside and she directed him to take her to the drawing room. Both Lord and Lady Westlake awaited them and he placed Miss Nicholls upon a large settee, seeing the pillow was placed under her tender ankle.

Then he looked directly at Lord Westlake, avoiding both women, and said, "I am afraid I will be unable to stay for tea, after all. I recalled that I was to meet with my steward this afternoon. I am certain you understand when the duties of your estate call."

The earl nodded sagely. "Certainly, Lord Kingston. Perhaps you can come another time for tea."

"That would be lovely," he said woodenly, knowing there would be no other teatimes for him and Miss Nicholls.

She deserved someone far more interesting than he could ever be. She was a shining light that would brighten any room.

Forcing himself to look her way, he saw the puzzled expression on her face as he said, "I hope you recover from your injury, Miss Nicholls, and are back to your usual walks sooner than later. Good day." He turned to Lady Westlake and echoed the same words.

Leaving the drawing room behind, Percy cursed himself for ruining his chances with the very beautiful Miss Nicholls.

CHAPTER SIX

"ARE YOU CERTAIN you don't want to go with us, Minta?" Aunt Phyllis asked.

"No," Minta said. "I believe I will stay here and do a little bit of gardening. You know how I enjoy being outdoors."

While she usually didn't mind accompanying her aunt and uncle on an errand, this one involved visiting Reverend Whitehead and his odious wife. How a sweet-tempered man could have married a tart-tongued woman such as Mrs. Whitehead baffled Minta. She would have done anything to avoid being in the woman's company. Besides, talking about a new roof for the local church held little interest for her. If she was fortunate enough to make a match during the Season, she suspected her aunt would want a smart town wedding for her and not one at Reverend Whitehead's small church.

"I will never understand that about you," her aunt said. "At least you are wise enough when it is sunny to wear a bonnet and have a parasol in order to protect your delicate skin from freckling. Redheads are prone to freckling, you know."

"I suppose we are off then," Uncle West said. "We will probably be several hours, Minta."

He dropped a kiss upon her head and said quietly, "Enjoy your time alone."

Minta flashed him a grateful smile. Although she loved her

aunt deeply, sometimes Aunt Phyllis was a little overbearing and Minta found she needed time to herself. Gardening and walking were two of the ways she escaped the house and had time alone. Her aunt had warned her there would be very few moments alone once they returned to town and the Season began. She had described the varied activities. Mixed with the social calls they would pay and the visitors they would receive—including potential suitors—meant that Minta would possibly only be alone when she dealt with her toilette and slept.

A warm feeling came over her as she sipped her remaining tea. Once again, her thoughts turned to Lord Kingston. They had done so repeatedly over the last week.

She wondered why things had gone astray between them. Their conversation had been good while in the carriage. What had even better been was the feel of his steady hands upon her ankle and leg, keeping her ankle secure as the carriage rolled along. The scent of his cologne had filled the vehicle and Minta had hoped that he might possibly kiss her.

She had never been kissed.

She supposed the influence of her parents had something to do with that fact. Mama and Papa were still deeply in love after many years and quite affectionate toward one another. Though Minta did not expect a love match for herself to occur, it always seemed to be in the back of her mind. She had attended some of the assemblies held in Ontario, especially the ones before the war began, and a few occasions had arisen where she thought a gentleman might kiss her. Somehow, she had always done something to discourage a kiss, however.

She wondered if Sera and Edward Marsh had kissed before he left for the battlefront. Usually, her twin shared everything with Minta but she had not been very forthcoming regarding any information about the time she'd spent with Captain Marsh. Surely, they had kissed. They had an understanding that when Edward returned from war that they would pursue a courtship and marriage. Whether they had kissed or not, though, Minta had no idea. She wished for the thousandth time that Sera was here so they could talk over this situation with Lord Kingston.

She left the breakfast room and went to her room, where she had Bertha help her change into her oldest gown, one from her early days in Ontario. Heading downstairs again, she went to the gardening shed, where one of the gardeners had left an oversized apron for her use. Minta placed it over her gown to protect it from the dirt. She also slipped workman's gloves on her hands before picking up a trowel.

Moving into the gardens, she knelt and began pulling weeds, something she found cathartic. Her thoughts drifted back to Lord Kingston and that day in the carriage. She had been right. He was shy, just as Sera was. He had admitted as much to her, saying he was uncomfortable around those he did not know. The marquess had said that he was close with his brother, which saddened her, knowing he had no more siblings to turn to. She wondered about his friend, Lord Danbury, and if Lord Kingston might have any other close friends to depend upon.

Her thoughts turned back to when their conversation took an ill turn. Everything had gone smoothly until they had begun to speak of marriage. She had mentioned it was natural for women to want to wed and have children. Suddenly, the tide had turned and Lord Kingston clammed up. They had not spoken anymore and the atmosphere in the carriage had been rife with tension. Minta had thought of what to say to him to break it and change things, to return to their earlier banter, but nothing came to her. And when they had arrived back at Westfield and he carried her inside, the marquess made a piddling excuse and departed, not taking tea with them.

They had heard nothing from him since.

Aunt Phyllis had merely remarked upon how odd Lord Kingston seemed and pressed Minta about what had occurred in the carriage between them. When Minta said they had only spoken for a few minutes, her aunt had proclaimed they must wash their hands of the marquess. She told Minta there would be plenty of eligible bachelors in London and not to worry about one foul-tempered marquess.

But Minta did worry about him and how he would react during the Season. She understood how crowds could terrify Sera. Just because Lord Kingston was a man did not make him immune to that same terror, especially since he had admitted his reserved nature. She wondered if she would see him at social events and if he would flounder in public or draw upon his military experience and push through.

One thing was true, however, and that was what Aunty Phyllis said about how society would look at him. Because of his lofty title and his extremely good looks, Lord Kingston would be in demand. She shivered, thinking of all the aggressive mamas who would push their daughters in his direction. It wouldn't surprise her—and she wouldn't blame him—if he fled every ballroom, knowing some of them might even give chase and try to track him down.

As she dug and pulled another weed up by its root, she told herself to stop thinking of Lord Kingston. He was not her concern. If anything, Lord and Lady Danbury would take good care of him. In fact, Lady Danbury probably had in mind a few unattached females to introduce him to.

Minta had liked both Lord and Lady Danbury quite a bit and she and Lady Danbury had already exchanged a letter apiece. Lady Danbury had reminded Minta of her promise to come to tea so that she might introduce her two cousins to Minta. She had shared the letter's contents with Aunt Phyllis, who was terribly excited that Minta would take tea with a duchess, along with two countesses. Her aunt told her those would be valuable social connections to make and that these women, especially the powerful Duchess of Camden, could help launch her into Polite Society even better than she and Uncle West could.

Minta, of course, hoped the three women could introduce her to some appropriate gentlemen, but she also longed to gain their friendship. She still sorely missed Sera's company. No one would ever replace her twin but she thought the friendly Lady Danbury and her cousins might give Minta the needed time with women close to her age.

She moved to a new section and began pulling weeds there, forgetting where she was as she let her thoughts meander. Then something changed in the air. Something so subtle that if she hadn't have been alone in the quiet, she would not have noticed it.

Turning, she spied Lord Kingston standing before her. Her heart slammed against her ribs at the unexpected sight as she looked at him. He was dressed as the perfect country gentleman, with tight, fawn breeches that outlined every curve of his legs, his feet encased in tall, polished Hessians. His coat of hunter green emphasized his broad shoulders. The slight wind ruffled his dark blond hair and she fought the urge to stand and sweep it back into place.

Finding her voice, Minta said, "Good morning, Lord Kingston."

She couldn't read the look in his eyes as he replied, "Good morning, Miss Nicholls. Your butler said that I might find you here."

Minta started to rise and the marquess took her elbows, pulling her to her feet. Wordlessly, she merely gazed upon him, thinking once again how he seemed to be a statue come to life, perfection in the flesh. She inhaled a whiff of the spicy cologne he wore and realized his hands still cradled her elbows. A warm rush raced through her and she wet her lips.

Lord Kingston released her but he did not step back. Minta could still feel his body's warmth so tantalizingly close.

"I have come to apologize to you, Miss Nicholls."

Confusion filled her. "Whatever for, my lord?" she asked.

He glanced about and said, "Might we sit upon this bench?"

"If you wish."

Taking her elbow in hand again, he led her to the bench. She placed the trowel at her feet and sat, slipping off the heavy gloves and placing them next to the gardening tool. He joined her and she realized just how small this bench was and how large he was. Their thighs and hips pressed against one another in the small space, causing a delicious frisson to ripple along her spine. A colony of butterflies seemed to explode within her belly and flutter madly inside her, leaving her breathless.

"You were right about me," he said softly. "You guessed my nature and how uncomfortable I am with most everyone."

"Is that why you refused to stay for tea?"

He pondered her question a moment and then replied, "Perhaps. I feel we were getting to know one another a bit. I would like to continue to do so if that is agreeable with you."

Her heart raced as she said, "I would like that, my lord. Very much. You and your friends, Lord and Lady Danbury, will be the only people I know once the Season begins. Lady Danbury has asked me to come to tea when I return to town with my aunt and uncle so I suppose I will meet her two cousins, as well. Because of that, I will admit that I am somewhat nervous about partaking in my first Season."

Minta hoped by admitting this that it was not just him who might be frightened about the events to come.

"That is kind of you to say, Miss Nicholls, though I doubt your nerves match mine. You are a most beautiful woman and have a spark that draws others to you. You will easily make friends and find yourself swamped with a bevy of suitors."

"I am not quite as certain of that as you seem to be, Lord Kingston. I have already mentioned my age to you. Even Aunt Phyllis has warned me that the new girls making their come-outs will probably have little to do with me."

He smiled. "That is because they will see you as a threat, Miss Nicholls. You have much to offer and they will be jealous of the attention you will receive."

"You also have much to offer, my lord."

He gave her a rueful smile. "Yes, I have the title Marquess of Kingston. That is all most people will see when we are introduced to one another. My friends' wives, whom I call the Three Cousins, have warned me that my title alone—let alone my great wealth—will attract women to me. Pushy mothers will thrust their daughters in my path, hoping to snag a marquess. The Three Cousins have told me that a majority of *ton* marriages occur between people who are, for the most part, strangers. Couples who have danced a handful of times. Spoken about the weather or a few other inane topics. They have said most marriages occur to unite families and strengthen political and social ties. I am not interested in that."

Intrigued, she asked, "Then what are you interested in? Love?"

He flinched and seemed to retreat within himself. Knowing she was about to lose him again, Minta placed her hand upon his forearm and squeezed it gently. The distant look in his eyes left as he met her gaze.

"I did not mean to frighten you off with such a bold question, my lord. Although my parents are a love match, I doubt that will be in the cards for me. Despite what you say, my age works against me and my dowry won't be as large as that of most women. In fact, it was but two hundred pounds, all my father could afford on his government salary. My aunt and uncle look upon Sera and me as their children, however, and Uncle West has added to my dowry. So hopefully, I might appeal to some gentleman."

She squeezed his arm again and added, "But what are you looking for? Please, share it with me."

A hopeless look entered his eyes. "What I am looking for probably does not exist. I, too, as you, do not think of making a love match. My parents had an arranged marriage and tolerated one another. I have seen love between my good friends, though. While I do not believe I am destined for that, I would like to find a wife who could be my friend as I see with the Second Sons."

"The Second Sons?" she asked. "Who are they?"

He seemed to relax but she continued to leave her hand upon

his forearm, enjoying the feel of the muscles under her fingers.

"The Second Sons are my merry band of close friends," he revealed. "Growing up, I worshiped my brother, Rupert, who was three years older than I and destined to claim the title one day. My closest friend was my cousin, Win, who lived on the estate next to us. Just as Westfield is to the east of Kingwood, Woodbridge lies to our opposite side. Both Win and I were born second sons and destined to go into the army. We went to school together and did everything together, spending all of our holidays with one another, as well. Win, like Rupert, was as a brother to me."

"When we enrolled at Cambridge, we wound up meeting three other good friends, men who were all second sons as Win and I were. The five of us were thick as thieves during our university days and we all went off to war together, being stationed in units close to one another. Our friendships only deepened through the years and the Second Sons became not only brothers but family to me.

"Then through several odd twists of fate, one by one, the Second Sons began leaving the battlefield as the first sons and heirs fell. First was Spence, who became the Earl of Middlefield. He married Tessa. The next to leave was Ev, who is now the Duke of Camden. Ev wed Adalyn, Tessa's cousin. You have met the third Second Son, Owen, who became Lord Danbury and married Louisa, a cousin to Tessa and Adalyn, thus, the Three Cousins. These three women are now as sisters to me and I am as close as ever to those three Second Sons."

A shadow crossed his face. "The only one of us left behind is my cousin. Who knows where Win will go and where his career will take him? I miss him terribly. I feel guilty returning to England, now close to my brotherhood of friends, while Win is all alone."

Minta told him, "You must accept the fact that you are now the Marquess of Kingston. Just as you served your king and country and were responsible for your men, you now have different responsibilities. You must always care for your tenants and servants. Assume your seat in the House of Lords and help make decisions for the good of England's people, based upon the experiences you have had. I know you miss your cousin. You always will. But keep your eyes on the present and look to your future, my lord. Be glad you have three wonderful friends to support and guide you."

She smiled gently. "And be happy you now have three sisters, as well. They will help see that you make a good match. While you may or may not find love as your fellow Second Sons have, I believe you are in good hands with the Three Cousins. You are intelligent and forthright when you are not hiding inside your shell. You will find a woman who is your equal. One you can share your life with. Trust your judgment, my lord, and if you have any doubts, you have people in your life you can turn to for advice and encouragement."

Minta wished she could be the one this man would choose. She grew to like him more each time they spoke. What better basis for a marriage than a friendship and respect for your spouse?

Oh, she wished he would kiss her. They sat so close together. Her hand still rested upon his sleeve. She knew, though, due to his nature that he would never be the first to act.

What if she kissed him?

It would certainly be bold. Bolder than she had ever acted before. It might cause him to flee. He might never speak to her again. It might cost her a chance with him.

Or it could possibly bring them together . . .

She swallowed, deciding she would make the move. She would kiss him—and see what happened.

Her decision made, she glanced up at him, her gaze meeting his, her arm tightening on his as she drew on her courage.

And suddenly—he kissed her.

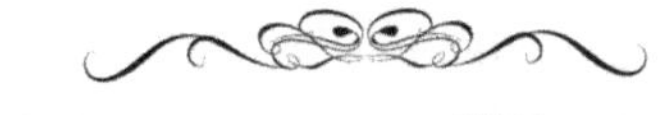

CHAPTER SEVEN

PERCY HADN'T COME to Westfield to kiss Minta Nicholls.

And yet he found himself doing that very thing.

He was conscious of so many things. The sweet smell of vanilla coming from her skin. The feel of her fingers, warm on his arm. The softness of her lips against his.

Raising a hand, he cupped her cheek, wanting to touch the smooth skin. His lips slowly brushed against hers, an aching sweetness pouring through him. Her hand left his arm and both her fists clutched his lapels, pulling him closer to her. His pulse thumped wildly in his throat as the blood rushed to his ears. His heart pounded so loudly he feared she would hear it and laugh at him.

But it didn't stop him. His lips continued to caress hers slowly as time slowed and then ceased to exist. All that mattered was this breathtakingly beautiful woman, who was far more than her pretty face and shapely curves.

He increased the pressure, his mouth asking more of her. His hand slid from her cheek to her nape and held her still. The other moved to the small of her back, moving her forward, anchoring her to him. Slowly, his tongue swept back and forth along the seam of her mouth and her lips parted, granted him entrance.

Into Heaven . . .

She tasted as sweet as she smelled. His tongue swept along

hers, mating with it. He could sense her surprise and wondered if she had ever been kissed. If she had, certainly not like this.

He grew bolder, demanding more of her, heat filling him. His fingers pushed into her hair, tangling in it, even as his tongue tangled with hers. She caught on quickly and though he barely knew what he was doing, instinct led him and she joined in with ease. With eagerness. Little sighs came from her, urging him on.

He had never kissed a woman for this long. His previous kisses had only lasted a few seconds. This kiss went on and on. Or was it one kiss which blended into another and another? He didn't know and didn't care. He simply let it continue, holding her near, kissing her until he was breathless and knew she had to be, too.

Percy broke the kiss, his lips hovering just above hers, and then he sank his teeth into her full, bottom lip which had driven him to distraction. She gasped, her fingers tightening, as he sucked on the lip, wanting to take and take and take every bit of her. Then he released it, gliding his tongue across it, soothing it. She whimpered, causing a rush of power to roll through him.

His lips went to her jaw, nibbling along it and down her throat, nipping it with tiny love bites and once again comforting her with his tongue. He moved down the slender column of her throat, reaching the swell of her breast as it peeked from her gown. Wanting—no, needing—to taste her, he slid his tongue along the curve. She whimpered again, pulling him closer. He cupped her breast, feeling it swell in his palm, as he continued to stroke its curve with his tongue, her skin slightly salty and yet sweet at the same time.

Slowly, his thumb circled her nipple, causing her to become restless. After teasing her a bit longer, he brushed his thumb against her nipple, feeling it pebble as her breath hitched. He swept it back and forth lazily, enjoying the little sounds she made in the back of her throat. He tweaked the nipple and she gasped.

What the hell was he doing?

Quickly, he released her. Minta Nicholls was as innocent as

they came. Here they were, alone in a garden. And he was ready to push her gown down and suck on her breasts as if she were some paid whore.

Percy leaped to his feet and stammered, "I am s-s-sorry, Miss Nicholls. I . . . I . . . goodbye!"

He quit the garden, racing back the way he had come, avoiding the house and going directly to the stables where he had left his horse. Trying to compose himself, he slowed his pace, taking deep, even breaths.

A stable boy fetched his horse and Percy mounted, taking off at breakneck speed and riding that way for some minutes. Finally, he slowed the horse and dismounted, walking along the lane, trying to give himself time to collect his thoughts before Kingwood came into sight. He cursed aloud, berating himself.

Going to Westfield had been a terrible idea. He had already decided he would never have a chance with Minta Nicholls after their carriage ride together. He lacked in everything a woman like her needed. Yet somehow, he had found himself heading to see her today. The past week, his head had been full of thoughts of her, despite telling himself that she would never be interested in a fellow such as himself.

It were those thoughts which had driven him to Westfield this morning. When he learned that Lord and Lady Westlake were not at home, he almost turned away. Until the butler had told him that Miss Nicholls was present. Actually, in the garden. When he had gone there, he had spotted her at once and watched her at first from a distance, then moved closer. She was pulling weeds, a dreamy expression on her face.

Percy had never seen a more lovely sight.

Their conversation had not been stilted at all. In fact, he had enjoyed telling her about the Second Sons and the Three Cousins. He was delighted that Louisa wanted to take Minta under her wing and help her find friends and become established within the *ton*.

Then talk had turned again to marriage. He supposed it must

be inevitable since they both would be attending the Season with the same end result in mind. She was so wise, encouraging him to come out of his shell and to listen to his friends. She made him believe that he could have a future with a woman such as her.

That was why he had kissed her. The sweetest kisses of his life, now and in the future. Percy could not fathom kissing another woman the way he had Minta. Yet his head and heart both told him that he was not worthy of such a woman. That he was too damaged by the war. That if they did wed, she would discover how weak and tired the war had left him. Minta deserved the world. The best Polite Society had to offer. A man of talent, looks, and wealth, one who was as wise as she and would love her.

Percy didn't think he could love. He believed that the ugliness of the war had seeped into his soul, burning it up until nothing was left. Minta may think she wouldn't find love but he believed she would. She needed a man who could give her all his love. One who would treat her with kindness and respect. A man who would give everything to her, laying his soul bare.

He couldn't let her see who he truly was. He knew he wasn't worthy of her. No matter how great a temptation she proved to be, he vowed to avoid her both now and in the future.

Though he was scheduled to leave for London in a week's time, he made the decision to leave today. Putting distance between him and Minta would be the first step in avoiding disaster.

Mounting his horse again, Percy galloped the rest of the way home. Arriving, he began issuing orders left and right, Bailey and Mrs. Bailey scurrying into action, Huston quickly packing, and Smith receiving final orders regarding the estate and harvest.

An hour later, he sat in his carriage as it turned from Kingwood in the opposite direction of Westfield and headed toward London.

HE WAS A bloody coward.

Percy had never thought himself one but he certainly did now after having fled Essex—and Minta Nicholls—for London. He wavered between regretting having kissed the copper-haired beauty and regretting leaving her side. He still didn't believe himself worthy of such a magnificent woman but he almost wished she had made the decision to push him away instead of him doing so, running with his tail tucked between his legs. How could he have faced such danger in battle for so many years and yet be frightened of one woman?

Percy didn't know if he would ever have an answer to that question.

His first two weeks in town had been spent mostly in solitude. He had visited his tailor's, getting fitted for an extensive wardrobe. When he'd first arrived from the war, Percy had been fitted for a few items. Adalyn had then arranged for the tailor to come to Kingwood as only a duchess—and Adalyn—could. The man brought some of the clothes Percy had been fitted for previously and had returned a week later with several more items. Adalyn made certain to speak to the tailor regarding patterns and materials so that when Percy arrived in town this time for his extended stay, he had even more fittings, which seemed outlandish, considering the number of pieces involved.

But Adalyn had stressed to him because of his position in society that he must have a wardrobe to match. It astounded him the number of coats he now possessed, not to mention shirts, trousers, cravats, hats, and pairs of boots. She had given specific instructions to the tailor, who also saw to the needs of the Second Sons. After wearing a uniform for most of his adult life, it seemed odd to be dressed so fussily in anything else but he was thankful she had seen to his needs since he would not have had a clue where to begin.

Huston had been delighted once all of the clothes arrived, telling Percy he would be the best-dressed peer in London. He was finally becoming comfortable with the valet inherited from Rupert. The London staff, however, was different. They were all strangers to him. At least at Kingwood, he had been familiar with Bailey and Mrs. Bailey from his years growing up on the estate. Now, however, he was surrounded by a houseful of servants who were strangers to him. He knew he acted aloof but didn't believe they would think anything of his behavior, as that is most likely how a marquess did behave with his servants.

Besides meeting with the tailor and others regarding his wardrobe, Percy had seen his solicitor twice. They had discussed his financial holdings and other business ventures in which he should invest. He had told the solicitor he would take things under consideration, including hiring a business manager. Rupert's had retired only two weeks before his brother's death and the position had not been filled. That was something Percy would see to during his time in town. He would wait, though, to get input from his fellow Second Sons, hoping possibly to even use one of theirs. Owen had spoken highly of his business manager and, hopefully, he might share the man with Percy.

The rest of the time, he had kept to himself, wandering the deserted streets of London in the early morning hours when they were empty, so as to avoid any kind of crowd. He also went riding some mornings but the rest of the day he had spent locked away in his study, looking over financial records or sometimes reading for pleasure. He had always enjoyed both history and architecture and had found many volumes on both topics in his large library in town.

Things had changed in the past week because the Second Sons and the Three Cousins had arrived in town with their children and servants in tow. His new sisters were seeing to wardrobes for the Season and spending several hours each day with Percy, tutoring him in the ways of Polite Society. He had learned about the plethora of unwritten rules he was to follow and the three women had told him about every kind of activity that would occur during the Season.

The thought of the Season still had him in a panic. So many people. So many new faces. And the expectation that when it ended, he would take a bride. Being on the battlefield had been different. Yes, there had been hundreds and sometimes thousands of soldiers fighting, but Percy had always had a strong sense of duty and he was able to issue orders and lead with ease. Social situations, however, were a different matter and, sometimes, he wished that the Three Cousins would tell him which young lady to wed, plan the wedding, and allow him to merely show up on that day and speak his vows.

Tessa had explained to him how he was expected to dance numerous times at balls since he was an eligible bachelor but that he was never to dance more than twice with a woman. Even dancing more than one with the same partner would have Polite Society's tongues wagging, as that was an indication of his interest in a female. He reminded them that he did not know how to dance at all and so afternoons this past week had involved dance lessons with his new sisters.

Adalyn, who could barely play the pianoforte, insisted one be rolled down to the ballroom, while Tessa and Louisa took turns playing. Both women played quite well and the three also were more than patient with him as they taught him and then led him multiple times through various dances. He had always been athletic and agile and found that he actually took to the lessons well. He had no doubt he could perform any of the country dances or reels, as long as he did not let being around so many others overwhelm him. Percy decided he would look upon it as a battlefield to be conquered and that might get him through evenings at balls. How he was to survive more intimate gather-ings, such as garden parties or routs, he would soon learn. Fortunately, he had the Second Sons and the Three Cousins on his side and they promised to attend any event that he did so he would always have familiar faces surrounding him, especially during suppers at the various balls.

The last two days had been devoted to the waltz, a dance which Louisa said many women looked forward to simply because a woman could actually hold a bit of conversation with her partner during it, due to its intimate nature. He practiced diligently until he had the steps down but dancing with one of these three women whom he knew was far different from dancing with a total stranger. He hated to tell them that he doubted any conversation would go on as he waltzed, merely because he would be inhibited being so close to someone he didn't know.

The idea of holding a strange woman in his arms while trying to make banal conversation was almost as bad as the nightmares of war that continued to plague him.

A knock sounded at his door and Tate, his London butler, entered the study.

"My lord, Her Grace, Lady Middlefield, and Lady Danbury have arrived. They went directly to the ballroom and requested that you join them there."

Percy rose. "Thank you, Tate."

He went upstairs and found not only the three wives there but another man with a violin in hand.

Adalyn came to him and said, "Today, we are going to practice everything you have learned, Percy. First, we will work on your waltzing so that the steps come so naturally that you will be able to speak as you dance. In an hour, the Second Sons will join us and we will have a chance to practice several of the other dances in a larger group."

He was grateful for that opportunity. He knew the steps of many dances but he had merely walked through them, pretending other dancers were there. This would certainly be a challenge to all he had learned during the week and better prepare him for his first ball.

Then he noticed someone else sitting in the corner and asked Adalyn, "Who is that woman?"

Adalyn said, "Abra is Tessa's lady's maid. She is going to join in the dances so we will be even in number and no one will have to sit out. As you know, many of them involve couples in groups of four. With Abra's help, this will allow us to practice both longways and closed sets fully, as well as reels."

The next hour passed swiftly as he took turns dancing with Adalyn, Louisa, and Tessa as the violinist played for them. He even took a turn with Abra and thought the servant might be the best dancer of them all because she was so light on her feet. She was cheeky enough to wink at him at one point, which made Percy laugh and enjoy the dance all the more.

He noticed movement at the door and turned, seeing the Second Sons had entered and now watched his progress. Once again, he said a silent prayer, thankful that he had these good friends by his side as he entered Polite Society. His only wish would be that Win could join them, which would be impossible.

Owen stepped up and clapped Percy's back. "You, my friend, are a born dancer," he declared. "I don't know if I have seen a smoother man on the dance floor."

Percy was thrilled at the praise and said, "If I am skilled, it is because I have had three of the best teachers in London. If they ever bore of being your wives and mothers to your children, they could open a dance school and be the most beautiful dance masters in town."

Everyone laughed heartily at his words and Adalyn went to speak to the violinist.

Soon, Percy found himself swept away in the various dances, actually enjoying himself far more than he thought possible. He knew circumstances would change, however, when the ballroom he danced in was packed with members of the *ton* and he was having to dance with strangers who would fawn over him in hopes that he would offer for one of them. Still, the Three Cousins had given him confidence, more than he thought he possessed.

After another hour of lively practice, Tessa asked if they could stop.

"I am famished," she declared. "And I could certainly use more than one cup of tea to quench my thirst."

"I spoke with your cook before we started this afternoon," Louisa said. "I told her we would all be staying for tea. We should head up to the drawing room now because I am certain it is ready."

They moved to the drawing room, where a lavish tea was being set up. Percy decided when it was done he would have to go and thank Cook for her efforts. He knew he needed to start making more of an effort toward his servants. They worked long, hard hours and as a former soldier and officer, he knew how appreciated it would be if they heard from him how well they were doing in their positions.

Tessa and Louisa poured out for the group as Adalyn made plates and passed them around. Teatime became quite lively and Percy hoped that the woman he chose as a bride would fit in well with not only the Three Cousins but also when the four couples would gather together in situations such as these. He looked forward to many times such as this throughout the years.

Tate entered the drawing room and came to him. "You have a visitor, my lord."

"A visitor? All my friends are here with me. Who has come calling?"

Percy couldn't imagine anyone calling upon him because he didn't know anyone in London. Of course, there would be a few acquaintances from his school and university days but he couldn't fathom them calling upon him now. It wasn't as if he had gone to White's and socialized, although Owen had insisted they go tomorrow afternoon and do that very thing, which Percy dreaded.

The butler said, "It is His Grace, the Duke of Woodmont."

"Woodmont? What on earth would he being doing here?" Percy said, shocked that his cousin would come calling.

"Who is Woodmont?" Louisa asked. "The name sounds

familiar to me."

"He is Win's older brother by eight years," he replied.

"Perhaps he merely wishes to welcome you to town and congratulate you on holding the title," Tessa suggested.

He laughed harshly. "That is not Woodmont's way. If he barely tolerated Win, he couldn't stand the sight of me. As a second son, I could do nothing for him. Woodmont is all about titles and positions and who can do something for him."

"He is also as wild as they come," Ev said. "Never comes to *ton* events because he's usually too deep in his cups."

Spence nodded. "He keeps a string of mistresses and has quite a nasty reputation. But you should see what he wants, Percy. After all, he is family."

He looked to his butler and said, "Please show His Grace in and have another teacup sent up in case he wishes to join us."

"At once, my lord," Tate said, quickly exiting the room.

Moments later, the door opened again and Percy supposed his cousin had been standing outside, probably impatient and in a foul temper now for having had to wait so long for admittance.

Much to his surprise, the man that entered the drawing room and strode quickly toward the group was not his older cousin, Terrance.

It was Win.

CHAPTER EIGHT

"Y OU ARE . . . Woodmont?" Percy asked, stunned.

Win smiled wryly. "I am now."

The cousins threw their arms about one another, pounding each other on the back. Percy's eyes stung with tears, knowing somehow, some way, his cousin was gone from the army and home.

For good.

The other Second Sons gathered around them, each wanting a turn to greet Win to London, followed by a flurry of introductions allowing Win to meet the Three Cousins for the first time. His cousin immediately charmed the three women and Percy couldn't help but feel a small pang of envy at how easily Win could enter a situation and feel comfortable with everyone present, immediately on a first-name basis with the wives he had previously only known through letters.

"Shall we have a seat?" he suggested and they all found a place to sit as a maid slipped in and placed a new teacup and pot of tea on one of the carts.

Win took in the tea before him as Adalyn poured out and handed over the cup and saucer.

"This is a veritable feast," he proclaimed. "I don't remember the last time I had a decent cup of tea, let alone scones and sandwiches. Oh, is that trifle? I must have some of that." He rubbed his hands in glee.

"Tell us what the devil you are doing here," Owen said. "And how you came to be Woodmont."

"Give me five minutes to eat something and then I will spill all," Win said. "I am ravenous and have only been in town but a few hours." He glanced down at his attire. "Forgive my stained uniform. It's been worn for quite some time and I literally have nothing else to my name."

"Take all the time you need," Louisa told Win.

As his cousin downed a vast amount of tea and ate everything in sight, they began sharing with him what was going on in their lives, especially with their children. Percy talked a bit about what Kingwood was now like and some of the improvements he was beginning to make on the property.

"I cannot believe I did not know of Terrance's death," he told his cousin. "After all, we are neighbors, even though our estates are twelve miles apart. What happened that led you here?"

Win wiped his mouth with a napkin and set his empty plate aside. "Terrance died in London last month, which is probably why you had no knowledge of his death. I received a vaguely-worded letter from his solicitor acknowledging the death and that I was the new Duke of Woodmont. The letter arrived hours before I was scheduled to leave on a ship bound for Canada, new orders in hand."

"Oh, that would have been terrible," Tessa said. "It could have taken months to catch up to you and then just as long for you to return."

"Exactly," Win said, sipping his fourth cup of tea. "I showed it to my commanding officer at once. He wasn't about to let a new duke step foot on the ship and quickly put into motion a scheme to help me sell out and return to London from Bristol. By the time I reached town, Terrance had already been buried. Not at Woodbridge, but here in London."

"That's odd," Adalyn remarked. "Why wouldn't he be buried in the family plot?"

Win frowned. "Because he was a bastard of the first class and hated our father. Mother rested on one side of Father and Terrance was supposed to be laid to rest on his other side. My brother was defiant until the end, insisting he be buried in town. He even had it drawn up in writing and made his wishes clear to his solicitor, should anything happen to him."

"How did he die?" Spence asked. "You haven't said."

"Is he the peer who perished in the fire at that gaming hell?" Ev asked. "I heard some talk about that at White's yesterday but there was no mention of names."

Win nodded. "Yes. The fire started after hours. I learned Terrance would often be too deep into his cups to leave and would stay over in the company of one of the tarts. I thoroughly questioned my solicitor and he led me to believe that Terrance himself most likely started the fire by smoking in bed. The woman he was with also died. Only two others were on the property at the time and they both escaped."

His cousin shrugged. "By the oddest twist of fate, it made me Woodmont. The solicitor has heard rumors that my brother may have left a bastard or two behind. I plan to put a Bow Street Runner on the case and see if these children—if they do exist—can be located. Obviously, Terrance wasn't seeing to them in any way but that is no excuse."

"If anyone can find them, it will be a Bow Street Runner," Owen agreed. "They are experts at tracking down lost people and stolen goods. Even murderers. It is admirable that you would hunt for these children, Win."

"It is the least I can do. My brother never cared much for anyone but himself. I fear I will find the estate in shambles. He spent a majority of his time in town and I believe Woodbridge was sadly neglected. That is why I am headed there immediate-ly."

"But what about the Season?" Adalyn asked. "You have just arrived and should remain here with your friends and family. I know how much the Second Sons have missed you."

Win shook his head. "Looking for a wife is the last thing on my mind. I need to get the estate in order. All of them, in fact. I learned that I own five of them scattered across England. My chief objective is to bring Woodbridge back to its former glory before I see to any of the other ones."

"Then I will return to Essex with you," Percy said.

A shadow crossed Win's face. "I cannot ask you to do that, Percy. You've spent months getting your own house in order. Now is your time to enjoy your title and take your seat in the House of Lords. And look for your marchioness."

"That can wait until next Season," he protested.

"No," Win said firmly. "It cannot. I know you, Percy. I know how you are dreading all the social activities." He glanced around. "You have a wonderful group of people here to support you. The Second Sons—and now their wives—are as family to all of us. By God, Percy, you are thirty years old. Don't be like your brother and put off finding a wife and starting a family."

He snorted. "You, too, are thirty, Cousin. And your brother was pushing forty and still hadn't wed. You should feel that same obligation to marry and provide an heir to the dukedom."

"I have a compromise," Louisa said quietly and all eyes turned to her.

Percy sat forward, eager to hear her suggestion. Louisa was the quietest of the Three Cousins but sometimes had the greatest insight of the trio.

"Win should leave for Woodbridge as soon as possible. His obligation is to his tenants, both there and on his other estates. Of course, there is much to learn as the four of you discovered when you came into your own titles. As a compromise, I think Owen should return to Essex with Win for a week and begin guiding him through that process. Then Spencer and Everett could follow and each stay a week. Since there are three weeks before the Season begins, it would allow Win access to their experience and valuable advice, while at the same time making sure they wouldn't miss any of the activities."

Louisa looked at Percy with kindness. "You are just learning things yourself, Percy, and you know you would like to find a bride during the Season. Let the other Second Sons help Win along, while we Three Cousins make certain you are prepared for what lies ahead. Then after the Season, we will meet up at the house party Owen and I will hold."

"We are hosting a house party?" her husband asked, a gleam in his eyes. "I seem to recall the last house party we all attended turned out very well." He took Louisa's hand and brought it to his lips, kissing it tenderly.

"My thoughts exactly," she said. "If Win would like to consider the idea of marriage, a house party is much more informal than the Season."

"And it gives ample opportunities to get to know people well in a short amount of time," Adalyn added. "Once the Season begins, I can work on a list of eligible young ladies to invite, as well as young men you might wish to become acquainted with."

Win guffawed. "I have heard about your matchmaking talents, Adalyn."

Adalyn ignored his remark and turned to Percy. "I should have thought about this before. If the large events of the Season prove too uncomfortable and prevent you from getting to know the women you are interested in, a house party would be to your advantage, as well, Percy."

It seemed as if the large boulder which had been pressing upon his chest, making him seem to fight for every breath of air, was suddenly lifted.

"That is a relief," he admitted. "While I will go ahead and participate fully, this house party allows me the freedom not to rush to choose a bride by Season's end."

"Then it's settled," Tessa said. "We will help Percy during the Season and if he needs an additional boost, the house party will accommodate both Win and him." She smiled broadly. "Oh, I do enjoy a good house party."

"Thank goodness it is being given by close friends who will

allow us to bring Analise and Adam along with us," Spencer declared. "I want Win to meet our children."

Win laughed. "I look forward to meeting the pair, as well as little Edwin and Margaret," he told the group. He looked to Owen. "Would you like to wait until tomorrow morning to leave for Woodbridge?"

"Yes, that will give my valet time to pack and allow me to spend some time with Margaret. It would also allow us to stop by and visit a tailor since you are sorely in need of clothes. Do you have a carriage?"

"I came in Terrance's. Or I suppose it is mine now." Win shook his head. "This whole becoming a duke overnight will take some getting used to."

Percy chuckled. "Oh, don't worry. The Three Cousins will prepare you for the social aspects of the position, while the Second Sons will aid you in adjusting to all the many duties you now hold." He thought a moment. "I suppose we are no longer Second Sons of London. All our lives have changed and the moniker no longer seems to fit. Perhaps we need a new one."

"No," Spence said firmly. "We might now all hold a title and lands and wealth—but we should never forget who we are and where we come from."

He rose and thrust out a hand and the four other men did the same, placing their hands atop one another.

"To the Second Sons of London!" they called out.

As Percy looked to his cousin and friends, peace settled over him. With the five of them together again, all seemed right with his world. All that was left was to find his marchioness and produce an heir.

Easier said than done.

CHAPTER NINE

TODAY WAS TEA with the Countess of Danbury and her cousins.

Minta was a jumble of nerves as Bertha fiddled with her hair. Her aunt looked on and nodded in approval.

"You look your absolute best, Minta, my darling," Aunt Phyllis said. "I am delighted that the modiste had this gown finished for you to wear to tea today."

She looked down and smoothed the gown of sky blue. They had been in town two days now and she had made her first trip to the dressmaker's shop, where she tried on a multitude of gowns that had already been made up for her for both day and evening wear. Very little needed to be done and so Madame Chevalier had sent over two dozen of the ready gowns. Minta was to return in three more days for another round of fittings.

Since she had spent so many hours at the modiste's shop, little else had been accomplished. She had sent a message to Lady Danbury, as promised, to let the countess know of their arrival in town. Lady Danbury had responded immediately, inviting Minta to tea, along with the Duchess of Camden and Lady Middlefield. She couldn't help but have high hopes for today's tea. Though she loved her aunt and uncle dearly, she had missed being around those her own age and especially missed her sister now that she was back in London. Sera had been more than a sister. She had been a confidante and friend to Minta over the years. Her twin had written once more, confirming that she would be on the late-April ship bound for London. Minta could not wait for her twin to arrive.

A knock sounded at the bedchamber door and Bertha answered it.

A footman appeared on the other side and said, "The carriage has arrived for you, Miss Nicholls."

"Very good," Aunt Phyllis said, linking her arm through Minta's and guiding her downstairs.

"I think it so very thoughtful that Lady Danbury sent her own carriage for you," her aunt remarked.

Minta had thought the same, which only made her wish to get to know the countess and her cousins even more.

Aunt Phyllis accompanied her outside, along with Bertha, and a footman handed her and the maid up into the vehicle. She gave a jaunty wave to her aunt and the carriage began in motion.

Aunt Phyllis had explained the rules in town differed from those in the country, being much stricter in nature. The carriage ride she had taken alone with Lord Kingston would never have been allowed in London. Her aunt had stressed that Minta was never to be alone with any gentleman at any time. She would always be chaperoned to events or calls that she made upon others. When her aunt wasn't available, Bertha would accompany Minta on these calls or errands, such as her appointments at the modiste.

She wondered for the hundredth time how Lord Kingston was faring. Their last conversation—and those incredible kisses— had her believing that there was potential in their relationship. The fact that the marquess had kissed her both startled and pleased Minta. She had relived those kisses every single day since they had parted, hoping to repeat the performance at some future point. Although from what her aunt said, she doubted she would ever be alone with Lord Kingston again. Even if he chose to become one of her suitors and called upon her, Aunt Phyllis and even Uncle West would always be present in the drawing room. She wondered how women did kiss a gentleman to decide if he would be a good husband or not if they could never be alone with a man and taste his kiss.

Her aunt said the rules slightly relaxed once a betrothal occurred. Only slightly, however. Minta didn't know if she wanted to commit the rest of her life to a man if she had not kissed him. She was also eager to compare Lord Kingston's kiss with that of others. She would have to be extremely careful in doing so, though. Aunt Phyllis had warned her if she were caught alone with a man—let alone kissing that man—it would mean an instant betrothal. If he were a true gentleman, her aunt said if she were caught in those circumstances, a gentleman of quality would immediately offer for her.

"But what if I don't wish for him to offer?" she had countered.

Aunt Phyllis had frowned, the crease in her forehead deep, and said, "You will not have a choice in that instance, Minta. If the man does not offer for you or if you do not accept his offer when he does, Polite Society's gossips would skewer you. You would be ruined. That is why I am warning you never to be alone with a man."

"But I have seen Mama and Papa kissing, Aunt. What if I do accept a gentleman's offer of marriage and then I do not enjoy his kiss?"

Her aunt's frown deepened and she finally had said, "Occasionally, you might be going for a stroll on a terrace between dances at a ball. On a rare occasion, you may find yourself in a situation—a darkened corner of that terrace—and your partner might steal a brief kiss. That should satisfy your curiosity. Hopefully, no one would see that occur. I warn you against such impulsive behavior, though, Minta."

Minta didn't believe a brief kiss would make up her mind, however. The kisses she had exchanged with Lord Kingston had gone on for who knew how long. She had marveled in the feelings a kiss could bring, both physically and emotionally.

She was desperate for the marquess' kiss again.

Though extremely reserved, he had made that bold move, which led her to believe the possibility existed that he had some feelings for her. He had acted upon the attraction between them before fleeing. She wondered if he had come to town or gone to one of his other country estates after leaving Kingwood. She would learn in the next few weeks if he was here in London or not since the Season would begin in a little over two weeks' time.

The carriage came to a halt and the door opened. A footman handed her down and then did the same for Bertha. Minta urged the maid to go with the footman and he led Bertha away, most likely to a servants' entrance, she supposed. Another of Lady Danbury's footmen escorted Minta to the door, where she was received by a smiling butler.

"Miss Nicholls, you are expected. Please accompany me to the drawing room."

She followed the servant up the stairs and into the drawing room, where he announced her. She moved forward, seeing a smiling Lady Danbury and two other beautiful blonds. The trio came to their feet and Lady Danbury took a step toward Minta.

"My dear Miss Nicholls, I am so happy that you could join us for tea this afternoon." The countess embraced her, kissing Minta's cheek, which surprised her.

"I am delighted to introduce you to my cousins, who are my closest friends since childhood."

She indicated the thin woman with hair the color of honey and sky blue eyes. "This is Her Grace, the Duchess of Camden."

Minta curtseyed as Aunt Phyllis had taught her to do and the duchess smiled graciously at her.

"My cousin has told me wonderful things about you, Miss Nicholls. I have looked forward to this tea and making your acquaintance."

She felt her cheeks heat at the attention from a duchess and said, "I, too, have been eager to meet you, Your Grace."

"And this is the Countess of Middlefield," Lady Danbury

continued.

Minta turned to the tall, lithe woman with golden blond hair and bright blue eyes, which danced with interest as she took Minta's hand.

"I have also looked forward to our meeting, Miss Nicholls. My cousins are my dearest friends and I spent years in the country nursing my ill parents so I have not been in society for very long. I hope a friendship will take root between us." The countess smiled sweetly.

"I am overwhelmed by such a welcome, Lady Middlefield," she said. "My sister and twin is my greatest friend. She is currently living in Canada with my parents. It is the first time we have ever been separated. I'll admit I have been a bit lonely and hoping to make friends with a few others in Polite Society once the Season begins."

"By the time the Season begins," Lady Danbury declared, "we shall be good friends, the four of us. Shall we have a seat?"

They settled themselves just as a servant entered, rolling a teacart. Minta's eyes widened at the lavish number of items, all looking scrumptious. Lady Danbury poured out for them and they each made up a plate for themselves.

"I know my cousin got to spend an evening in Essex with you when she and her husband were visiting Lord Kingston," the duchess began. "She must know a few things about you but I wish to learn about you, as well. Would you please tell us about yourself?"

Minta nodded. "I would be happy to do so, Your Grace."

She told them a bit of what her life had been like in London before her father received the promotion to assist the Administrator of Upper Canada.

"Papa was thrilled with his new position and Sera and I accompanied him to North America. Mama stayed behind because her father hadn't long to live and she wanted to nurse him during this time. It led to a lengthy separation, however."

"Oh, the war with the Americans," Lady Middlefield said.

"That conflict went on almost three years. Did your mother remain in England that entire time?"

"Yes, my lady. She stayed with her sister, Lady Westlake, so at least she was with family. We wrote constantly to her and she did the same but the letters delivered were few and far between. Mama arrived in Ontario last summer, once traveling the Atlantic was safe again and the weather was cooperative."

"It must have been wonderful to be reunited with her," Her Grace noted. "The three of us were all close with our mothers."

"I was happy to be with Mama again but my twin especially was. Mama and Sera are very much alike, both shy in nature. It is one of the reasons Sera remained in Canada instead of coming back to England with me."

She swallowed. "Sera had become friendly with an officer posted to the army in Ontario. Unfortunately, Captain Marsh was killed in action two years ago. That incident, along with Mama's absence, left Sera feeling quite fragile. I am happy to report, however, that I have received a letter from her. She regrets our separation and has booked passage on a ship leaving near the end of April. She should arrive in London from mid to late-June."

"Will she become active in the Season once she arrives?" Lady Danbury asked with interest.

Shaking her head, Minta said, "No, Sera doesn't wish to do so although I hope she will reconsider and accompany me to a few events. We are similar in size and she could wear anything in my wardrobe that she chose." She paused and then added, "Lady Danbury may have shared with you that I am seeking a husband during this Season. Since Sera is my closest confidante, I would like her opinion on any suitor that I might be interested in."

"I am happy for you that your sister will be joining you, "Lady Danbury said. "Even if she chooses not to partake in events of this Season, she—and you, Miss Nicholls—are invited to the house party my husband and I will hold in August after the Season concludes."

"A house party?" she asked. "I am unfamiliar with that, my

lady."

Her Grace chuckled. "Miss Nicholls, there is nothing like a good house party. They usually last ten days to two weeks and are full of so many activities that your head will spin."

"What kind of activities?"

Lady Middlefield smiled. "Things that are usually done in the country. Riding and walking and sometimes hunting. Picnics and boating. And all kinds of lawn games."

"It sounds wonderful," she said, awed to think of Sera and herself in such exalted company. "I am grateful to think you would ask Sera and me to attend."

"House parties are more than amiable gatherings," the duchess told Minta. "While the activities are delightful, the true purpose of many house parties is to encourage a match between eligible men and women. The relaxed nature and small numbers in attendance guarantee the chance for those seeking a spouse to get to know one another in a more intimate atmosphere."

Lady Middlefield added, "It is hard sometimes to get to learn much about a gentleman during the Season. Do not feel compelled to commit to anyone unless you truly know his nature. A house party is ideal for deeper conversations. You might choose to put off accepting any offers and go into this house party with an open mind."

"Since you mentioned your sister is shy, she might be more comfortable stepping into Polite Society at a house party instead of being overwhelmed at a ball or some other *ton* event," the duchess said. "Who knows? Your twin might find her perfect match and avoid having to hunt for a husband next Season." She looked to Lady Danbury. "You must let me help you prepare the guest list, Tessa. I will keep in mind which bachelors might make for good husbands for the Misses Nicholls."

Minta found this information fascinating and eye-opening. Sera would certainly prefer a setting involving a smaller group of people.

"Rest assured that Lord and Lady Westlake are also welcomed to come," Lady Danbury said. "My cousins and their husbands and children will be there, as well. Also someone you have met, Miss Nicholls. Lord Kingston and his cousin, the Duke of Woodmont."

Minta's cheeks burned at the mention of Lord Kingston. Then she realized what Lady Danbury had said regarding the marquess' cousin.

"You mentioned the Duke of Woodmont."

Lady Danbury smiled radiantly. "Yes, the final Second Son is now home from the military. Lord Kingston's older cousin recently passed and so his younger cousin and great friend has returned after selling his commission. His Grace has gone to Essex and his country seat to adjust to his new role in life but he has promised me he will come to our house party."

The duchess looked at Minta with interest. "So, you have met Lord Kingston. What did you think of him?"

The question startled her and Lady Middlefield chuckled, saying, "My cousin can be quite direct, Miss Nicholls. I hope you don't mind her boldness."

"I was direct before I was a duchess and now that I am one, I can get away with so much more." Mischief twinkled in Her Grace's eyes. "I noticed you blushed when Kingston's name was mentioned, Miss Nicholls. He is like a brother to the three of us and a brother to our husbands as well."

"Yes, he has told me of the Second Sons."

"Has he?" Lady Danbury asked. "That means you must have seen him since my husband and I departed from Kingwood."

"I have, my lady," she told the trio. "He came to visit me after I sprained my ankle, bringing me flowers. He came another time to visit, as well."

She felt her face flame as she recalled the marquess' fervent kisses.

Her Grace leaned over and took Minta's hand. "Tell us every-thing, Miss Nicholls." She squeezed her hand encouragingly.

Hesitantly, she said, "I believed we formed a small attachment. Sera, my twin, is quite shy. Especially around those she has just met. Lord Kingston was extremely quiet the night he and Lord and Lady Danbury came to dine with my aunt, uncle, and me. I guessed his nature was much like Sera's and we spoke of it."

"You did?" Lady Middlefield asked. "Why, that is wonderful. Percy does not open up to many people. He must trust you greatly to have done so."

Percy. She had not known the marquess' Christian name until now and smiled, thinking it fit him well.

"He's kissed you, hasn't he?" Her Grace suddenly asked.

Color and heat flooded Minta's cheeks and the duchess said, "I knew it!"

"I did not say Lord Kingston had, Your Grace," she protested.

The duchess smiled triumphantly. Squeezing Minta's hand again, she said, "Percy is notoriously reserved. To have shared a kiss with you and told you about the Second Sons means a great deal, Miss Nicholls." She paused. "I have a feeling the two of you will get to know each other much better as the Season begins. Or even before," she mused.

"What are you thinking?" Lady Middlefield asked. When the duchess did not immediately reply, the countess told Minta, "Her Grace was known as a matchmaker before her own marriage to the Duke of Camden. She recommended certain young ladies to a handful of eligible bachelors each year."

"And was quite successful at it," Lady Danbury added.

The duchess finally released Minta's hand and looked at her sagely. "Since Percy is so comfortable in your company, Miss Nicholls, we will have to see that he is in it more often—even before the Season begins. By the time it arrives, he might have already made up his mind regarding a bride."

"What do you suggest?" Lady Middlefield asked. "A dinner? A trip to the theatre?"

"Why not both?" Lady Danbury said. "I do not mind hosting Lord and Lady Westlake at dinner tomorrow evening. Of course, we are down in numbers with Owen having gone to Woodbridge for the week with Win." She glanced to Minta. "Each of our three husbands is spending a week with the new Duke of Woodmont, tutoring him in estate matters and the duties of a duke."

"Then we must invite an extra gentleman to balance the numbers." Looking at Minta, Her Grace added, "It must be a bachelor, of course. No sense in having another male unless he is someone new we can introduce Miss Nicholls to. We can't have her putting all her eggs into one basket in case she and Percy do not suit."

She shook her head. "I am not certain that Lord Kingston is quite ready to see me," Minta shared. "You see, he left Essex rather abruptly. After he kissed me. He apologized—and was gone."

All three women looked at her knowingly and Lady Danbury said, "Then it is imperative that we bring the two of you together as soon as possible to end any awkwardness." She grinned. "And encourage him to possibly kiss you again."

"That would be wonderful, my lady," she said to her hostess.

The door opened and Minta looked up to see two very dashing gentlemen entering the drawing room.

And Lord Kingston trailed after them.

CHAPTER TEN

P ERCY LEFT HIS solicitor's office with two recommendations regarding a business manager. He would bring up the subject when he saw Ev and Spence in a few minutes. He directed his coachman to the Camdens' townhouse and climbed inside his vehicle, settling against the plush cushions.

Closing his eyes, he lost himself—again—in his kisses with Minta. The young woman haunted him by day. Percy only wished she would invade his dreams and banish the nightmares that continued to grow in both length and severity. He awoke in the middle of the night, terrified, afraid to go back to sleep. When he finally did, usually dawn was breaking and what little rest he did receive did not leave him refreshed. With the odd hours of the Season approaching, he hoped he would be so exhausted that he would fall into bed in a dreamless sleep.

He arrived at Ev's townhouse and went inside, finding his friend in his study along with Spence.

"Have a seat, Percy," his friend told him. "Spence and I were discussing Win."

"I still cannot believe Win is back among us," he admitted. "I hope Owen is doing a good job of showing him the ropes at Woodbridge."

Spence chuckled. "Who would have thought Owen would have become so responsible? Louisa has done a world of good for him. He has settled nicely into his role as Earl of Danbury and even more so into the roles of husband and father."

"Who is the next of you to travel to Essex?" Percy asked.

"I have decided it will be me," Ev stated. "Adalyn is becoming increasingly busy with the Season about to begin. She definitely is looking upon you as her next project, Percy."

He flushed, uncomfortable with the attention being focused upon him, especially regarding marriage. Although he saw how happy his friends were in their marriages, he still believed himself to be poor husband material. He had even toyed with the idea of not attending the Season and merely waiting for the house party Owen and Louisa would host in late-August.

"I see that look in your eyes, Percy," Spence said. "Do not even think of backing out of attending the Season. Not after all the work the Three Cousins are putting in on your behalf."

Spence's astuteness did not surprise Percy. "You know I am not fond of social situations," he said.

"You don't have to be," Ev declared. "You have three Second Sons and our wives in your corner. We will help you through any situation that comes up. That includes introductions to the right women. Trust Adalyn and the others in this matter, Percy. She really does have a knack for putting the right people together."

But Percy didn't want to be put with any women.

Because he yearned for Minta Nicholls.

Pushing that thought aside, he asked, "When are we leaving for White's?"

Both his friends looked startled and Spence said, "We were only waiting for you to appear before we left. I am surprised you wish to go. Owen had to drag you to the club the other day."

Owen had taken Percy to White's and introduced him to a handful of peers. They had settled into deep, leather chairs, called for a brandy, and Percy had picked up a newspaper, keeping his nose in it the entire time they were there. Occasionally, he would give surreptitious glances about the room and was relieved that no one seemed to be paying a bit of attention to him.

"We might as well take my carriage," he offered. "It is waiting outside. I just came from my solicitor's office. He recommended two different business managers to me but I wanted to talk it over with the two of you. And Owen, when he returns to town since he seems pleased with his man."

They left the townhouse and talked business in the carriage. It pulled up at White's and they descended from it, entering the gentlemen's club.

Mr. Orr greeted them and asked if there was anything special they might like. Ev looked to his companions and then told the host, "Only coffee for Lord Middlefield and me. Please bring tea to Lord Kingston."

They went inside and Ev introduced Percy to a few other peers in the room. They took a seat and Percy started to reach for the newspaper on the table. Spence shook his head. Their beverages arrived and already White's knew exactly how Percy took his tea. He supposed that was one of the many perks of being a peer of the realm and member of the most exclusive club in London.

"Your Grace, Lord Middlefield, how good to see you here."

He looked up and saw two men standing nearby and rose as his companions did the same.

"It is good to see you, my lords," Spence said. "The last time we truly spoke was when we attended the house party given by Their Graces." Spence turned and indicated Percy to these newcomers. "Might I introduce you to a dear friend of ours, the Earl of Kingston. This is Viscount Boxling and the Earl of Markham."

Percy greeted the two men with his usual reserve and they joined them, both asking for a brandy, which appeared almost immediately. He supposed it was the usual drink of the pair and had already been poured before they'd even requested it.

The handsome viscount met Percy's gaze and said, "I am sorry for your loss, Kingston. I was friendly with your brother. We boxed several times in bouts at Gentleman Jack's. He was an incredibly honorable man."

His throat tightened with emotion. "Thank you for your kind words, my lord."

Talk shifted to Percy's estate and both Viscount Boxling and Lord Markham asked about it and his tenants. Boxling mentioned he had come into his title just over two years ago and still mourned his father's passing deeply.

"Will you be attending the Season, Kingston?" Lord Markham asked.

"Yes, I have already made a commitment to a few events."

"I am certain your two friends here will take excellent care of you, along with Lord Danbury. Their wives, also, will make sure you have an enjoyable time," Boxling said.

Lord Markham gazed intently at Percy and asked, "Are you considering perusing the Marriage Mart, my lord?"

Taken aback by the frank question, Percy merely nodded.

Lord Markham nodded. "Both Boxling and I will be doing the same."

Talk shifted away from the Season to politics and Percy retreated within himself, listening but adding nothing to the conversation. When Ev announced they needed to depart, both noblemen shook Percy's hand again and told him they looked forward to spending more time with him.

In the carriage, Ev said, "Both of them attended our house party two summers ago. Boxling was very interested in Louisa and almost wrested her away from Owen."

"Truly?" Percy asked. "I cannot see Louisa choosing anyone else but Owen. They are so perfect together."

Spence chuckled. "Oh, Owen was hellbent on not wedding for a good five years or more," he revealed. "He said that he had spent so much time away from England and civilized company that he was going to enjoy working his way through all the pretty women in Polite Society before he ever bothered choosing a wife and settling down. It almost cost him Louisa, however."

"We all knew they were meant for each other," Ev said. "But

Owen was his usual hardheaded self. Thank goodness he came to his senses and offered for Louisa. I have never seen him happier and I have known him practically from the cradle."

Percy had not known of Owen's reluctance to wed and yet he was glad his friend had chosen Louisa for his countess. Once again, he wondered if he would find a woman willing to put up with his many shortcomings.

The carriage slowed and Ev said, "Come in with us, Percy, and see the Three Cousins. Adalyn and Tessa took my carriage here and the four of us can ride back in it together."

He protested. "No, go in without me."

Ev's brows shot up. "And tell my duchess that you refused to come in and say hello? I know what battles to pick—and none of them are with my wife. You are coming in to say hello and since it's teatime, you can drink a cup of tea and be on your way."

"All right," he agreed reluctantly.

As they exited the carriage, Spence said, "You usually have a dance lesson in the afternoons. Perhaps after tea, you can work in a short one."

The idea of practicing his dancing appealed to Percy and he entered the Danbury townhouse with a lighter step. Following his friends up the staircase, they moved down the hallway and entered the drawing room.

As they crossed the room, Percy's heart hammered wildly in his chest.

Minta was here . . .

His gaze met hers and her jaw dropped slightly, letting him know that she had not been aware of the subterfuge organized by his friends. Both Spence and Ev strode quickly to their wives, kissing their cheeks, and Ev asked for Louisa to ring for three more teacups.

As she did so, Percy joined the group, quietly greeting every-one.

"I hope we are not inconveniencing you, Louisa," he said, feeling the flush fill his face.

"Not at all, Percy. I had invited Miss Nicholls to join us for tea today in order for her to meet my cousins."

He glanced quickly at Minta and saw her cheeks burned bright red, as well.

"We were discussing just a moment ago about how I wished to repay the kindness Lord and Lady Westlake showed Owen and me when we were visiting you at Kingwood. I have decided to invite them for dinner tomorrow evening, along with Miss Nicholls, of course. I hope that is acceptable to the three of you."

Ev and Spence nodded, with Spence saying, "Tessa is in charge of our social calendar. If it agrees with her, we are happy to come to dinner."

Louisa said, "With Owen in the country helping Win, our numbers will be uneven. I would like to ask another gentleman to join us. Do you have any suggestions? Did you see anyone at White's?"

Ev spoke up. "As a matter of fact, we saw Lord Boxling and Lord Markham and even talked about the house party we had all attended together."

Adalyn smiled. "That was a good time, bringing Louisa and Owen together. Do you think either of them might like to attend the dinner?"

Percy bit back his response, which would have been to invite neither man. Lord Markham had proved quite friendly and jovial, while Lord Boxling was far too good-looking. Percy didn't want either man around Minta.

He had to stop thinking of her that way. Merely because they had kissed, it did not mean they should be on a first-name basis. *Miss Nicholls*, he told himself. *Think of her as Miss Nicholls.*

"I think Boxling would be a good addition," Spence said. "That is, if you are comfortable inviting him, Louisa."

Louisa looked confused. "Why would I not want to invite Lord Boxling to dinner? He is most charming and affable."

"Well, he did pursue you," Spence said. "I don't know how Owen would feel having the viscount under his roof."

"First of all, Owen is not here. Second, Viscount Boxling is a friend of ours. He and I came to an understanding regarding my feelings for Owen. In fact, he is so kind, perhaps Adalyn would consider taking Lord Boxling under her wing this year and helping him find that bride he is looking for."

As long as Boxling did not want Miss Nicholls as his bride, Percy would be fine with the viscount coming to dinner.

"Then it is settled," Louisa declared. "I will write to him after tea and invite him."

"What of Percy's dance lesson?" asked Tessa. She looked to Miss Nicholls and said, "The three of us have been teaching Lord Kingston to dance since he did not already possess that skill and it is necessary for anyone attending the Season."

"We can do so after tea," Adalyn said. Looking at Miss Nicholls, she added, "Would you mind staying on and helping out? We have practiced with a few couples recently and I think it would be good to continue to do so. And you must dance the waltz, Miss Nicholls. Percy is getting tired of the Three Cousins as one of his partners. It would do him good having someone new to partner with."

Percy cursed inwardly. Adalyn had just sent him into one of Dante's circles of Hell.

CHAPTER ELEVEN

MINTA WAS THRILLED that she had been asked to stay and dance with the group, especially with the Marquess of Kingston.

The only problem was that she did not yet know how to waltz.

Mama had told her daughters of this beautiful, intimate dance and they were to learn it once they returned to London to make their come-outs years ago. The waltz had yet to arrive in Upper Canada and so the handful of assemblies she and her twin had attended had not seen it danced. Before she left Ontario, Mama had said Aunt Phyllis would hire a dance master in order for Minta to properly learn the steps.

When she had brought this up with her aunt, Uncle West had immediately spoken up, telling her that she didn't need any dance master when he could easily teach her to waltz, something he enjoyed. They were supposed to start their lessons once they returned to town but she had been so busy the past few days they had yet to do so.

Now, she was confronted with an awkward situation. Though she longed to be in the marquess' arms, how could she when she had no idea of the steps of the dance?

Before she could speak up and reveal her lack of dance knowledge, the Duchess of Camden had everyone on their feet, practically marching them to Lady Danbury's ballroom as if she were an officer leading soldiers into battle.

They entered the ballroom and Minta saw a pianoforte sitting there.

Lady Danbury said, "I will play for you today since Owen is missing." She made her way to the instrument and sat, starting to play a series of scales to warm up her fingers.

Drawn to the speed and complexity of the scales, Minta left the group and went to stand by Lady Danbury, watching her fingers fly across the keys. After a few minutes, the countess stopped, looking up and smiling.

"Do you play the pianoforte?" she asked.

Minta nodded. "I do both sing and play."

"Then you will have to do so for us after dinner tomorrow night."

Her Grace appeared and asked, "Are you ready, Louisa?"

Lady Danbury nodded and Her Grace led Minta back to the others. The duchess then elaborated on which dances they would practice and Minta noticed His Grace's lips twitching in amusement. More than that, however, she saw the look of love the duke bestowed upon his wife. Minta had seen such a look pass between Lord and Lady Danbury and many times between her parents. It made her think that perhaps she should be open to finding love this Season. Mama had given up the many luxuries that a title would bring in order to marry Papa but Minta knew just how happy her parents had been over the years.

His Grace cleared his throat and said, "I think we understand the battle plan, my love." He glanced to Minta and said, "My wife can be what the rest of us call a force of nature. She can become swept up in her plans. I hope you are not feeling overwhelmed, Miss Nicholls."

Before Minta could reply, Her Grace said, "Miss Nicholls is a woman of quality, both intelligent and understanding. Of course, she is ready to face any situation, and that includes dancing."

The duchess called out to her cousin, "The reel first, if you would, Louisa."

They took their places, Minta standing beside Lord Kingston, and the music began. A few of the dances they ran through were meant for four couples and so they merely pretended another couple was there and danced with air during those few times.

They practiced another reel, followed by two country dances, and Minta was feeling slightly out of breath when a maid rolled in a cart. On it were glasses of lemonade and the servants distributed them to everyone. Minta tried to sip but wound up greedily guzzling her beverage instead.

"Now that we have had some refreshments, it is time for us to practice the waltz."

Minta cleared her throat and said, "I am afraid I won't be able to participate in this, Your Grace. I have yet to learn how to waltz. My uncle was to teach me once we came to town but we have only been here a short time and I have been involved in a flurry of dress fittings. I am sorry to disappoint you."

Instead of disappointment, she saw the duchess' eyes gleam with interest.

"Oh, that is even better," Her Grace proclaimed.

Confusion filled her as the duchess smiled at her.

"The best way to test if you truly know something is to teach it to another," Her Grace declared. Looking to Lord Kingston, she added, "You have learned how to waltz and now you are going to teach Miss Nicholls how to do so, Percy."

Minta watched as the marquess' face turned scarlet. She felt herself blush to her roots, realizing they both were mortified.

Lady Middlefield patted Minta on the back and said, "That is a lovely idea. But I believe it will go better if you do not have an audience watching your every move." Turning to the others, she said, "Shall we return to the drawing for an hour and allow these two to have their lesson in private?"

By now, Lady Danbury had joined them and she agreed it was an excellent idea. The group exited the ballroom, leaving Minta alone with Lord Kingston.

"I . . . am sorry," he sputtered. "Adalyn has a tendency to take charge of every situation. If you are uncomfortable with this idea, she did not give you a chance to express your opinion. I will understand if—"

"I am fine with the idea if you are, my lord," she interrupted. "I have to learn at some point and the sooner that occurs, the more I will be able to practice and become comfortable with the dance. Since you yourself have just learned it, I believe you will make for a fine teacher."

She hadn't thought he could turn any redder, but he did.

"If you insist," he said.

"I don't insist, my lord," she told him. "I merely thought since you had recently learned the waltz yourself, you would make for a good teacher and be able to give me a few hints as my short-comings arise."

His gaze penetrated her and he said, "I doubt you have any shortcomings at all, Miss Nicholls. Not a one."

Warmth filled her at the compliment. She swallowed and managed to say, "Shall we begin?"

His brow creased a moment in thought and she remained quiet and still, letting him work out whatever was going on inside his head.

Then he looked up and smiled.

Her heart slammed against her ribs.

"I think I've got it now," he said, looking confident. "I just needed to think about how to do things in reverse since we perform opposite steps from one another." He paused. "Thank you for trusting me with this task."

She would trust him with anything at this moment.

He came to stand beside her. "May I take your hand?"

She offered it without speaking. His fingers wrapped around hers, sending the most delightful ripple through her. She blinked a few times, fighting to concentrate on his words.

"This isn't how we will stand when we partner but I want to help guide you along as I teach you."

"Thank you," she said softly. "I believe I will need all the guidance you can offer to me."

"The foundation of the waltz is a box step. Our movement creates a square on the floor. You will move backward, step to your side, and then step again to close your feet so they end up together. Like this."

The marquess had her step back with her left foot, sweep her right foot to the side, and then had her left foot join the right. They practiced the motion several times.

"It is a backward half-box," she decided.

"Let us add to that movement," he said.

They repeated the steps, her hand held in his, and then he had her move forward, completing another half-box, her right foot moving forward, the left going to the side, and the right foot joining it again, closing out the box.

"I see," she said, eagerness filling her as she caught on to the steps.

"It is done to a count of three. Slow, quick, quick. Slow, quick, quick," he explained.

Once again, Lord Kingston helped Minta move through the backward steps, followed by the forward ones. They repeated them several times.

"I like this," she said. "It is not nearly as difficult as I had imagined."

"We should concentrate now on being light on our toes. It is toe and heel action."

He released her hand and demonstrated to her, speaking aloud as he did.

"Toe, heel, toe-toe, heel. Then heel, toe, toe-toe, heel."

Minta frowned. "Could you do it again, please?"

"Yes, but only with you. Come."

He offered his hand again and she took it, thinking how right it felt to hold this man's hand.

"Say it aloud with me as we move," he suggested.

She did so, moving with him as they spoke together. He

urged her to continue and they repeated the action multiple times, moving across the ballroom.

"That's excellent, Minta," he praised.

He had called her Minta . . .

She held her breath, afraid he would realize he had done so and find the moment ruined. He didn't, however, and turned to face her.

"I think we are ready to try together," he told her. "Place your left hand on my shoulder."

Moving closer, she lifted her hand and rested it on his coat. He slipped his right hand to her back, and she realized just how close they stood. Her heart hammered wildly as he clasped her right hand in his left. They stood motionless, their gazes fixed, no words between them. She inhaled the spice of his cologne. Felt the warmth of his body, so close that it almost touched hers.

The marquess blinked, breaking the spell, and said, "I will begin counting now. Count along with me if you choose to do so. I will count to three and then we shall begin. One, two, three."

Then they began moving as one as he guided her through the steps, slowly at first. She made a few mistakes, colliding with him, but they both laughed and shrugged it off, taking their places again and starting from the beginning. Her pulse raced as she looked up into his chocolate brown eyes, which gazed upon her in approval.

He stopped counting but still held her. "I think you are ready to try a turn."

"There are turns?" she squeaked.

He chuckled. "Yes. You have mastered the steps. We'll merely turn a quarter and rotate the box we form. Are you game to try so?"

Wanting to please him, she told him, "Yes."

"This time, I alone will count," he informed her.

He began the count and they took off. Before she realized it, he eased her into a turn. Then another and another. A thrill shot through her.

"This is marvelous," she proclaimed.

He grinned boyishly. "Wait until we are dancing to music."

Minta didn't think any dance in a ballroom full of others would ever be as good as the one right now. Lord Kingston continued to count but his voice grew softer and softer until he wasn't counting at all and they simply moved to an unheard beat they both sensed.

"That is marvelous," a voice called out and she heard applause.

Looking across the ballroom, she saw that the others had returned. Lord Kingston brought them to a halt and released her. Immediately, she felt bereft and clasped her hands in front of her, gripping them tightly.

The duchess glided toward them gracefully, almost as if she danced across the ballroom floor to them.

"You moved together as one," she said, her tone awed. "I can't remember anyone I know picking up the steps of the waltz so flawlessly in such a short amount of time."

Her cheeks heated as she said, "Lord Kingston is an excellent teacher. Methodical and easy to understand. His instructions were very clear and he is quite light on his feet. I merely followed his lead."

Lady Middlefield smiled. "There is much more to a waltz than merely following your partner, Miss Nicholls. I do agree it helps if you have a partner who is skilled, however." She smiled at the marquess.

"It will be even better when I play for you," Lady Danbury told her. "You play yourself so you understand how you can feel music in your soul."

"You play?" Lord Kingston asked.

"And she sings," Lady Danbury said with a smile. "I have already asked Miss Nicholls if she would entertain us after dinner tomorrow night and she has agreed."

"It sounds as if dinner tomorrow evening will be quite enjoyable," His Grace said. "In the meantime, I am ready to waltz with my wife."

The duke slipped a possessive arm about his wife's waist and took her hand in his, smiling at her with great affection.

"You always have loved to dance," the duchess purred, cradling his cheek.

Minta turned away, feeling as if she intruded upon an intimate moment between the couple but saw Lord and Lady Middlefield also coming together, a tender smile on his face as he gazed down at his wife.

She whirled and saw Lady Danbury moving to the pianoforte.

"It gets a bit uncomfortable," Lord Kingston said softly. He glanced at the two couples and back at her. "Seeing them behave so affectionately toward one another. I don't know if they do so when in Polite Society but they are forever making me blush at their antics."

He chuckled and she bit her lip. "It is quite different from how others seem to behave."

The marquess offered her his hand. "Shall we, Miss Nicholls?"

He was back to addressing her formally and she realized he had not picked up on his earlier slip of the tongue.

"Yes, my lord," Minta said demurely.

He clasped her hand and his other hand settled upon her back. Heat shot through her.

Lady Danbury began to play and he said, "No counting aloud. Simply feel the music."

Then he swept her away.

Minta didn't know how long the waltz went on, only that by its end, her entire body tingled with the excitement of being held close by this handsome man as he guided her about the ballroom floor, twirling her with ease.

The music came to a halt and he held her a moment longer, their gazes connected. She licked her lips and saw his eyes drop to them. Oh, how she wished they were alone so that he might kiss her again.

Lord Kingston released her and bowed. "You are the best pupil I have had the pleasure of tutoring, Miss Nicholls."

She dropped him a curtsey. "And I have never enjoyed learning anything more than the waltz, my lord. Thank you."

He escorted her back to the others, where Lady Danbury praised how the two of them had moved as one.

"You looked as if you were meant to dance the waltz together," she declared. "Others will think so, as well. I think you should commit to dancing the waltz at the first ball of the Season. It will be hosted by Lord and Lady Blakeney."

"I concur," His Grace said. "You dance the waltz as it was meant to be danced. And just think—this was your first time."

"Perhaps the two of you should practice again before the Season begins," suggested Her Grace.

"That isn't necessary," Lord Kingston said quickly. "Miss Nicholls knows exactly what she is doing."

Disappointment filled her and she wondered why he would not want to dance with her again.

"But I would be happy to claim a waltz with you at the Blakeney ball," he added, the tips of his ears going red.

"Then the dance will be yours, my lord," Minta promised.

CHAPTER TWELVE

Minta dismissed Bertha and tried to quell the butterflies in her belly. She glanced to the mirror, seeing her image and knowing she looked her best in the emerald green evening gown. She'd had Bertha style her hair simply, sweeping it into a low chignon, and Minta was pleased with the results.

A soft knock sounded and she bid her visitor to enter. It surprised her to see her uncle there.

"My dear, don't you look lovely this evening?" he said before closing the door behind him.

"Thank you, Uncle West. I would not look this way if not for you splurging on my wardrobe for this Season. I cannot convey my gratitude enough. Not only for me, but what you will do for Sera when she arrives in England."

She had shared the contents of Sera's letter with her aunt and uncle and they all eagerly looked forward to her twin's arrival in London come summer.

Her uncle handed her a small box, saying, "I meant to give these to you on the opening night of the Season but I think you should have them now."

Curious, she opened the velvet box and found a pair of diamond earrings. Raising her eyes, she asked, "These are for me?"

"Yes. Every woman needs a good piece of jewelry that will enhance both her beauty and wardrobe."

"But . . . this is too much," Minta protested.

He placed his hands on her shoulders. "Please accept the earrings, Minta. You and Sera are the closest I will ever have to having children of my own. I want to do for you when I can."

A moment of sadness touched her, knowing her aunt and uncle had not been blessed with children of their own. Uncle West's title would pass to his younger brother upon his death—or his nephew. Neither man was a good one and Uncle West had been estranged from them for many years. Selfishly, Minta hoped she would not be barren as Aunt Phyllis and provide the expected heir to her future husband.

Smiling, she leaned up and kissed his cheek. "I will wear them each night of the Season—and tonight. After all, we will be dining with a duke and duchess."

She turned and sat at her dressing table, placing the box upon it and lifting the first sparkling earring from its resting place before attaching it to her earlobe. She did the same with the other and admired herself in the mirror a moment before rising again.

"They suit you," her uncle said. "Phyllis said you were at tea quite a long time yesterday."

"It was actually more than tea," she explained. "After it, I had a dance lesson. I learned the steps of the waltz."

"You did? I thought I was supposed to teach you."

"You will need to practice with me before the Blakeney ball," she insisted. "But the Duchess of Camden was most insistent."

He chuckled. "Yes, she can be quite insistent. She was headstrong before Camden wed her and she is unstoppable as a duchess."

"She and her two cousins have been teaching Lord Kingston how to dance."

"The marquess did not know how to dance?" her uncle asked, aghast.

"Apparently not. You must remember that he was in the army for almost a decade. I don't think much dancing occurred as the Anglo-alliance marched all across Europe engaging Bonaparte and his forces."

"I suppose not," he mused. "So, you danced with the marquess?"

She hoped she wouldn't blush as she said, "Those at tea practiced several group dances and then Her Grace said Lord Kingston and I should waltz. I told her I did not know how."

"Who taught you the steps?"

Heat filled her cheeks as she said, "Actually, Lord Kingston did, at Her Grace's suggestion. She said by him instructing me in the dance, it would help firm up his own lessons."

"I see." Uncle West studied her a moment. "Did you learn from him?"

"He made it very easy for me. He was an excellent tutor. Lady Danbury played the pianoforte and we all wound up waltzing together."

Minta thought it wise not to mention that she and the marquess had been alone for a good hour during their lesson since she didn't think her uncle would like that idea very much.

"Let's see if the lessons stuck."

Uncle West held out his arms and she stepped to him, assuming the position the marquess had taught her. Humming, her uncle guided her smoothly about the bedchamber. He was an accomplished dancer but she thought Lord Kingston moved more gracefully.

Coming to a halt, he released her and gruffly said, "Kingston did an adequate job. We will practice tomorrow morning after breakfast in our ballroom."

"That would be wonderful," she agreed. "The more I can practice, the better I will be at the steps."

He smiled at her. "A good waltzer is always in demand. We'll find you a husband for certain, Minta. We should get downstairs, though. Your aunt will be waiting."

After the short carriage ride to the Danbury townhouse, they entered, the butler greeting them by name and leading them upstairs to the drawing room. She spied Lady Danbury, along with the Duke and Duchess of Camden. The others apparently had yet to arrive.

"Lord and Lady Westlake, how good of you to come this evening," Lady Danbury said. "And Miss Nicholls, always a delight to see you again."

They exchanged pleasantries as Lord and Lady Middlefield entered the room, accompanied by Lord Kingston. Minta took several deep, slow breaths, hoping her pounding heart wouldn't run away and cause her to faint.

The marquess looked so handsome tonight in his dark, formal clothes, which were impeccably tailored. His shoulders looked even broader than usual.

More greetings were exchanged and she saw he made a point of looking her aunt and uncle in the eyes and making a few remarks instead of tersely saying hello and turning away. It touched her at the effort he made.

Then he looked to her and her heart caught in her throat.

"Miss Nicholls," he said, his voice deep as he claimed her hand and kissed her fingers. Even with both of their hands gloved, she felt the scorching heat and swallowed.

"Lord Kingston," she said, her voice quivering just a bit.

He held her hand a moment longer than he should have and then released it as a newcomer joined them. Minta caught the slight frown before the marquess composed his features.

"Ah, Lord Boxling," Lady Danbury said. "I am so happy you could join us for dinner."

"I know I am no substitute for Danbury," he said affably. "I hear your husband is off in the country helping his friend."

"Yes, the Duke of Woodmont," Lady Danbury confirmed. "He recently came into his title and my husband is spending a week in Essex with him at Woodbridge, the ducal country seat."

"Then I will take my turn," His Grace said. "Middlefield will finish up. We are each spending a week with our old friend, helping him find his way through the mountain of responsibilities."

"I think you know everyone present except for Miss Nicholls," the countess continued, glancing at Minta. "Viscount Boxling, may I introduce Miss Araminta Nicholls, niece to Lord and Lady Westlake."

The viscount turned his gaze on her. He was six feet, with dark hair and eyes, and one of the most handsome men Minta had ever seen.

Taking her hand, he held it a moment as he gazed at her, then kissed her fingers. "The pleasure is all mine, Miss Nicholls. I do hope you are in town to attend the upcoming Season."

"I am," she said breathlessly, taken aback by his good looks.

"Boxling and I knew each other from university," the duke said. "He is one of the smartest individuals I have encountered—and that includes Wellington."

"Is anyone as clever as Wellington?" the viscount asked.

Minta saw Lord Kingston frown slightly and wondered why he didn't seem to like Lord Boxling.

Two footmen came around with trays of drinks and she took one, sipping on it, glad to have something to do with her hands. They talked as a large group for the next few minutes until the butler announced dinner.

"Cook has promised us a surprise," Lady Danbury said. "Shall we go in?"

The married couples paired up quickly, leaving her and Lady Danbury to be escorted by the two single gentlemen.

Lord Kingston said, "Might I escort you in to dinner, Miss Nicholls?" and offered her his arm, leaving Lord Boxling to do the same with Lady Danbury.

Minta took it and they were the last to leave the drawing room.

"Why don't you like Lord Boxling?" she asked quietly.

"I made no such statement."

"You didn't have to," she pointed out.

"He . . . was interested in Louisa—Lady Danbury—at one time."

"But you were still at war, my lord. And Lady Danbury married Lord Danbury. It is easy to see they adore one another."

"I am loyal to my friends," he said succinctly. "I did meet Boxling the other day at White's."

"Did he make an ill impression upon you?"

"No, he was rather agreeable," the marquess admitted. "Just don't let his oozing charm dazzle you."

She bit her lip, realizing the marquess might be just a tad jealous of Lord Boxling's presence tonight. Since she was the only unattached female present, it gave her a slight thrill that Lord Kingston might not wish her to show any interest in the viscount.

"It takes more than charm to interest me, my lord."

They reached the dining room and he led her to her seat.

Which was right next to Lord Boxling.

And Lord Kingston was on her right.

Oh, this was going to be a very interesting meal.

PERCY THOUGHT DINNER would never end.

He had never experienced jealousy before tonight. Oh, he had upon occasion been a bit envious when one of his friends scored better on an exam than he did but that had been fleeting. He had never truly had any type of relationship with a woman, much less one he cared for.

And he had come to realize that he cared deeply for Minta Nicholls.

While he still believed she deserved a much better man than he could ever be, he did not like her paying attention to Lord Boxling. Under any other circumstances, Percy might have actually tried to make friends with the viscount. He had seemed interesting the other day at White's. Now, however, Percy saw the man as a competitor. Unfortunately, if tonight was a race?

He would be losing by a good amount.

Miss Nicholls had done her best to include him in conversation but Percy had been reluctant to enter it. Eventually, she turned her attention to her left, where Lord Boxling sat. The viscount occupied a good portion of her time during dinner. He wanted to kick himself, wishing for the thousandth time that his nature was different and he could be open and charming as Rupert had been.

Louisa said, "It looks as though it is time for the men to have their port. Shall we withdraw to the drawing room, ladies?"

The females rose and the countess added, "Don't be long, gentlemen. Miss Nicholls has agreed to sing and play for us once you join us."

"Do we really need a glass of port after such a lavish meal?" Lord Boxling asked. "I, for one, would be happy to forego it and head straight to the drawing room to hear Miss Nicholls play."

Ev rose. "That would be fine with me." He looked to Louisa. "My compliments to your cook. She outdid herself. Owen will be upset he missed such a wonderful meal."

The other gentlemen rose and Lord Boxling quickly claimed Miss Nicholls, leading her from the dining room. Glumly, Percy watched the others do the same and offered Louisa his arm.

"You did so well yesterday, Percy," she encouraged. "You talked with Miss Nicholls. You did a remarkable job of teaching her the waltz. Do not let your progress be stymied by anyone."

"You mean Lord Boxling," he said petulantly, as an angry child might.

Louisa halted. "Do not be sullen, Percy. It is not an attractive quality on anyone, man or woman. If you are interested in Miss Nicholls, then you must let her know."

"I thought I had."

He recalled kissing her and felt his ears grow warm.

"One time isn't enough. A woman needs to know of your interest in order to encourage your further interest in her. Remember, Miss Nicholls may be older than those making their come-outs this year but she has never been in Polite Society before. She might be feeling as lost as you are right now."

As they entered the drawing room, he heard Miss Nicholls' laugh.

Giving Louisa an eye roll, he said, "I don't think she's a bit lost. Why did you invite the fellow?"

"Because he is charming company. And if you aren't going to fight for Miss Nicholls, I think Lord Boxling would make for an excellent husband for her."

Her words angered him. "You want me mad, don't you?" he realized.

Louisa smiled. "All is fair in love and war." She lifted her hand from his arm and crossed the room.

This wasn't war. It certainly wasn't love. Yet Percy disliked the fact that Boxling was entertaining Miss Nicholls.

He watched as the viscount escorted her to the pianoforte before taking a seat directly in her line of view.

Suddenly, he had an idea and made his way toward her.

"Will you be using music, Miss Nicholls?" he asked. "If so, I would be happy to turn the pages for you."

Not that he read music. But he didn't want Boxling to be the one close to her.

Louisa said, "I have sheet music here for you to choose from, Miss Nicholls." She glanced questioningly at Percy.

"I have volunteered to turn the pages for Miss Nicholls," he informed her.

"Have you?" Louisa asked. "Why, that is certainly thought-ful." Turning to Miss Nicholls, she placed the stack on the nearby table. "Glance through this and see if there is anything here you wish to play for us."

"Thank you, my lady," Miss Nicholls said as she began perus-ing the pile. She pulled out two different pieces and returned to the pianoforte.

"Where would you like me to stand?" he asked.

"You may sit next to me, Lord Kingston. It will be easier, I believe. I will softly say 'now' when it is time for you to turn the page."

She took a seat and he sat beside her, inhaling the wonderful scent of vanilla. Percy glanced out and saw Lord Boxling frowning slightly.

Let him frown the rest of the night.

Percy was exactly where he wanted to be.

CHAPTER THIRTEEN

MINTA FOUGHT THE nerves filling her as Lady Danbury's guests looked on. She couldn't help but feel elated at Lord Kingston singling her out, wishing to sit with her at the pianoforte. At the same time, Lord Boxling sat directly across from her, nodding encouragingly.

Who would have thought she would have two such attractive men interested in her?

She knew it to be true. Lord Boxling's conversation throughout dinner was sparkling, causing Minta to laugh and feel free. And Lord Kingston had already kissed her and now sat possessively next to her, his large frame crowding her a bit. Oh, why couldn't Sera be here? She needed her twin's advice. The Season had yet to begin and already Minta believed she had two men vying for her hand.

She placed the sheet music before her. She had chosen a piece which she had practiced this afternoon, knowing Lady Danbury would ask her to play tonight. In truth, she did not even need the sheet music since she had the composition memorized. But the opportunity to have Lord Kingston sit next to her and turn the pages was too good to pass up.

She flexed her fingers a few times, not wanting to attempt any fancy scales to warm up as Lady Danbury had yesterday.

Taking a deep breath, she began to play.

Music could always transport her to another place but she made certain she remained aware of her surroundings. Something told her that Lord Kingston did not read music and so she would be able to tell him to turn the page whenever she chose. Her confidence grew as she continued playing and Minta found she nodded as a cue rather than telling the marquess to turn the page. He was in tune to her and reached up, flipping it with ease. She finished the sonata after several minutes and the invited guests all applauded enthusiastically. She felt the flush creep up her neck and spill onto her cheeks.

"Saying you play remarkably well would be an injustice," the marquess said quietly to her. "I enjoyed listening to you play very much."

His words caused a warm glow to fill her.

The Duchess of Camden said, "You must sing and play for us." Pausing, she added, "Oh, I have a better idea. Your voice, Miss Nicholls, is so high and sweet, while my cousin's is so low. Perhaps the two of you would care to perform a duet for us?"

Her Grace turned to Lady Middlefield. "Tessa, would you please accompany them?"

Lady Middlefield rose. "I would be delighted to do so."

Both Lady Middlefield and Lady Danbury moved toward the pianoforte and the three of them began discussing which song to perform. The marquess made an attempt to leave but Lady Middlefield said, "No, Percy, stay. You may turn the pages for me since you proved so skilled in doing so." The countess smiled at the marquess.

They decided what they would perform and Minta moved from her place, Lady Middlefield sliding next to Lord Kingston.

Lady Danbury took Minta's hand and squeezed it. "I have never sung with anyone else and am looking forward to this," she revealed. "I hope our voices will blend well together."

Minta glanced to Lady Middlefield and nodded and the countess began to play. Minta started singing and realized she did so alone. She gave a questioning glance to Lady Danbury, who merely shook her head. After a few moments, however, the countess joined in the song in a rich contralto.

She had never performed with anyone else either and was overjoyed by the end of their song, thinking their voices sounded as if they were meant to sing together. The gathered guests all rose and heartily applauded their effort. She glanced and saw Lord Boxling smiling warmly at her and then looked to see Lord Kingston doing the same.

"I think we should quit while we are ahead," Lady Danbury said. "It is always better to leave an audience wanting more than to overstay your welcome."

"I agree," she concurred.

They rejoined the others and talked for another hour about acquaintances they had in common and some of the early invitations that had been received for the Season.

She saw her aunt stifle a yawn and Uncle West, aware of that, said, "It has been a most delightful evening but we should take our leave."

Everyone rose and Lady Danbury escorted her guests downstairs.

"I am so sorry we did not have Lord Danbury's company this evening," Aunt Phyllis remarked. "Perhaps once he has returned from the country, we can have you come for dinner."

"This has been one of the most delightful evenings I have experienced in a long time," Lord Boxling noted. "Thank you for including me, my lady."

Minta saw the look in her aunt's eyes and knew what would be coming next.

"It was enchanting to make your acquaintance, Lord Boxling. Perhaps you would care to come to tea tomorrow afternoon." Then seeing her invitation might be awkward, Aunt Phyllis looked to the marquess and added, "You are also welcome, Lord Kingston."

Quickly, the marquess said, "I will be there, Lady Westlake. Thank you for the invitation."

All eyes turned to Lord Boxling and the viscount said, "I, too, would be happy to come to tea. I also have a new curricle I am ready to test." He faced Minta and said, "Perhaps you would care to go for a drive in it with me after tea, Miss Nicholls."

Not knowing if that was allowed or not under Polite Society's rules, Minta turned to her aunt. "What do you think, Aunt Phyllis?"

"I think it a marvelous idea, my lord. Of course, my niece will accompany you for a drive after tea. It was quite thoughtful of you to ask, my lord."

Minta saw the satisfied smile on Lord Boxling's sensual lips and the flash of anger that sparked in Lord Kingston's eyes. She bit back a smile, thinking it wouldn't hurt if the marquess was just a tiny bit jealous.

Uncle West escorted them to their carriage and once inside the vehicle, he said, "That was a most enjoyable evening."

"It was beyond enjoyable," Aunt Phyllis insisted. "Why, I do believe that Minta has garnered her first suitor even before the Season has begun. Viscount Boxling is everything a gentleman should be. Handsome. Attentive. Friendly. Any woman would be happy if he chose to court them."

"It doesn't matter what you think of him, my dear," Uncle West pointed out. "Besides, you already have yourself an attentive husband. I believe it is Minta who should be deciding whether or not she is interested in the viscount's company."

He winked at her and Minta couldn't help but chuckle.

"Well, what do you think of him?" insisted her aunt. "Do you have an interest in Lord Boxling after this evening's dinner?"

Not wanting to commit, Minta merely said, "I find both Lord Boxling and Lord Kingston to be appealing."

Her aunt sighed dramatically. "I do not see how you can compare the two and find them equal. However, your uncle is right. It is for you decide, Minta darling."

She only wondered how tomorrow's tea would turn out with both men seemingly in pursuit of her—and what her carriage ride with Lord Boxling would reveal.

THE SCREAM TORE from Percy's throat as he quickly muffled it in his pillows. His body was drenched in cold sweat. He had hoped the nightmares would recede, replaced by sweet dreams of Minta Nicholls, but that had not been the case.

Seeing light pouring from the window, he rose and splashed cold water on his face.

He would have liked Lord Boxling under any other circumstances. The man had proven to be intelligent and amiable, as much at White's as he was at last night's dinner. The fact he was interested in Minta, though, let any idea of friendship between them fly out the window. He knew he could not compete with the friendly, outgoing viscount and shouldn't even try to do so. His head told him that Boxling would be an ideal match for Minta.

Yet stubbornness filled him, his hackles raised. He didn't want to think of wooing Minta as a competition but he realized most likely that was what the Season was all about. Bachelors becoming interested in women they wished to take as their brides. Sometimes, there would be no competition and other times, it might become fierce. Knowing the copper-haired beauty would draw much attention, it seemed ridiculous that he would try to vie for her hand. But he felt compelled to do so, even knowing in his heart he wasn't the best candidate for her. Instead, he should choose some fresh-faced girl straight out of the schoolroom and remain polite but distant, both in courtship and marriage.

He wanted more, though. Much more. He wanted what his friends had.

He wanted love.

He had not felt an ounce of love from his parents, only seeing they did their duty toward him. He did experience fraternal love from both Rupert and the Second Sons but he yearned for more. He needed a strong partner who would help guide him through Polite Society and share his life with him.

He wanted—no, needed—Minta Nicholls to be that woman.

But how was he supposed to compete with a man such as Lord Boxling? Or the countless other bachelors of the Season, knowing how many would be attracted to Minta. Frustration filled him and yet determination did, as well. He would do his best in the two weeks leading up to the Season and see if he could make any progress with her. If he saw it was hopeless and Lord Boxling took the advantage, he would withdraw gracefully and direct his attention to other candidates.

Ringing for Huston, he asked for hot water to be sent up for a bath. Percy wanted to cleanse the nightmare from his body, mind, and soul.

An hour later, he was feeling refreshed as he headed downstairs to breakfast. He opened the newspaper resting beside his plate and perused it as he ate. Just as he finished his meal, Tate arrived with the post. The butler also said, "My lord, Bailey is waiting in your study. He says it is imperative to speak with you at once."

Worry filled him. Bailey coming all the way from Essex to London meant bad news.

"I will see him at once," Percy said, collecting the post and heading straight to his study.

He arrived and saw his country butler standing stiffly, hands clasped behind his back as he gazed out the window.

Turning, he greeted Percy.

"My lord, I hope things are well with you here in town."

"Have a seat, Bailey," he said, taking one himself, thinking it better to receive bad news sitting down. "What brings you to town?"

"It regards Mr. Smith, my lord. He has suffered a heart attack, one so severe that the doctor said he will not survive but a day or so. With so much going on at the estate, I felt you should hear this news in person and act accordingly."

Guilt flooded Percy, as he thought how the steward had wished to retire and stayed on as a favor to Percy. Now the man would never enjoy his golden years.

"I will accompany you back to Kingwood," he stated. "Give me a few minutes to let my valet and the staff here know. Why don't you go to the kitchens and let Cook feed you?"

"Thank you, my lord," the butler said, rising. He left the room.

Percy's first thought was not about all the work to be done once he returned to Kingwood but rather how he would have to miss today's tea with Minta.

Removing a piece of parchment from his desk, he wrote a carefully worded note to Lady Westlake, informing her of the circumstances and that he could not make today's tea since he would be returning to Essex indefinitely.

He also composed a quick note to Louisa, telling her what had occurred and asking her to share the news with the others. If he sent word to Ev or Spence, they would dash over and either insist on accompanying him home or tell him he couldn't go because of his obligation to attend the Season.

Ringing for Tate, Percy gave the butler both pieces of correspondence and asked that they be delivered immediately. Then he explained the situation and how he did not know if or when he might return to London.

"I understand, my lord. Everything will be taken care of here. Please do not worry." The butler hesitated and then said, "Might I be so bold as to tell you of my cousin, a Mr. Rowell?"

"What of him?"

"He recently wrapped up employment as the steward for the Earl of Newcombe's estate. I know he is very good at what he does, my lord."

"Then why is he out of work?" questioned Percy.

"It is a delicate situation, my lord. The earl passed away and his son, the new earl, claimed the title. He has a younger brother who has a tendency to . . . run a bit wild. And so the new earl, in order to keep an eye on his brother, has made him the estate's manager."

Awareness filled Percy. "So, your capable cousin is out of a job."

"Exactly, my lord."

"I will consider him for the position, Tate. Where is Rowell now/"

"He is staying with his sister here in London, my lord."

Percy thought a moment and then said, "Write a note to him and have him come here at once. He can travel to Kingwood with me. We shall talk on the way and I will pick his brain and see exactly what he knows. If I am pleased, I will take him about the estate and hear his opinions regarding it. I cannot guarantee him employment."

The butler's face lit with a smile. "You don't have to do so, my lord. Rowell is so competent that I believe he will convince you he is the man for the position."

"Very well. I shall work in my study until he arrives and we will depart immediately. Inform Huston of my plans and let the rest of the staff know as you see fit."

Percy sat behind his desk, regretting several things. That he had pushed Smith to his limits. That he would miss today's tea with Minta. That Lord Boxling would now have the advantage. But his tenants and Kingwood must come first. It was an obligation he took seriously.

He only hoped Tate's cousin would be the answer he sought and allow Percy to return to London so that he might have a ghost of a chance with Minta Nicholls.

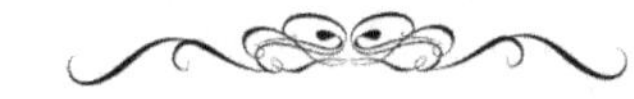

CHAPTER FOURTEEN

MINTA PACED HER bedchamber, nerves flitting through her. She finally forced herself to stop and went and stood in front of the window that gazed out upon the square below. Soon, their two guests would be arriving for tea and she was eager to see both men. She knew relatively little about Lord Boxling but he was most attractive and interesting. She would like to get to know more about the viscount.

Then there was Lord Kingston, an enigma to her. He seemed to blow hot and cold where she was concerned and Minta did not know if she liked that about him or if she should move on to someone who displayed his feelings more plainly and consistently. The fact she already had two men interested in her bolstered her confidence. She might find others interesting as well, once the Season began. However, she felt she might sort out at least some of her feelings once today's tea concluded.

She saw movement and noticed a carriage had pulled up in front of her uncle's townhouse. Moments later, out climbed Lord Boxling and she knew she should hurry to the drawing room in order to be there in time to greet him.

Entering the drawing room, she found Uncle West and Aunt Phyllis already there.

"I was about to send a maid to summon you, Minta," her aunt gently chided. "I did not want you to be late to tea."

Before Minta could respond, the butler appeared and announced, "Lord Boxling is here, my lord."

"Please show him in," her uncle told the servant and the viscount moved through the doors gracefully.

He crossed the drawing room to them, bowing first to her aunt and then to Minta before shaking hands with Uncle West.

"It is so lovely that you could come today," Aunt Phyllis said brightly. "Won't you please have a seat, my lord?"

The four of them took a seat and Minta found herself next to Lord Boxling, wondering where Lord Kingston might sit when he arrived. They spoke a few minutes about the weather, talking of how the heavy rain had finally dissipated.

"The skies were clear when I left," Lord Boxling said. "I hope that they will remain that way for our drive in Hyde Park."

A maid rolled in the teacart, leaving it. Much to Minta's distress, her aunt started pouring out.

Knowing Lord Kingston was tardy to tea, she still asked, "Aunt Phyllis, should we wait for Lord Kingston to arrive?"

Her aunt handed a cup and saucer to their guest, giving him a smile. Then looking to Minta, she said, "Lord Kingston will not be coming for tea today. He has been called away from town and has returned to his country estate in Essex."

She stiffened. "Called away? Why did you not share this with me?"

She saw the warning look in her aunt's eyes. "He did not know when—or if—he would be returning to town. All he mentioned was pressing business at his estate."

Minta felt herself deflating. It was bad enough the marquess would miss today's tea but to miss the Season itself?

"I am sorry to hear that," Lord Boxling said. "Lord Kingston seems to be a fine man."

Her aunt took charge of the conversation and Minta withdrew into herself, allowing the others to converse. Finally, she realized the viscount might find her silence rude and off-putting and she made more of an effort to entertain him.

When they finished with tea, Lord Boxling looked to her and asked, "Are you still up to going for a drive in my new curricle, Miss Nicholls? If you aren't, I understand."

Aunt Phyllis said, "Oh, Minta would not disappoint you, my lord. Naturally, she will drive with you, won't you, my dear?"

"Yes," she said with determination. "I have been looking forward to doing so, my lord."

"Good," said the viscount. "It's fortuitous the skies have cleared and we finally have sunshine. You might want to call for your shawl, however. It is still a bit chilly outside though I do have a blanket in the vehicle that we can place across your lap."

Minta excused herself and returned to her bedchamber, where she placed a new bonnet on her head and wrapped herself in a cashmere shawl. Returning downstairs, she found Lord Boxling waiting for her in the foyer.

He escorted her outside and she saw the gleaming curricle, with a beautiful pair of matched bays.

"I don't know which is more beautiful, the horses or the vehicle."

Lord Boxling smiled. "The horses are new, as is the vehicle. Let me climb aboard and I will lift you up."

He did so, raising her by the waist and placing her on the seat, taking his next to her. Taking the reins in hand, he clucked his tongue and they set off for the park.

She had not felt anything unique when he touched her. Unlike when Lord Kingston had clasped her hand and placed his other hand on her back to waltz. She tried to shake off the thought and turned her full attention to the viscount as they pulled from the square. He told her a little bit about his curricle and the horses, which he had purchased at Tattersall's. From the way he spoke, she could tell he was quite interested in horseflesh and that Tattersall's appeared to be the best place to purchase horses in London.

"Hyde Park will seem empty," he said. "There will not be but a scattered handful there now but come a few weeks when the

Season is in full swing, the park will be teeming with others at this time of day."

"Aunt Phyllis told me that five o'clock is the fashionable hour to drive in the park."

They entered through the gates and only saw one other carriage for several minutes, along with a nanny who led her two charges along the path next to the Serpentine.

"Might I ask you a personal question, Miss Nicholls?"

"I suppose so," she said guardedly, wondering what he considered personal.

"You seemed rather upset when Lady Westlake revealed that Lord Kingston would not be joining us for tea today. Are you in love with the marquess?"

Minta jumped as if he had slapped her. "No, of course not. I mean . . . that is . . . I don't know!" she exclaimed, frustration filling her.

Surprisingly, Lord Boxling chuckled, a reaction she would not have predicted. "My father—who was in love twice—said that love could be confusing, frustrating, and yet the most satisfying thing on the planet. It seems you do hold Lord Kingston in high regard. Have you known him for long?"

"Not really," she admitted. "He is a neighbor of my aunt and uncle in the country and they invited him for dinner, along with Lord and Lady Danbury, who were visiting him at the time. He did call upon us a few other times before he left for town."

"He seems to be a good man. I know the set he travels in is a group of honorable men and if you do have feelings for him, I hope they will amount to something and that he will return your love."

"I don't know about love," Minta said. "My parents were a love match. Mama married well beneath her, disappointing her parents. Aunt Phyllis married a peer of her father's rank. Though she did not love Uncle West, they seem to have gotten along well over the years."

"Because my father found love, I wish to do the same," the

viscount stated.

Curiosity filled her and she asked, "Were you in love with Lady Danbury?"

He smiled ruefully. "I thought so at the time. I was physically attracted to her and found her to be rather sweet and kind. I do know that unrequited love is not truly love at all, though. Even if what I felt for Lady Danbury was love, it never could have flourished if she did not return that love. Besides, Lord Danbury is her perfect match in every way. She and I had an honest conversation about it, even before Danbury admitted his feelings for her, and we have fortunately remained friends. I count Lord Danbury as a friend of mine, too."

He looked at her beseechingly and said, "I do feel attracted to you, Miss Nicholls. It seems your heart is already engaged, however."

"Kiss me," she said impulsively. "That should let us know if this is something we should pursue or not. It would give me something to compare . . ."

Then Minta realized what she had admitted to this lord and felt the scalding heat sting her cheeks.

He chuckled low. "So, the reserved Lord Kingston has already kissed you." It was a statement and not a question on his part.

"Yes," she admitted. "I thought I should compare his kiss to see if I felt the same with another or not."

The viscount grinned at her. "I have never been one to pass up the opportunity to kiss a beautiful woman," he told her.

He turned his full attention to the road ahead without speaking, which thoroughly confused her. A few minutes later, they arrived at a lane and he turned off the main thoroughfare onto it. After driving for a full minute, he halted the horses and glanced about.

"No one can see our grand experiment, Miss Nicholls. If you are willing to share a kiss with me, I am willing to do so."

Anxiety filled her but Minta knew this was an opportunity she could not pass up. Viscount Boxling was marvelously handsome and also very kind to want to kiss her after her admission that she had already kissed Lord Kingston.

"Yes, my lord. If you would please kiss me, I would appreciate it."

He cupped her nape with his gloved hand, bringing his lips down upon hers. Slowly, he brushed his lips against hers and eventually pressed them more firmly against her mouth. He did not, however, kiss her using his tongue. She broke the kiss and said imploringly, "That is not exactly how Lord Kingston kissed me. He started out this way but it became . . ." Her voice trailed off as she had no idea how to put into words what she wanted to say.

Understanding lit his dark eyes and he said, "He used his tongue, did he? That devil."

Alarmed, she asked, "Was it wrong of him to do so? I had never been kissed before and so I did not know." Worry filled her.

This time, Lord Boxling laughed aloud. "No, it is not wrong at all. In fact, when done properly—and with passion—it feels quite right."

He studied her a moment and then added, "I do not believe that passion exists between us, Miss Nicholls. I am willing to try but I believe you will be disappointed."

"I would rather be disappointed and know for certain than have a lingering question in my mind, my lord. I am sorry if that sounds bold and causes you to think less of me."

His hand took hers and he said, "Not at all, Miss Nicholls. If anything, I hold you in an even higher regard." He paused and added, "Shall we?"

She nodded and he lowered his lips to hers again, kissing her briefly before urging her to open to him. The viscount kissed her for a good full minute. That told Minta right away he was not the one for her if she was aware of the time involved in the kiss.

He broke the kiss and smiled sadly. "You didn't feel much of anything, did you?"

"No. Did you?"

"No, not a bit," he declared, laughing merrily. He sobered and then said, "But I do like you quite a bit, Miss Nicholls. I have two younger half-sisters, as well as an older, married one. I almost feel as if you are a sister to me. If you want my help with Lord Kingston, I will do whatever I can to help bring the two of you together. And if that proves to be unsuccessful, I have a few other friends I am happy to introduce you to."

She placed her hand on his forearm and squeezed it. "You, my lord, are a wonderful man. I don't know of any gentleman who would be so understanding with my predicament. I will take any help you are able to give me, however. I did not think I wanted or needed love as I looked for a husband but perhaps I have been wrong. My feelings for Lord Kingston are strong. I hope, however, they will not be unrequited as you found with Lady Danbury."

He gave her a winning smile. "Well, you see I survived that. It took a while to get over my bruised feelings but I am ever the optimist. I know love is out there, waiting for me and that I will find it one day. I hope the same for you, Miss Nicholls."

Minta squeezed his arm again and the viscount took up the reins. They finished their drive through the park, as he described to her different events of the Season and even some of his friends he would introduce her to once it began.

The curricle pulled up in front of her uncle's townhouse and Lord Boxling helped her from it, escorting her to the front door.

Taking her hand, he lifted it to his lips and kissed it, a twinkle in his eyes. "Thank you for accompanying me on my drive today, Miss Nicholls. If I do not see you before the Season begins, then we will dance together at the Blakeney ball." He grinned. "Perhaps a little rivalry between Lord Kingston and me would benefit you."

"Thank you again, my lord. It is nice to have you in my corner."

CHAPTER FIFTEEN

P ERCY GREW RESTLESS as his carriage approached the outskirts of London. He had been gone two weeks and a day.

The Season opened tomorrow night.

Fortunately, Tate's suggestion that his cousin, Mr. Rowell, become the new estate manager at Kingwood had been a blessing. From the moment Percy had met Rowell, he sensed the man to be quite accomplished. On the carriage ride to Essex, he had asked a few questions but mostly let Rowell discuss his previous experiences, both at the Earl of Newcombe's estate and two other positions prior to it.

By the time they had arrived at Kingwood, Percy had made up his mind to hire Rowell at whatever salary the man requested because he knew he had a gem in hand. The two had ridden the estate part of that afternoon and talked late into the night about not only the improvements Percy had started on the property under Smith's leadership but also ones Rowell believed to be both important and necessary for Kingwood to thrive.

The following day, both men had attended Smith's funeral. The former steward had passed away only hours after the heart attack that felled him. Thoughtfully, Rowell went to the funeral and Percy had requested that Kingwood be opened for mourners after the funeral service. He watched Rowell work the room, always sympathetic, and yet gradually learning names and forming opinions of the tenants who had turned out for the service and afterward.

The two men had spent the entire day after the funeral out on the estate again, hatching plans and speaking to tenants regarding their needs. Percy realized the elderly Smith had let up and not pressed as he should have on some matters. The much younger Rowell subtly let the tenants know that the time for lassitude had ended and that much would be required of them. He did it so calmly, however, that Percy believed the new steward would quickly gain the trust of those working at Kingwood.

After another two days of implementing his plans, Rowell had asked Percy about his other estates. He shared what he knew, having visited them when he had returned to England, and the new steward suggested they tour the other properties together, putting into place some of the new reforms which Rowell would implement at Kingwood. They traveled to them and met with the stewards at each place, with Rowell outlining what was to be done and what the marquess expected in the months and years to come. Once again, Rowell so smoothly discussed matters that it seemed the transition to new practices would come easily.

They had returned to Kingwood yesterday and Rowell had encouraged Percy to return to London, telling him things were well in hand now and that he should go and enjoy his first Season.

"You've spent your entire adulthood on the battlefields, my lord," Rowell had said. "It is about time you kicked up your heels a bit and relished your title. Perhaps you will be able to find a lovely woman to be your marchioness. A woman's touch would be welcomed, both here at Kingwood and your other estates."

Agreeing that things were well in hand, Percy had chosen to return to town today. He knew three of the Second Sons would be back by now, having taken an afternoon to ride over to Woodbridge and visit with Win, who was settling in nicely, and Spence, who was the last of the three to spend a week in Win's company, helping him along.

He had shared with his friend and cousin his decision to hire Rowell and many of the things the new estate manager was implementing. Win, impressed by what Percy was saying, had even risen and collected ink and parchment, making a few notes as they discussed things. Percy had gotten his cousin's promise to attend the house party Owen and Louisa would hold.

Percy wondered if it was possible that he might be betrothed by then.

And if it would be Minta—or another lady he had yet to meet.

He knew Spence, upon his return to town, would have shared with the others Percy's plan to arrive in time to attend the Blakeney ball tomorrow night. He only wished he had the opportunity for a final dance lesson before the social swirl began, especially time dancing the waltz. He wondered if Minta remembered her promise to dance it with him and hoped she had not fallen hopelessly in love with the ever-charming Viscount Boxling over the past two weeks. Knowing Boxling had been given ample opportunity to woo Minta with him gone to the country, he hoped for the best.

And continued to imagine the worst.

The carriage slowed and he saw the traffic surrounding them, eager now to arrive at his London townhouse and send a message to his friends that he had arrived. Finally, the coach pulled up next to his townhouse and the door opened. Percy descended the stairs and saw Huston, who had ridden next to the coachman, already on the ground and ordering footmen to retrieve the trunks.

Percy entered his home and was immediately greeted by Tate.

"Good day, Lord Kingston. I trust you had a pleasant journey from Essex."

"Not only a pleasant journey," he told the butler, "but one that gives me peace of mind. I cannot express my gratitude to you in recommending your cousin for my employ."

The butler smiled broadly. "I told you, my lord. Rowell is

efficient and organized. He has already written to me, thanking me for making the introduction to you. I told him that was all it was, a mere introduction, and that he had won you over wiltz his brilliant ideas."

"Indeed, he did. Rowell is everything you promised, Tate, and even more."

"I am glad you are so pleased, my lord. Would you like a bath drawn? Tea?"

"Both," he replied. "Have the tea sent up with the hot water. I feel like a good soak."

"Very good, my lord. In the meantime, I have placed the post upon your desk. Invitations to upcoming events have been pouring in. You also received a note from Lady Danbury this morning. It is atop the stack on your desk."

"Then I will see to it now."

Percy retreated to his study, knowing it would take some time for the water to be heated for his bath. Huston would be scurrying about the bedchamber as he unpacked. It would be nice to have a little peace and quiet in the meantime.

He entered the room and went to sit behind the mahogany desk, spying Louisa's handwriting. Taking her note, he broke the seal.

Percy—

Spencer informed us you would be returning sometime today. I hope it is early enough that you can take tea with us. If not, please come for dinner. All the Second Sons, minus Win, will be there with the Three Cousins and we are all eager to hear about your new steward and what the two of you have been up to since you left us.

Don't be put off by me revealing this, but I have asked Miss Nicholls to join us for tea today. She is already committed to dinner with her aunt and uncle. I hope you will wish to see her. I like her, Percy—and I know you do, as well. Taking tea with her would be a good thing since you could renew your ac-quaintance, as well as remind her that she promised to waltz with you tomorrow night.

I hope this finds you in good spirits and that we will see you shortly.

Fondly, Louisa

Postscript – Owen says hello—and that he will darken your doorstep from three o'clock on in order to see that you come to us once you arrive back in town.

He chuckled, imagining Owen lurking in the shadows, ready to pounce and force him to come to tea and dinner.

No force would be necessary at all.

Percy was willing—and very ready—to be in Minta's company again. Especially before the Season opened.

MINTA CHANGED INTO a light pink gown for tea. Though she had never worn the color before, thinking it clashed with her copper hair, Madame Chevalier had corrected her misconception. Minta found she quite liked the color on her, thinking it made her skin rosy and her blue eyes stand out.

She decided to leave her hair as Bertha had styled it this morning and dismissed the maid. She still had another quarter-hour before she needed to leave for Louisa's and took that time gathering the packages she would bring with her this afternoon. The past two weeks had been happy ones for her as she got to know the Three Cousins, whom she now called her new friends, just as the Second Sons referred to them in the same manner. The women had taken Minta under their wings and she had spent much of her free time with them, shopping for hats and gloves, visiting bookshops, taking strolls, and gathering for tea almost daily.

Lady Danbury had asked Minta to dinner this evening, as well, but she decided she should stay home with her aunt and uncle since she hadn't spent much time with them lately. Uncle West had said they could practice their waltzing tonight for the last time. He had given her a brief lesson each morning after breakfast and her confidence now soared as she danced it.

It saddened her, though, to think her first waltz in front of Polite Society at tomorrow night's ball would not be with Lord Kingston. She had promised it to him before he had left town. Due to her budding friendship with the Three Cousins, Minta had learned that the marquess' steward, a longtime family employee, had died from a sudden heart attack, leaving the estate in turmoil. Lord Kingston had given the steward a long list of things he wished to see accomplished at Kingwood. With the man's death, the marquess would have to see to the job himself, at least until a reliable, experienced manager could be found and hired.

She had mentioned the situation to her uncle and he had told her it was actually quite hard to find a competent estate manager. He claimed them worth their weight in gold. With sad eyes, he had warned Minta that she probably would not see Lord Kingston for much—if any—of the Season since he would most likely be tied up in the country.

"It is perhaps for the best," he had said gently. "The marquess is new to the title. Working out matters on his estate will give him time to settle better into his role. He seemed a bit uncomfortable in polite company. By next Season, he may be better equipped to enter the ballrooms of the *ton*."

That thought had depressed her. She didn't want to wait around for him. Even if she did ignore any suitors from this Season, there was no guarantee that Lord Kingston would be interested in offering for her next Season. She was already two and twenty and felt life was passing her by. Waiting for him was not an option and Minta resolved to forget about the handsome marquess and look to her future.

Placing the wrapped packages in a box she'd had Bertha locate and bring upstairs, Minta now carried it with her. This time, she would be taking Uncle West's coach to tea.

"Let me get that for you, Miss Nicholls," a footman in the foyer said and quickly hurried to Minta, lifting the box from her.

"It isn't very heavy," she protested.

"I will take it to the coach for you," he insisted.

They went outside and another footman handed her up. She took a seat and the footman with the box rested it on the floor of the carriage by her feet.

"Do not try to carry it in, Miss Nicholls. Have one of the Danbury footmen do so for you," the servant warned.

She agreed and he closed the door. Moments later, the vehicle rolled into motion.

Minta hoped her presents would be well received by her three friends. The women had been so welcoming to her, insisting that she call them by their first names when in private. She had met their four children, as well. Tessa had two, Analise, who was just over two years of age, and Adam, who had recently turned five months. Adalyn's boy, Edwin, was fourteen months old. Louisa's daughter, Margaret, was eight months. Minta had played with Analise and Edwin and held the other two babes, which brought a deep longing within her. Again, she hoped she would not turn up barren as Aunt Phyllis had. She had sympathy for her aunt, who had seen many of her friends have several children while her own nest remained empty.

After the short distance, the carriage pulled up at Louisa's townhouse. Her box was taken from her and she was ushered inside, being led up to the drawing room, where the Danburys and Camdens were already present. The footman placed the box on a table as her friends greeted her.

Adalyn's curiosity was obvious. "What have you brought, Minta?" the duchess asked.

"Presents for the Three Cousins," she said cheerfully. "And you may not open yours until Tessa arrives."

His Grace roared with laughter and he bent and pressed a kiss to the top of his wife's head. "It will probably kill you to wait," he teased.

Minta loved how playful all three Second Sons were with their wives although sometimes she did squirm a bit at the open affection they displayed. She never saw Uncle West and Aunt Phyllis behave in such a fashion and she doubted she would see members of the *ton* doing so tomorrow night. Still, she appreciated the fact that her new friends all had husbands who adored them.

It would be lovely if she could find a man who showed her the same affection.

Again, her thoughts turned to Lord Kingston and she quickly banished them. She would pin her hopes on Adalyn finding her a match, which the duchess had promised to do. Lord Boxling had also promised to introduce his friends to her. Surely, between the two of them, they could help Minta find a good husband.

Tessa entered on the arm of her husband, sailing in with a smile on her face as everyone greeted the new arrivals.

"Minta has brought gifts for us," Adalyn exclaimed. "Now that you are here, Tessa, we can open them."

She reached into the box and handed each woman the package designated for her. Minta had come to know bits and pieces of each of them and had gone to a bookstore, choosing a book that each one might enjoy.

"I would have rather embroidered something for you because I like how personal a gift of that nature is," she explained. "The three of you have kept me far too busy, however, and I had no time to do so."

"You did not have to get us anything," Tessa said. "Your friendship is quite enough."

Minta smiled. "I appreciate you saying that, Tessa. I did want to show you a bit of appreciation, though. You have welcomed me to London with open arms."

"And I will find you a husband," Adalyn chimed in as she undid the string and tore away the brown paper.

She watched as the packages were opened. For Tessa, she had chosen a book on gardening. Adalyn, who was known for her keen fashion sense, had received an illustrated copy of women's fashions during the Renaissance. Louisa was mad for Bach and Minta had found a biography of the composer which had recently been released.

All three exclaimed how delighted they were with their books, giving her warm embraces.

Then Minta sensed something different in the room and turned. Standing to the side was the Marquess of Kingston looking on. Somehow, he had slipped in during the chaos of the packages being unwrapped.

He took a few steps and joined her. Her pulse beat wildly as she inhaled his cologne.

"I see you have made the Three Cousins quite happy," he noted.

"I did not know you were returning to town," she said faintly, the blood pounding in her ears.

"I was fortunate to find—through my butler—a remarkable man who has proven to be the perfect estate manager. I have so much confidence in him that I decided I could return to town and partake in the Season."

Minta swallowed, her mouth dry. She couldn't think of a single thing to say.

Lord Kingston's gaze pierced her. "I hope you have not forgotten that you promised to waltz with me at the Blakeney ball tomorrow night."

"No."

One eyebrow cocked up. "No, you haven't forgotten—or no, you won't dance with me?" he asked.

She dug her fingernails into her palms. "No, I had not forgotten," she said quietly.

"I have been gone for a few weeks. I was worried you had. Or that you might have promised it to another gentleman. Say, Lord Boxling."

Her heart sped up. He *was* jealous of the viscount!

"I have promised no dance to any gentleman," she told him.

"However, you must arrive in time to sign my programme if you wish to waltz with me at the ball, my lord."

Again, one brow shot up. Then the marquess smiled. "I wonder if Lady Blakeney minds if I join them for breakfast tomorrow morning."

"Why would you do that?" she asked, puzzled by his odd remark.

He grinned. "Why, the better to stake my claim by being first in line at their ball, Miss Nicholls."

Minta turned red to her roots.

CHAPTER SIXTEEN

MINTA STOOD IN her bedchamber, ready for tonight's ball. She had finished dressing early and dismissed Bertha, wanting time to collect her thoughts before tonight's affair. The ball would kick off the beginning of the Season and she knew from what Aunt Phyllis had said that she would be swept away in a whirlwind of events. She wanted to reflect upon what was to come.

And what may occur by Season's end.

At tea yesterday, Lord Kingston had surprised her. He had been the most talkative she had seen him ever since she had made his acquaintance. It hadn't taken her long to understand she was seeing the true Lord Kingston. Comfortably ensconced among his friends, he relaxed completely and his demeanor changed. Teatime had been full of good conversation, interesting tidbits about Polite Society, and quite a bit of teasing between the Second Sons. Minta had enjoyed herself immensely, knowing she was among good friends. Hope filled her that she might continue to count this circle among her friends. The only question now was whether she would be a member of it as Lord Kingston's marchioness or the wife of another peer.

She decided to make her way downstairs and found Uncle West waiting in the foyer at the bottom of the staircase.

He smiled in approval. "You are wearing your diamond earrings."

"I told you I would wear them every night of the Season. You and Aunt Phyllis have made this possible for me. I won't forget it, Uncle West."

He cupped her cheek and smiled fondly at her. "I hope that this Season will be everything you wish for, Minta. Moreover, I hope you find a man who will be a good partner in marriage to you, just as your aunt has been to me."

"Do you love Aunt Phyllis?" she asked.

"I didn't when we first wed," he admitted. "I still don't in the way you mean. You have had the example of your parents, who were wildly in love from the moment they laid eyes upon one another. Throughout the years, your aunt and I have settled into an understanding. We are better with each other and quite fond of one another. Some might even say that is love."

He paused and added, "I want more for you, however. I want you to experience that grand passion if at all possible, Minta. You are a woman full of life and I believe when you find the right man, you will love him fiercely."

He dropped his hand and steadily gazed at her, saying, "Perhaps you have already discovered who this man is. If so, remember that I act in your father's stead in these matters. Your young man will need to come to me to ask for your hand in marriage. I will be responsible for negotiating the marriage contracts on your behalf. I will make certain you are taken care of, Minta."

"I know you will, Uncle."

Her aunt came down the stairs and joined them. "Don't you look lovely this evening, Araminta? I cannot wait to introduce you into Polite Society this evening. You already have an excellent start with the friends you have made. The Duchess of Camden has a powerful influence in the *ton* and her two cousins are well thought of, as are all three husbands. You are traveling in lofty circles, my dear, and that will attract the attention of others."

The butler came toward them and informed them, "Lord Danbury's carriage has arrived, my lord."

Louisa had insisted that Minta and the Westlakes accompany them to the opening ball, which Aunt Phyllis had readily agreed to. They now joined the earl and countess in their carriage.

"I cannot thank you enough, Lady Danbury, for the kindness you have shown to our niece. She values your friendship and that of your cousins."

Louisa smiled graciously. "We are the fortunate ones, Lady Westlake. Minta has been a delight and I know we shall remain friends for many years to come."

They arrived at the Blakeneys' townhouse and joined the throng of people entering it. Inside, she saw the receiving line that had formed and they joined it. She looked about, taking in all the beautiful gowns and jewels worn by the women of the *ton*, glad her uncle had gifted her with the pair of diamond earrings. It made her feel as if she truly did belong to this society.

Minta did not see Lord Kingston anywhere and wondered if had already passed through the receiving line or if he had yet to arrive. She worried about how he would react being in a ballroom made up mostly of strangers to him. Sera would be quaking in her slippers at the thought of being around so many she did not know. A wave of sadness washed through her at the thought of her twin. She wished that Sera could have joined her this evening so that they might have taken these first steps into Polite Society together. At least with Minta making her come-out first, she would have a clear understanding of how the Season worked and be able to share that with her sister. She knew launching Sera into society would be a little more difficult because of her twin's aversion to crowds. Once again, Minta wondered if by next Season she might have a husband as she introduced Sera to other members of Polite Society.

They reached their hosts, who greeted Lord and Lady Danbury first, and then turned to the Westlakes and her.

"My lord and lady, allow me to introduce our niece, Miss

Araminta Nicholls," Uncle West said. "She is making her come-out this Season."

She made her curtsey and the couple nodded approvingly at her.

"I hope you enjoy dancing, Miss Nicholls," Lady Blakeney said to her. "There will be plenty of that at the numerous balls you attend this Season."

"I have always enjoyed dancing, my lady, and have recently learned how to waltz. I look forward to that dance most of all."

Lord Blakeney chuckled. "The waltz is a favorite of my wife," he revealed. "She asks that it be played twice tonight. Once as the supper dance and again as the final number of the evening."

Minta tucked away that information, knowing she would share it with Lord Kingston when he asked her to dance. Aunt Phyllis had explained that a gentleman rarely asked a lady to partner with him more than once in an evening. If he requested a second dance, it signaled to the *ton* his interest in the woman. She wondered if the marquess would claim one waltz—or both.

They left the receiving line and moved to the entrance of the ballroom, which sparkled with lights. Her eyes roamed the room, looking for Lord Kingston. She located him standing with Adalyn and the duke. She knew Adalyn had promised the marquess that she would help him find his marchioness this Season and tried to tamp down the jealousy she experienced at that thought.

Suddenly, his gaze met hers and a thrill of anticipation rippled through her.

Louisa steered them to the left, where they joined Tessa and her husband. Still looking at Lord Kingston, she started to pull away but her aunt gently clasped Minta's elbow.

"No. You must not go to him. He must come to you," she whispered. Then her aunt smiled brightly. "We will leave you with your friends, my dear. I know they will take good care of you and introduce you around to those of your own age."

As her aunt and uncle moved away to join their friends, Minta's heart beat rapidly as Lord Kingston approached her. Then from the corners of her eyes, she saw Lord Boxling also making his way in her direction and suppressed a smile. The pair arrived at the same time.

Lord Boxling spoke first. "It is a pleasure to see you here tonight, Lady Danbury." He kissed Louisa's hand. Turning to Minta, he did the same.

She smiled at him, wanting Lord Kingston to also speak up and greet her. Glancing in his direction, she saw him looking tongue-tied.

Then he seemed to swallow his fears and he greeted both her and Louisa.

A footman arrived and offered her a dance card. She accepted it and, immediately, Lord Kingston said, "Miss Nicholls, you have promised me a waltz. Might I sign your programme?"

She handed it to him and said, "Our host informed us two waltzes will be played at tonight's ball. One for supper and one to close out the ball."

Minta watched as he scribbled his name and returned the programme to her. She noted he had signed for the supper dance. She tamped down her disappointment of him not claiming both waltzes and smiled at him, knowing that being his supper partner meant they would dine together, giving her additional time with him.

Lord Boxling said, "Since Lord Kingston only claimed one waltz, Miss Nicholls, I would be pleased to take the other."

She gave him her programme and he scrawled his name on the last slot. As he returned it to her, the viscount winked. She hoped no one had witnessed that as she bit back a smile.

By now, Adalyn and her duke had joined their circle and her friend said, "Come along, Kingston. I have several ladies I wish to introduce you to before the dancing begins."

Lord Kingston nodded to Minta and said, "Until later, Miss Nicholls," and left with the duke and duchess.

Lord Boxling said, "I have several friends who are eager to meet you, Miss Nicholls. May I bring them to you?" He looked to

Louisa for approval and she nodded.

Tessa told Minta, "The viscount is one of the most handsome, eligible bachelors in Polite Society. He has a pleasing manner, as do his friends."

"To dance the final number with him will certainly bring attention to the two of you," Louisa added. "Dancing the last dance of the evening with Lord Boxling will certainly let other gentlemen know that he is most interested in you. I only hope it does not discourage any particular gentlemen."

Minta knew Louisa referred to Percy.

Once the viscount left, others made their way toward her and Tessa and Louisa introduced her to a good number of gentlemen.

Lord Boxling reappeared with three men in tow and made the introductions, each friend of his also signing her dance card. By now, it was filled and Minta relaxed, relieved she would not be a wallflower.

Minutes later, Lord and Lady Blakeney opened the ball and she joined her first partner, a Lord Markham. Fortunately, she had a knack for recalling names, as her father did, and the one time she did not remember an upcoming partner's name, she merely glanced at the programme to confirm his identity.

Once, as she danced a reel, Lord Kingston and his partner were a part of their set of four. The marquess was light on his feet and seemed to be enjoying the dance, unlike when she had caught sight of him earlier as Adalyn ushered him about the ballroom, making introductions. At least he enjoyed dancing.

The supper dance arrived and she watched as he confidently strode her way.

He arrived and said, "I see we have an orchestra this time to play for us as we waltz, Miss Nicholls."

He led her onto the dance floor and they assumed their positions as the musicians struck up the first note. The instant his hands touched her, joy filled her. He stepped close, closer than he had during their dance lesson, so close that her breasts grazed the front of his waistcoat, causing her nipples to stand out. She licked her lips and his eyes dropped to her mouth, making her mouth grow dry as he began guiding her about the ballroom.

Dancing with the marquess was like floating through the clouds. Although she had become quite familiar with the steps of the waltz, thanks to the additional practice with Uncle West, Minta simply gave herself over to the music and his guidance as he twirled her about the ballroom floor. She wished the dance could have gone on forever but the final strains sounded and then the music ceased.

Lord Kingston released her and took her hand, tucking it possessively into the crook of his arm.

"Shall we go in to supper?"

She nodded and they made their way along with the masses to the supper room. She might have known the Second Sons would take care of their friend because he led them directly to a large table where they were taking their seats.

Lord Kingston seated her and asked what she might like from the buffet.

"Since I have never gone through a midnight buffet before, you may surprise me," she said playfully.

He smiled at her and left with his fellow Second Sons. Immediately, Adalyn turned to her and said, "You looked divine dancing that waltz, Minta. I think every bachelor's eye was upon you during the dance."

She felt the blush warm her cheeks. "It was all Lord Kingston," she told her friends. "He is a marvelous dancer and partnering with him made me appear to be better than I am."

"Are you enjoying your first ball?" Tessa asked.

"I am. But I have never danced so much in my life," she declared. "I will be quite worn out by the time this ball ends and will probably fall asleep as I tumble into bed."

Louisa laughed. "I always find that I am exhausted after a ball myself. I noticed you will close the evening by dancing with Lord Boxling."

"Yes, he claimed the final dance of the night. I have not seen him since he came for tea and we took a drive in his curricle a couple of weeks ago. It was thoughtful of him to ask to dance with me this evening."

Minta recalled the wink the viscount had given her and wondered if Lord Kingston would be jealous of Lord Boxling ending the evening with her.

CHAPTER SEVENTEEN

PERCY HAD SPENT most of the evening waffling between misery and enjoyment. It had been miserable being dragged about the ballroom by Adalyn, who knew everyone present and constantly stopped in order to introduce him to people. Where the men who served under him had all appeared different to him, despite the fact they all wore the same uniform, these perfectly dressed and coiffed members of the *ton* all seemed to look alike.

Adalyn did a good job of introducing him to not only his fellow peers but a good number of women, some making their come-outs this Season and others who were unattached. His face got tired of plastering on a social smile, his cheeks aching. And he couldn't seem to recall a single name once they had moved on. No one, man or woman, seemed to make much of an impression upon him.

One woman deliberately stepped into their path as they made their way about the ballroom. She was in her early forties and had a young girl with her, most likely her daughter.

"Oh, Your Graces," the woman said, her eyes glittering. "It is so wonderful to see you. Have you met my daughter, Lady Eve? She is making her come-out this Season and would make a perfect bride."

Percy looked at the sullen girl who stared at the ground as Adalyn said formally, "Good evening, Lady Vickers. Lady Eve. I hope you enjoy your Season."

"Aren't you going to introduce us to your friend?" the older woman pressed, looking from Adalyn to Ev.

"This is Lord Kingston," Adalyn said brusquely.

"How do you do?" Percy said, reluctant to engage them in conversation because of Adalyn's odd behavior.

"Curtsey," Lady Vickers commanded and her daughter dropped into a curtsey.

"If you will excuse us," Ev said and led them away.

"Who was that?" Percy asked as they made their escape.

"Lady Vickers is the worst gossip of the *ton*," Adalyn shared. "She is on the hunt for the highest title she can command. Avoid her—and her daughter—like the plague, Percy. That is one family you do not wish to marry into."

He nodded in agreement and they paused again, once more making small talk with people whose names he would never recall.

Twice, he looked about, spying Minta as she also was being introduced to other members of Polite Society. Percy longed to stay by her side. If it were up to him, he would have danced every number with her. That, however, was taboo. Adalyn had explained that dancing twice with a partner was quite enough and rarely done, while three times would be considered a terrible faux pas.

At least the dancing had been fun. He had always enjoyed movement, be it running or fencing or riding. While every dance started off awkwardly as he claimed his new partner and tried to think of something casual to say as they moved to the dance floor, the dancing itself was what he liked.

But what he looked forward to the most was waltzing with Minta.

He hated that he had not signed his name beside both waltzes but he had thought that would be too presumptuous. He noticed that she danced every time the orchestra played and supposed her entire programme had filled quickly, as he knew it would. Self-doubt began to plague him and, once again, he felt himself not good enough for her.

When the time came for them to dance, however, his confidence returned as he claimed her. Enveloping her in his arms, he moved to the beat, the count of three echoing in his head as he guided her about. He could tell she had practiced since their session together for she moved with ease. He hoped it had been her uncle who had worked with her and not Viscount Boxling.

The waltz ended far too soon but Percy would remain in her company, thanks to this being the supper dance. Adalyn had reminded him to join the rest of the Second Sons for supper and he led Minta to where they now gathered. He noticed the beautiful flush to her cheeks as he asked her what she wanted from the buffet and then set out with his friends to make up plates for the table.

"Is it as bad as you thought it would be?" Ev asked. "Or better?"

"A mixture of both. Meeting so many people at the beginning was a blur."

"You actually said a few things. I was proud of you," his friend praised.

"I am having trouble thinking of anything to say when I meet up with each of my dance partners. Fortunately, the dances are so lively that conversation is all but impossible during them."

"You seemed to be very relaxed in Miss Nicholls' company yesterday," Owen commented. "You didn't clam up once. I think she is the one for you."

Percy didn't say anything and busied himself with collecting two plates.

"The Three Cousins have certainly taken to Miss Nicholls," Spence added. "Yesterday's tea was delightful."

"I thought so, as well," he admitted. "But I fear Miss Nicholls is far out of my league."

"What?" Spence asked, confused. "You are a marquess now, Percy. Your title and wealth speak for itself but you are a good man. Any woman, including Miss Nicholls, would be a fool if they did not see who you are." Spence smiled encouragingly. "I do believe Miss Nicholls sees something in you. Even if you do not see it in yourself."

Spence was right. He was a marquess, albeit an incredibly shy one. He didn't seem to be shy around Minta, though, and he thought that a good sign. For a moment at tea yesterday, he had imagined what it would be like if she truly were his wife and they had come to call upon Owen and Louisa and enjoyed tea with all their friends.

He needed to kiss her again. No shying away. He should mark his territory. Kiss her. Call upon her. Offer for her. Eventually, at least. He didn't think it smart to propose marriage a day into the Season. Still, he needed to let her know of his interest in her. Already, he believed Lord Boxling had tried to stake his own claim with Minta though she hadn't treated the viscount with any special regard as he signed her programme earlier this evening.

Finishing with their plates, he returned to the table. Tessa was finishing up a story and the other three women burst into laughter as he joined them.

Percy placed a plate in front of Minta. "I hope I found some things to your liking."

She looked upon it, a slow smile crossing her face. "You did quite well, my lord. I am a fool when it comes to sweets and I see several here. I also adore deviled eggs with ham."

"Then I am glad to have pleased you."

A footman brought wine to their table, pouring the rich, red liquid into goblets sitting there.

"A toast!" cried Owen. "To the Second Sons—and a Season to remember."

Everyone raised their glasses and echoed Owen's words. Percy shook his head as he took a sip of wine.

"What are you thinking of, Lord Kingston?" asked Minta.

He sighed. "Just how different my life is now than what it was a year ago. It was just last spring that Bonaparte escaped and gathered a new army. Waterloo had yet to occur."

"I suppose you were in the thick of that battle."

He nodded, not speaking, flashes of the cannon fire in his head.

"You do not have to speak of it, my lord. I know many men prefer to leave those memories on the battlefield."

He saw no sympathy but empathy in her eyes. "Thank you. War is difficult to explain to those who have not been in the thick of it."

She placed a hand on his forearm, causing a jolt to run through him. "Your past year has been difficult. You lost a beloved brother. You gave up a promising career. You returned to England and found yourself with a dizzying amount of responsibility. But you have weathered all of those storms, my lord. I cannot guarantee it will all be smooth sailing ahead but you are home, where you belong, with good friends. You have a new purpose in life, caring for the people on your various estates, just as you cared for your men."

Removing her hand, she took a bite of custard and smiled. "This is marvelous."

He tried some. "I agree."

"I heard that you lost your steward. Have you replaced him?"

They continued speaking only to one another throughout supper, as if they were dining alone. Percy told her about Smith's passing and the availability of Rowell, brought to Percy's attention by his butler. He spoke of Kingwood and some of the changes that were being implemented this spring and over the next year, as well as what would be done and changed on his other two estates.

Before he realized it, supper had ended. He had cleaned his plate without remembering he had done so.

Embarrassment filled him. "I am afraid I have dominated most of our conversation, Miss Nicholls," he apologized.

"I didn't view it that way, my lord. I asked questions and you answered them. I was fascinated by what you spoke of. You must remember that my father owns no country estate and I lived in London for the majority of my life before we departed for Upper Canada. I enjoy hearing about the inner workings of an estate and life in the country."

"Did you visit your aunt and uncle often?" he asked.

"They actually prefer town to country life," she told him. "I saw them frequently during the year and my family would go down to Westfield and spend a few days at Christmas with them each year."

"They think quite a bit of you."

"They look upon Sera and me as their children since they had none." She touched a hand to her ear. "Uncle West gifted me this pair of earrings for the Season. Papa would never have been able to afford them. I am fortunate to have them hosting me during this Season."

"When will your family return from Canada?"

"My twin is coming sometime in June. From Mama's last letter, she believes Papa will wrap up his assignment early next year. They will probably return to England in the spring once the harsh winter weather is gone and a sailing across the Atlantic is more palatable."

"You must be quite happy to know your sister—and your parents—are returning home."

"I am, especially reuniting with Sera. Aunt Phyllis wants Sera to make her come-out next Season but, in the meantime, Louisa has asked that both Sera and I attend the house party she is giving at the conclusion of the Season." She paused and looked at him hopefully. "Might you be attending this as well, Lord Kingston?"

He planned to do so. With Minta as his wife.

"Yes, Miss Nicholls. I have been pressed by the Three Cousins to attend. I will drag my cousin, the Duke of Woodmont, with me."

A slight fear ran through him. Win, with all his charm and winsome ways, would be drawn to Minta like a moth to flame.

Percy better do what he could to see her attached—to him—before the house party ever took place.

"Would you care to go for a stroll before the dancing resumes?" he asked, praying she would accept.

Before she could reply, Ev caught his eye and said, "We don't want you to miss the announcement."

He and Minta turned their attention to the center of the table.

Ev smiled broadly. "We wanted you to know that Edwin is going to be a big brother."

Percy frowned a moment and then he realized what that meant.

"Congratulations!" echoed around the table.

"When?" Louisa asked eagerly.

"Most likely mid-November," Adalyn replied. "I am to see both a doctor and a midwife tomorrow at Ev's insistence."

The duke beamed at his wife. "I am so pleased with Addie. I hope, this time, it will be a girl."

His words surprised Percy for a moment. He was used to men only being interested in heirs and possible spares, with no consideration given to females who were birthed. Then again, his circle of friends had proven most unusual, with the fathers actively involved with their babies, even the girls. Spence treated Analise as a princess and Owen never seemed to put down Margaret.

He glanced to Minta and suddenly wished that she carried his child, a girl who would have the same copper hair and sweet soprano voice as her mother. He shook it off, not wanting to get ahead of himself. His current mission was to kiss Minta again and let her know of his interest in her. One step at a time, he reminded himself.

"We should go to the retiring room before the dancing begins again," suggested Tessa.

The four women rose and disappointment filled him. By the time that occurred, he was sure Minta would need to be returned to the ballroom for the next set.

She surprised him, however, leaning over and saying, "Would you wait for me in the foyer, my lord? Perhaps we could get in a small stroll."

He beamed. "I would be happy to."

The women left the table and Percy also excused himself, taking his time reaching the foyer. On his way, he was stopped three times. Twice, the faces looked familiar and he recalled meeting the gentlemen at White's. The third time, Lord Boxling claimed his attention.

"Enjoying this evening, Kingston?" the viscount asked.

Percy shrugged. "I suppose so."

"You landed the best partner in the room for the supper dance. Do you have plans of calling upon Miss Nicholls tomorrow afternoon?"

"I do," he said quickly, thinking Minta would be the only lady he visited. "And I plan to ask her to drive in the park with me afterward," he added, hoping to beat the viscount to the idea.

Boxling merely nodded. "I will see you at the Westlakes then." He strolled away.

He wondered if this was Boxling's way of telling Percy that they would be directly competing for Minta's affections.

In the foyer, he studied a suit of armor to pass the time, thinking how cumbersome it must have been to wear into battle.

"Lord Kingston?"

Turning, he saw Minta next to him. Offering her his arm, he led her back to the ballroom, slipping out a set of French doors that led onto the terrace. Frustration filled him as he saw several couples strolling the length. Then he spied a stone staircase and moved toward it, leading her down it. He brought them around the corner of the house until they were out of sight. Percy found himself trembling at the thought of kissing Minta.

Looking at her, he saw her brow knitted and bent, kissing it gently. Her quick intake of breath indicated her surprise.

He placed his hands on her bare shoulders and lowered his mouth to hers, the scent of vanilla enveloping him. He would forever associate the smell with her.

Percy kept the kiss chaste and tender, unlike the previous time he had kissed her with growing passion. It would not do to return her to the ballroom and allow others to guess what they had been up to. Still, his lips lingered on her mouth, his fingers kneading her shoulders.

Breaking the kiss, he gazed down upon her, seeing her cheeks flushed with color.

"Might I call upon you tomorrow afternoon, Miss Nicholls?"

"Yes," she said breathlessly.

"And would you also take a drive with me through Hyde Park?"

She smiled radiantly. "I would like that very much, my lord."

"So would I."

He couldn't help himself. He bent and kissed her again, hard and fast, yearning for the taste of her but wise enough to break the kiss quickly.

"Let me return you to the ballroom," he said.

Leading her back up the stairs, they entered the doors and he delivered her into Adalyn's care.

Taking her hand, he brought it to his lips and kissed it. "Until tomorrow."

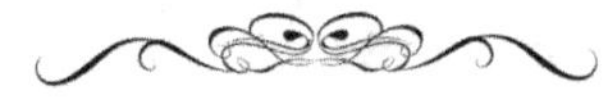

CHAPTER EIGHTEEN

THE SCREAM TORE from Percy's throat, ripping him from a terrible nightmare. He rolled swiftly to his side and found no pillow to muffle the horrible sounds coming from him. They continued to pour forth and he wadded up the bedsheet and stuffed it into his mouth, his body trembling violently.

The nightmares had only grown stronger over the last few weeks. He had thought being away from the battlefront would ease his mind but, apparently, he was growing worse.

A sudden pounding sounded on his door.

"My lord, are you all right?" shouted Huston.

Percy froze. Before, he had always been able to quiet his screams. No one had a bedchamber along the corridor where he slept. Huston's arrival only meant that his shouts had been loud enough to go as far as the servants' quarters.

Huston beat on the door again. "My lord! Open up!"

A new voice joined in. "Lord Kingston, please open the door. We must see if you are all right."

That was Tate, his butler. God only knew how many others had been awakened and disturbed.

He yanked the bedclothes from his mouth and barked out, "I am fine. Leave!"

Silence was the response for a few moments and then Tate called out, "We just want to see if you need anything, my lord."

"I said I was fine—and I meant it!" Fury filled his body, which still quaked.

"Very well, my lord," the butler shouted.

Percy listened, hoping to hear their steps retreat but did not, thanks most likely to the thick carpeting that lined the corridor.

His body continued to shiver as if he had no control over it. He realized he did not and curled into a tight ball, beginning to weep. His tears turned to gut wrenching sobs and, once more, he tried to quiet the noise so as not to alarm any more servants. He had no idea how long the sobbing went on, only that he felt he was slowly losing his grip on sanity.

Finally, they subsided and the tremors running through him receded, leaving him chilled and spent. He located the pillows, which had somehow been knocked to the floor, and brought them to the bed again. Bringing the bedclothes to his chin, he wrapped them securely about him, wondering why he had thought he could have a normal life. The life meant for Rupert. The life of the Marquess of Kingston.

He cursed aloud, blaming his brother for not having wed and producing an heir, causing that responsibility to fall upon his shoulders. Percy realized in this moment how unsuited he was, not only to hold the title but to think he should wed Minta and have children with her. He knew he could never relinquish the title. It was the albatross that would hang about his neck until his death. He could, though, see that it was passed beyond him. Surely, there was some cousin or distant relative who could inherit it upon his death. If there were no such heir, the title would revert to the crown.

Resolve filled him. That is what should happen. He would retreat to the country and live a solitary life, tending to his tenants and responsibilities and withdrawing from all social life in London.

That meant giving up his dreams of a life with Minta Nicholls.

A fresh wave of tears assaulted him. He let them run their

course, deciding it would be the honorable thing to tell her in person. She deserved someone whole, not a broken man who would never be put right again. She needed a husband who could make her laugh. One who would cherish her.

But Minta was a determined young woman, not one who would take no for an answer without a fight. Percy believed in order to save her from him, he would have to hurt her. The thought of doing so nearly broke him but, in the end, it would be for the best.

Sleep must have come again for he awoke as light filtered into his bedchamber. The bedclothes were sticky with sweat. He rang for Huston and the valet appeared quickly. Huston did not bring up the events of the previous night and neither did Percy. Instead, he called for a bath and allowed the valet to scrub him from head to toe. His body might now be clean but he knew his mind never would be. It carried the scars of war. His damaged soul was his cross to bear. He would never burden Minta—or any other woman—with his shortcomings.

He went downstairs to breakfast and pretended to read the newspaper as he ate. Everything was tasteless to him. He merely put food into his mouth to give his body fuel for the battle that lay ahead.

Retreating to his study, Percy closed the door and sat in it for hours, brooding. When it was time to leave and call upon Minta as he had promised, he prayed for the Herculean strength it would take to end things between them. He promised himself not to argue with her nor be swayed by tears. He regretted how deeply he would need to hurt her but, in the long run, he would be doing her a favor.

He rang for Tate and asked for his carriage to be readied. When the butler returned and said the carriage awaited him, Percy went outside. Before boarding it, he gave instructions to the driver.

"Take me to Lord Westlake's townhouse. Once I have left there, you are to drive."

The coachman's brow furrowed in confusion. "Drive where, my lord?"

Percy shrugged. "I will need time to think. Drive for an hour—no, two—before you return here."

The coachman still had an odd look on his face but he nodded. "Yes, my lord."

Percy climbed inside the vehicle and it set off. His belly roiled at what he was about to do and dread permeated every pore. He knew he was right, though. To save Minta, he would need to wound her gravely. Push her so far away that she would not ever be able to stand the sight of him again.

⟫⟫⟫✕⟪⟪⟪

MINTA CAME DOWNSTAIRS after dressing in one of her favorite morning gowns, a pale yellow the color of soft sunshine. She entered the drawing room half an hour before the time suitors would come calling. The sight and scent of flowers overwhelmed her.

Aunt Phyllis smiled at her, waving her hand about. "Look at all the beautiful bouquets you have received today, my darling."

Dumbfounded, Minta went to one and pulled the card from it. She recalled dancing a Scotch reel with the gentleman.

Looking about, she said, "How many arrangements have arrived?"

Her aunt grinned triumphantly. "Twenty-seven in all."

"But I did not dance with twenty-seven gentlemen. Far from it, truth be told."

"Whether you danced with them—or even met them—you made quite an impression on many eligible bachelors, just as I knew you would."

She went from bouquet to bouquet, reading the attached cards. She smiled when she came to a rather large arrangement of lilacs, which Lord Boxling had sent.

When she came to the last floral arrangement and read the card, disappointment filled her.

Percy had not sent flowers to her.

She turned and Aunt Phyllis shook her head in disgust. "I know what you are looking for, Minta. The Marquess of Kingston did not send anything to you, despite having danced the waltz with you and supping with you."

She wanted to give him the benefit of the doubt and said, "Perhaps Lord Kingston is not aware of the custom of sending flowers to a lady he is interested in. Remember, Aunt Phyllis, he is new to the *ton* and its ways."

Her aunt shook her head. "No, I will not have you defending him. The Duchess of Camden has taken the marquess under her wing and she would have made him aware of what Polite Society expects. He did not send you a bouquet because he is not interested in you, Minta."

She remembered the tender, sweet kiss he had bestowed last night. "No, Aunt, you are mistaken. I am certain it is merely an oversight. Perhaps the florist has yet to deliver all the arrangements about town. Besides, Lord Kingston told me he would be calling upon me this afternoon. He is not a man who would break his word to me. I know that."

Aunt Phyllis glared in disapproval a Minta's words. "Say what you want, Child, but I doubt he will show his face this afternoon."

Minta returned to her bedchamber, where she knew she would not be disturbed. She sat and thumbed through the cards she had collected from each bouquet, thinking of each gentleman and trying to recall his face. Other than Lord Boxling, however, they all seemed to be a blur now.

The only face that mattered was Percy's.

He would prove Aunt Phyllis wrong when he called today. She knew it. She believed it.

A knock sounded at her door and Bertha quickly entered. "You must come downstairs at once, Miss Nicholls. Your suitors are arriving."

Minta stood, squaring her shoulders. Returning to the drawing room, she saw both Uncle West and Aunty Phyllis now in attendance, thinking it sweet they both wished to chaperone her on this first day of callers.

The butler entered and announced three names and the arrivals entered. Soon, the drawing room was full of gentlemen, each staying about a quarter-hour, which Louisa had told her was an acceptable amount of time for a visit. Every time the butler entered the room, Minta found her heart in her throat as she waited to hear Lord Kingston's name announced.

Finally, she did hear it and turned to give her aunt a triumphant smile, only seeing disapproval on the older woman's face.

As he entered, Minta immediately knew something was wrong with the marquess. She couldn't put her finger on what it might be and then decided he must be uncomfortable with several suitors still present. He did not do well in large groups and most likely never would. It was all right. He had come and her heart sang as he moved toward her.

"Good afternoon, Miss Nicholls," he said with no emotion, nodding his head.

It surprised her that he did not take her hand, much less kiss it, as every other bachelor who called this afternoon had done.

Swallowing her disappointment, she said, "Thank you for calling today, my lord."

When he said nothing more, Lord Boxling began a new conversation, joined by two of his friends who had accompanied him. They spoke several minutes, with nary a word uttered by Lord Kingston.

Abruptly, he said, "I will take my leave. Would you care to walk me out, Miss Nicholls?"

His request was unusual but Minta knew he must have something he wished to say to her in private.

"Of course, my lord," she said graciously. Turning to the circle around them, she said, "I will return in a few minutes, gentlemen."

She turned and found Percy had already left the drawing room without her and she moved to the door.

He strode down the corridor and she lengthened her own stride, trying to catch up with him. She did so as he reached the staircase.

"What is wrong, my lord?" she asked.

He did not bother answering her and moved down the stairs. Minta followed, a sick feeling growing in her belly. They reached the foyer and he paused, looking about. Only a footman stood in the foyer, on duty at the door.

"Please come outside," he ordered and she followed him, concern growing within her.

On the pavement, he turned and faced her.

"I owed it to you to come in person today, Miss Nicholls."

She tried to smile and said, "You did promise you would call upon me, my lord. Remember, we are to go for a drive in Hyde Park."

He frowned deeply and met her gaze. "I was wrong to have promised that and given you false hope."

"False hope?" she echoed faintly, feeling disaster was striking.

"I have determined that we do not suit, Miss Nicholls, and that we never will. There are things I am looking for in my marchioness and you possess none of those qualities."

Tears stung her eyes. "What? Why are you saying this, Percy?"

He flinched at her use of his Christian name. She saw his eyes harden. She was losing him—and didn't understand why.

"I know very well that we *do* suit," she told him. "I know the kind of man you are. That I am a better woman when I am around you. We bring out the best in one another, Percy. You know that. I know that."

His eyes narrowed. "You think you know me but you do not. Our acquaintance has been very short and must end now."

Anger flared within her. "You would throw everything away? Everything we have? You are different with me and you know you are, Percy. You speak openly with me. The reserved, retiring man the world sees is not the one I see. You open up to me. We have things in common. I know we could build a good life together."

She touched his forearm. "Tell me you do not sense that spark between us. Tell me the kisses we have shared mean nothing. Tell me there is another woman in Polite Society you would be more comfortable with." Minta snorted. "You can't—because there isn't. We are right for one another, Percy. I beg you, do not do this."

He shrugged her off. "You do not have the right to question me, Miss Nicholls," he said coldly. "I am trying to let you down as gently as possible but you are being obtuse. I will speak plainly so that no misunderstanding will arise. You are not the woman for me. I was mistaken about you in every way possible. Go back to your bevy of suitors because you certainly have acquired enough of them. Lord Boxling would be a good choice for you. But under no circumstances do I have any interest in you nor will I vie for your hand. This will be the last conversation between us," he stated, his voice flat and unemotional.

"You don't mean a word you are saying," she said, tears streaming down her cheeks.

Anger sparked in his eyes. "I meant every word of it," he snapped. "I am not like the Second Sons in that I do not wish to have a marriage similar to the ones they have."

"But they are so happy," she stated firmly, seeing him slip away from her.

"They may want to be friends—as well as lovers—with their wives. I have no interest in that type of marriage. You are far too meddlesome to ever be my wife. I would not have a moment's peace around you. You would demand too much of me—and I have too little to give."

His words pierced her. "You are saying you do not wish for good conversations? Shared happiness?"

"They have nothing to do with a marriage. Marriages are

about dowries and social connections. You simply are not up to snuff, Miss Nicholls. I can do far better than you."

"Then go ahead and do so," she lashed out, anger filling her. "Marry some empty-headed fool. Get her with child. Carry on with your selfish life. I hope I never see you again."

His eyes turned wintry. "I hope the same thing, Miss Nicholls. If we do run into one another in the future, since we do have acquaintances in common, I will be polite but distant and expect you to do the same."

Minta slapped him. Hard.

Shaking, she said, "Go to Hell, Lord Kingston. I hope you will enjoy it there."

Whirling, she hurried back into the townhouse, rushing past the startled footman and racing up the stairs. She paused on the landing, unsure where to go. She couldn't return to the drawing room with her bodice stained with tears and her eyes practically swollen shut. Yet she had left visitors with the promise that she would return to them.

And return she would. She would not let Percy's atrocious behavior make her behave poorly. She had more than manners. She had kindness and a regard for others, unlike the selfish, frustrating marquess.

Quickly, she went to her bedchamber and washed her face. It would take too long to wait for Bertha to come and help her into a new gown and so Minta grabbed a colorful shawl and wrapped it about her. She glanced into the mirror and grimaced at her reflection. Still, she determined to return to her suitors.

Making her way downstairs, she inhaled a deep breath and held it a moment before letting it out and stepping into the drawing room again. She saw the three gentlemen still present, though they had all taken a seat and now spoke with her aunt and uncle.

Aunt Phyllis looked up, dismay crossing her face. "Minta, my dear, whatever is wrong?"

She launched into a quick lie as she took a seat. "I had something in my eye that hurt fiercely, Aunt. I returned to my room and was able to wash it out but I spilled quite a few tears since it was so painful."

"And you are better now?" Lord Boxling asked, his deep voice filled with concern.

"Very much so, my lord." She smiled at him. "In fact, I was hoping you and your friends might stay and join us for tea if Aunt Phyllis and Uncle West do not mind."

"Not a bit," her uncle declared.

Her aunt beamed. "We would be delighted if you could stay."

The viscount glanced to his friends, who both nodded eagerly.

"Then stay we will," Lord Boxling said.

She rang for tea and spent the next hour with a smile pasted upon her lips. She fought every urge to think about Percy, shoving it away, as she focused upon their visitors.

When teatime ended, Lord Boxling asked, "Will you be attending tonight's musicale, Miss Nicholls?"

This time, Minta gave the viscount a genuine smile. "Yes, Lord Boxling. And I hope you will be present, as well."

"Good," he said. "I will claim the seat next to yours. I believe we have much to speak about."

CHAPTER NINETEEN

PERCY HAD NEVER been more miserable in his entire life.

He took a swig from the whiskey bottle, draining the contents, letting it fall from his fingers on to the floor. The last couple of days had gone by in a haze as he had drunk himself into oblivion. He knew he was going to have to tell the Second Sons at some point about his decision not to wed. He realized he should have quickly retreated to Kingwood before he hit the bottle but he hadn't. Last night, he was to have attended a card party. Only Ev and Adalyn were scheduled to go and they were supposed to pick up Percy in their carriage. Fortunately for him, Adalyn had a horrible bout of nausea and Ev had sent word they would be unable to go, urging him to attend without them.

Percy had no intention of going to any further *ton* events. Ever.

While he still had a cohesive thought within him, he scrawled a note to Owen and Louisa regarding tomorrow night's ball, writing that he had somehow eaten a bad portion of meat and his belly and bowels were in ruins. He instructed Huston not to deliver it until tomorrow afternoon. That way, they would not expect him at that evening's ball. He hoped by then he could pull himself together enough and get out of town and return to the country, where he planned to stay the rest of his life.

He had asked Huston to keep the liquor bottles coming as he

tried to drink away his problems. If he drank enough, hopefully the nightmares would recede, as well as Minta's image. The look on her face stayed with him and would until his dying day. Wounding her had been the hardest thing Percy had ever done but it was for her own good. The Season was only beginning and it would give her time to find a good man as her husband.

And forget she had ever met him.

He reached for another bottle and opened it, pouring the amber liquid down his throat. It burned a trail of fire to his empty belly, which growled in rebellion since he hadn't eaten in who knew when. He continued drinking until he did not know if it was day or night. He drank to forget the dreams which had withered and died, knowing in his heart he had done the best thing for the woman he loved.

That admission had startled him. He hadn't known himself capable of love but realized that was exactly what he felt for Minta. He tortured himself by wondering if she had those same feelings for him and tried to shove those painful thoughts away. He'd spent hours passed out and then awakened, drinking again, and repeating the process all over. The few times a knock sounded on his door, he shouted obscenities at the top of his lungs and, soon, whoever was there ceased trying to enter.

Hurt hung over him like a dark storm cloud. He would do his best to get dressed the next time he awoke and leave London for good.

Percy came to with a start, drenched in icy water. He sat up quickly, gripping his skull in his hands as pain exploded through his head.

Glancing up, he saw Owen hovering over him, a stormy look on his face. Huston stood nearby.

Turning his wrath upon the valet, he shouted, "Traitor!" Huston flinched at the accusation.

"What the bloody hell have you done to yourself?" Owen demanded.

"It is none of your business, Owen. Stay out of it."

Percy fell back against the pillows, exhausted, his head throbbing violently.

"You don't know me as well as I thought you did," his friend said, glowering at him. "You are going to drink the coffee Huston brought you and we are going to put you in a tub." Owen's nose crinkled. "Because you stink to high Heaven."

He squeezed his eyes shut and moaned. "Leave," he begged.

"No," Owen said flatly. "Coffee, Huston."

Percy found himself lifted from the bed by the two men and placed into a chair. Owen tore open the curtains and bright sunlight flooded the room, instantly causing Percy to wince.

"You may drink the coffee yourself or I will pour it down you," Owen threatened.

Knowing he hadn't the strength to fight back, Percy gave in to defeat and took the cup offered to him by Huston. The hot brew was just what he needed and it began to clear the cloud which had descended upon him. Once the haze disappeared, only the dull thud remained, throbbing in his temples.

Not to mention the pain in his heart.

Signaling to Huston, Owen said, "Bring the concoction now."

The valet went to the table and brought back a large container to Owen, who handed it to Percy.

"Drink," his friend ordered. "The stuff is horrendous but it will help your head."

He took a sip and his face scrunched. He spit it out.

Owen's hand gripped Percy's shoulders and he said, "This isn't something to sip, my friend. Down it quickly. It may taste vile but it is highly effective."

He did as he was told, not having the energy to protest. Drinking the entire contents, he dropped the cup and shuddered.

The door opened and a bevy of servants brought in buckets of hot and cold water. Owen had two of them strip the bed as the others filled the tub. Once all the servants were gone, Owen helped Huston remove Percy's clothes and they half-carried him to the tub since his legs gave out.

Once in the bath, both men worked on scrubbing him. Owen was more gentle as he lathered Percy's hair and rinsed it, probably knowing just how violent the headache was. It did seem to recede as the bath continued and he didn't know if it was the hot water or the horrible concoction he had drunk but he was feeling a bit better.

They helped him to stand and dried him off, getting him into his banyan. His belly grumbled and Owen nodded. Huston went and rang for a servant who must have already been given instructions because she appeared with a tray. He spied a pot of tea and dry toast on it. Owen got Percy to move to a chair and he collapsed into it. Owen nodded and Huston left the room.

"The tea is strong and overly sweetened with honey, which will aid in your recovery. Tear the toast into tiny bits and go slowly."

Percy did as ordered and it took a good hour to get the entire pot of tea and two pieces of toast in him.

"What is wrong?" Owen asked. "You seemed so happy the opening night of the Season. I believe that happiness was due to Miss Nicholls."

He flinched upon hearing her name and said flatly, "There is nothing between us, Owen. Don't push it."

Fire sparked in Owen's eyes. "I will push, Percy. Hard. It is obvious to the Second Sons and the Three Cousins that Miss Nicholls and you are made for one another. I want to know what happened. She was at last night's ball and I know she wasn't happy. What passed between the two of you?"

He sighed. "I called upon her and told her that we had no future together."

Surprise filled Owen's face. "Why would you do something so foolish, Percy?"

"I did it *for* her. I am not good enough for her, Owen. She deserves a whole man, not half of one."

"Is it the nightmares?" his friend asked quietly.

"You know of them?"

Percy had shared a tent with Win while at war and he had thought only his cousin knew of the nightmares.

"Yes, Win shared his concerns with us. They still linger, I am assuming."

He nodded. "They are worse than they ever have been," he admitted. "I thought being away from the battlefield would cure me of the nightmares. Instead, they have grown in intensity and frequency." Sadness draped him like a cloak as he said, "I could not let an angel such as Minta be stuck with a broken man. She needs love and laughter in her life."

"Don't you think she could bring those things to *your* life, Percy?" Owen asked pointedly.

He shook his head. "No, I will not subject her to my deficiencies. I did everything in my power to shove her away as hard as possible. The things I said to her, Owen. If she ever lays eyes upon me again, she would probably spit in my face. As it is, she slapped me before we parted."

Sympathy filled his friend's eyes. "Oh, Percy. You aren't giving her enough credit. I think all of us came back from the war much different men than when we left. The love of a good, kind, strong woman would be the beginning of your healing."

Could it be true? Could he have a future with Minta? Would she take him, knowing how damaged he was?

"I don't know if she would even speak to me, much less consider, marrying me after the hateful things I said to her."

"You should trust more in her, Percy. She is meant for you and you for her. At least try to see her and discover if a future together is possible. Either she will forgive you—or she won't—but either way, you must try or you will live with regret the rest of your life."

Shakily, Percy rose from the chair. "I will do as you ask," he said quietly. "I don't carry much hope of her bestowing forgiveness upon me, but it is worth a try."

Owen stood and smiled, placing his hand on Percy's shoulder and squeezing it in support. "Good. We should get you dressed.

There is a garden party this afternoon and Miss Nicholls told Louisa that she would be attending it. Perhaps you can steal a private moment with her and see where you stand."

Owen himself helped to dress Percy and the pair left the bedchamber and went outside, where Owen's carriage had just pulled up. Louisa sat inside it and beckoned for Percy to join her. He sat beside her and she took his hand, threading her fingers through his. He saw no judgment on her face.

"It is good to see you again, Percy. We have missed you."

Those were the only words spoken as the carriage made its way through the streets of London and delivered them to the garden party.

MINTA RODE WITH her aunt and uncle to the afternoon garden party. She hoped today she might make a new start as far as the Season went. Uncle West had invested heavily, not only in her wardrobe but her dowry, and she owed it to him and Aunty Phyllis to put forth her best effort in finding a husband.

The card party she had attended had been a disaster. She had told Lord Boxling of the vicious things Percy had said to her and even the viscount was puzzled by Percy's sudden shift. They had partnered in cards and Minta had needed to excuse herself three different times to rush to the retiring room and weep.

Each time she emerged, Lord Boxling was waiting for her. His steady presence truly comforted her and she wished she could have more than a sisterly affection for him.

Last night's ball had been only slightly better. Though Minta looked her best and her dance card had filled quickly, she felt as though she were sleepwalking through the entire event. Fortunately, conversation was not required during most of the active dances. Lord Boxling had danced the supper dance with her and she had supped with him and three of his friends, getting to know a few other young women making their come-outs.

When she had arrived home, Minta cried herself to sleep, awaking with swollen eyes. Seeing her image in the mirror, she resolved to quit shedding tears over a man who cared nothing for her. Today would be the day she would make a new start and put forth her best effort in order to land a husband. It wasn't only for her but for Sera. She wanted to be able to help in launching her twin into Polite Society. Sera had been so glum after receiving news of Captain Marsh's death. She'd had enough time to grieve, however, and Minta knew her sister's beauty and goodness would help her find a good man as her husband.

"Are you looking forward to the garden party?" Aunt Phyllis asked, concern in her eyes.

For the first time in days, Minta's smile was genuine. "Yes, I am. I hope this occasion will give me a better chance to get to know some of the gentlemen I have met during these first few days of the Season."

She saw the obvious relief sweep through her aunt and her uncle even winked at her, saying, "Good for you, Minta. I have always enjoyed the conversation at a garden party. I heard our hosts' gardens are the envy of everyone in the *ton* and look forward to seeing them."

Their carriage arrived and they entered the townhouse, passing through to a receiving room, where they were greeted by an older couple she had not met before. Minta followed her aunt and uncle out the doors to where others gathered on the lawn. She spied Tessa and Adalyn.

"May I go visit with my friends?" she asked.

"Of course, my dear," Aunt Phyllis said.

Making her way toward them, she accepted a glass of champagne from a passing footman.

"Don't you look wonderful?" Tessa said.

"The peach silk suits you well, Minta," Adalyn agreed. "How have you been?"

"I am looking forward to this garden party and tonight's

outing to the theatre," she told her friends.

"Oh, who is going to the theatre with you?"

"Viscount Boxling invited me. We will go with him and two of his friends. Uncle West and Aunt Phyllis are accompanying us as chaperones."

"Do you know what play you will see?" Tessa asked.

Minta giggled, not recalling the last time she had done so. "No, I haven't a clue. I am still looking forward to the outing and a light supper afterward, all the same."

She realized it felt good to feel lighthearted and knew she had much to be grateful for. Her parents, who had allowed her to come to England for this Season. Her aunt and uncle, for taking her in and treating her as their own. Her new friends she had made. And this Season, in which she had the opportunity to find a man to share her life with and build a family together.

Yes, her world had been turned upside down by the rejection she had experienced at Percy's hands. No, Lord Kingston. She must never think of him as Percy again.

Minta took another sip of her champagne and glanced across the scene, seeing all the beautiful, light-colored gowns and tables filled with sandwiches and petit fours. The sun was shining and the day was cool, with a slight breeze in the air. A perfect English day.

Until she sensed someone's gaze upon her and turned.

Lord Kingston had arrived—and was headed in her direction.

A huge lump formed in her throat. She reached out blindly, finding Tessa's hand and clutching it tightly.

Then he was in front of her.

He looked ashen, as if he had been ill. He appeared unsure of himself. He started to speak and hesitated, staring at her.

"May we speak, Miss Nicholls?" he finally got out, sounding as if someone were strangling him.

Minta surprised herself when she said, "No, we may not."

The marquess winced, looking like a kicked puppy. She held fast, though.

"You shredded my heart, my lord," she said frankly. "I am done with you."

With that, Minta walked away.

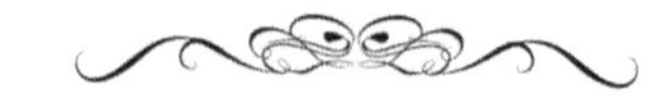

CHAPTER TWENTY

MINTA MOVED AWAY and accepted another glass of champagne from a footman. She downed the entire flute, immediately regretting it as she became lightheaded. A wave of dizziness swept over her and she was loath to take even a single step.

Suddenly, someone clasped her elbow and took the champagne flute from her hand.

It was Lord Danbury.

He smiled and placed the empty flute on a tray and turned back to her.

"Why don't we stand here just a moment, Miss Nicholls? Champagne has a way of sneaking up on you."

She frowned at him. "If you are here to defend your friend, I don't care to hear what you have to say."

He slipped her hand into the crook of his arm and, slowly, they moved about the party.

"I do not speak for Lord Kingston. No one can do that except Kingston himself."

She eyed him with suspicion. "You may say that, my lord, but I am certain that you wish to whisper into my ear all of the wonderful things about him. Well, I don't find him wonderful at all."

"I agree with you."

His words startled her. "You do?"

As they strolled, he said, "Do I know that he was deliberately cruel to you? Yes. Should he make his apologies to you? Most certainly."

Lord Danbury gazed steadily at her. "But you would need to be open to hearing such an apology, Miss Nicholls."

They continued about the party without further conversation. She was glad to be on his arm since she still felt a bit shaky.

Then he returned her to her aunt. Bowing, he said, "My wife thoroughly enjoys your company, Miss Nicholls. Thank you for the friendship which you have extended to her. Good afternoon."

Minta watched the earl retreat and Aunt Phyllis said, "My, what a perfect gentleman Lord Danbury is. You are fortunate to count Lady Danbury among your friends, Minta."

Distracted, she merely nodded.

Lord Markham asked if she would care to take a turn about the party. She agreed to do so and took his offered arm. For the next hour, they spoke to a good number of guests, Minta trying her best to focus on the party and not wondering what Lord Danbury had meant by saying Lord Kingston had been deliberately cruel to her. She had no idea why the marquess would have gone out of his way to hurt her as he had. Perhaps she did owe it to him to listen to whatever apology he was willing to give. That did not mean, however, that he would be back in her good graces. She decided to allow Lord Kingston to apologize so there would be no further awkwardness between them, especially since she was bound to run into him while she was visiting one of the Three Cousins.

Viscount Chatsworth approached her and said, "Are you enjoying yourself this afternoon, Miss Nicholls?"

She had met him the previous evening through a friend of Lord Boxling's and had danced with Chatsworth once. The viscount was tall, blond, and had a sunny smile.

She smiled in return and said, "Yes, my lord. This is a delightful garden party."

"Have you had a chance to stroll the gardens yet?" he asked.

"No, I haven't."

He brightened, a bit of mischief in his eyes. "Then would you care to see my father's gardens with me?"

His words surprised Minta. Both their hosts were dark-haired. Lord Chatsworth resembled neither of them.

He must have seen the question in her eyes because he chuckled and said, "I am the only child from my father's first marriage. My mother died giving birth to me. I am told I favor her and her side of the family."

"I am sorry for your loss, my lord."

He shrugged. "It is hard to miss what one has never known. Shall we?"

She took his arm and he tucked her hand into his, placing a hand over hers, and leading her toward the gardens.

They strolled for a few minutes and he pointed out various blooms to her.

"You seem quite knowledgeable about flowers," she noted.

"They are something I enjoy," he told her. "But there are some exquisite tulips if we go along another path. Would you care to see them?"

"I would be delighted to do so, my lord."

They strolled leisurely, passing several couples, and then Lord Chatsworth turned. Minta grew concerned when they did not run into anyone else. She thought to the warnings Aunt Phyllis had given her about never being alone with a gentleman at any given moment.

However, Viscount Chatsworth had proven to be charming and interesting. She would see the tulips and then casually suggest they return to the others.

Moments later, they came across an array of colors.

"See? I told you that you would like this."

He pointed not only to the tulips but also to the anemone and crocus. She nodded occasionally, simply listening to the timbre of his voice, wondering if he could be someone she might possibly spend the rest of her life with.

"You are late making your come-out, Miss Nicholls," he said.

"Yes, I am. I spent several years in Ontario, where my father assisted the Administrator of Upper Canada. It was impossible to return to England during the war years."

"I see." He smiled again. "It is a pleasure to speak to a lady who is a bit older than the girls making their come-outs. They all seem to be silly geese."

She laughed. "I have met several of them and I understand what you mean, my lord. They are quite young and some of them a tad immature."

He faced her, an intensity in his eyes, giving her a chill.

"Being a mature woman, Miss Nicholls, you must know exactly what you want."

She felt her cheeks heat and said, "I am not quite certain what you mean."

His hands gripped her shoulders and he said, "This."

Suddenly, he yanked her against him and his mouth came down on hers, hard. There was no finesse to the kiss. It was brutal and overpowering. She placed her palms against his chest, trying to push him away, but he wrapped his arms about her so that she was imprisoned within them. He forced her mouth open and thrust his tongue inside as she continued to struggle. Not knowing what else to do, Minta bit it as hard as she could.

Immediately, he broke the kiss, a string of obscenities pouring from him.

"You are a tease, Miss Nicholls," he told her, anger in his eyes, which caused a chill to run through her.

"I am nothing of the sort, Lord Chatsworth. I never asked for your kiss or gave you indication I wanted one from you. Please release me. Now."

A gleam entered his eyes. "Why should I? When I now need to punish you for your wanton behavior."

Fear filled her as his mouth came down hard on hers again. Minta tightened her lips, denying him entrance, sensing the rage that filled him.

Then he was suddenly torn from her and she was free.

She saw Percy had hold of Lord Chatsworth. The marquess landed a strong blow to the viscount's jaw. It was so forceful, Chatsworth would have been felled if Percy had not been gripping the viscount's coat. He slammed a fist into Lord Chatsworth's nose and blood spurted. He struck the viscount repeatedly and she saw his fist becoming bloodied.

"Stop!" she cried. "You will kill him if you don't."

Percy shoved the viscount and he stumbled, falling to the ground.

Percy took two steps forward and hovered over the man, contained rage in his face and fisted hands.

"You were a sneaky little bastard in school. It doesn't surprise me that you would try and take advantage of an innocent. You better thank the stars that Miss Nicholls kept me from beating you to a pulp, Chatsworth. Get up and leave. You are never to speak to Miss Nicholls again, is that understood?"

Minta saw the fear on the viscount's face as he nodded rapidly. Percy took a few steps back and Lord Chatsworth scrambled to his feet, blood dripping from his nose onto his snowy white cravat.

"Go," Percy ordered quietly and the viscount scurried away.

He took a few steps to her and clasped both her elbows in his hands to steady her.

"Are you all right? Did he hurt you?"

Tears brimmed in her eyes as she shook her head. "No, he did not hurt me. He did scare me, though. If we had been seen by anyone of the *ton*, then he would have had to offer for me." She shuddered. "I cannot imagine what it would be like having to wed a man I have only spoken to twice. One so dishonorable and fiendish as to attack a guest invited to his home."

He cupped her cheek with one hand, his thumb brushing away the tear that fell.

"He will not come near you again. I guarantee it." He

frowned. "I am sorry you had to witness such brutish behavior."

Minta gazed up at Percy, seeing the hard look in his eyes, wondering if this was how he appeared when on the battlefield. "Thank you for saving me."

"I am so sorry that I hurt you, Minta," he said huskily. "What I said to you was inexcusable."

But she did not want to hear apologies from his lips. What she wanted was his lips on hers. Somehow, her unspoken thought became clear to him and he lowered his mouth to hers.

The kiss was incredibly tender, soothing her, making her feel safe and protected. She clutched the lapels on his coat and pulled him closer to her.

That was all it took—and the kiss heated up considerably. She opened to him and his tongue swept inside, finding hers, gliding along it. They began a game as their tongues danced along each other's. The spice of his cologne filled the air as he continued to kiss her.

She wished this kiss could go on forever.

As Percy kissed her, he cursed inwardly, feeling he was taking advantage of Minta. She had looked so sad and lost that he had only meant to take her into his arms and hold her close a moment, just to reassure her that everything would be fine.

The look in her eyes had changed, though. He knew she desired him as much as he desired her. She might regret this kiss.

But he never would.

He took and took from her and she gave to him readily. Their passion heated their skin and he broke the kiss, trailing his lips along the slender column of her throat. He longed to nip it but restrained himself from doing so, knowing the cut of her gown would not hide what they had been up to.

Moving his lips back up, he seized hers again, pouring every-thing he felt for this woman into the kiss. He would kiss her until she was breathless—and then he would beg for her forgiveness. He could only pray she might bestow it upon him.

Because he didn't think he could live without Minta in his life.

A loud gasp sounded.

And it didn't come from the woman he was kissing.

Percy broke the kiss and glanced up to see Lady Vickers standing only a few feet from them. This was the woman Adalyn had advised him to steer clear of, the woman she had called the biggest gossip in the *ton*. He had taken Adalyn's words to heart and had avoided being around Lady Eve, the daughter of Lady Vickers.

"Well, I am shocked to my core," Lady Vickers said, her eyes roaming up and down both Minta and him. "You are quite disheveled, Miss Nicholls, and pink from all that kissing. Why, the gentlemanly thing to do, Lord Kingston, would be to offer for and wed this poor girl immediately."

Then a sly look crossed the countess' face and she smiled. "Or . . . perhaps you should wed *my* daughter instead . . . and I will overlook this unfortunate incident I have witnessed."

Minta sucked in a quick breath. "Why, that is blackmail!" she proclaimed.

Lady Vickers shrugged. "True," she agreed, "but I find it effective in obtaining what I want." She eyed Percy. "I believe I want a marquess as my son-in-law."

He would not stand for this. Knowing it would be fruitless to try and deal with this appalling woman, Percy grabbed Minta's hand and strode away.

Lady Vickers called after them. "I will ruin her, Kingston. You know I will do it."

He continued, pulling Minta behind him, his mind racing as he tried to think of a way to quell the diabolical woman's ugly whispers that would destroy Minta's reputation.

They reached the edge of the gardens and he turned, his hands finding her waist, pulling her to him. His mouth descended upon hers, knowing there would be no turning back from what he now did. Percy kissed Minta with everything he had, a long, drugging kiss that sealed their fate.

All he had to do was keep kissing her until someone discovered them together.

It didn't take long. Enough couples had been strolling along the path. He heard the rustling of skirts. Then whispers. And he knew he had accomplished his mission.

Raising his lips, he said softly, "We have been seen."

Minta's head whipped around and Percy looked as well, seeing three couples had halted and watched them with interest.

"Oh, Percy. What have you done?" she asked, her expression pained.

"We have been caught kissing in public," he said. "It is obvious what comes next."

"No," she told him. "It is not right. You were done with me. You said I was unsuited to be your marchioness. I will not see you unhappy, forced into a marriage with me."

He gazed at her a long moment, hearing the other couples titter as he did. "Trust me."

Taking Minta's hand, he slipped it into the crook of his arm and escorted her to Lord Westlake, who stood with his wife and two other couples.

"My lord, I would like to make an appointment with you for tomorrow morning."

Lady Westlake's jaw dropped. "What is this about, Minta?" she demanded, her eyes flicking from her niece to him.

Percy turned to the countess. "I will be asking Lord Westlake for his niece's hand in marriage." He pivoted to the earl. "If you would be so good as to have your solicitor present, my lord, I will bring mine as well. That way, we can draw up the marriage contracts."

Lady Westlake gasped. Lord Westlake merely nodded and said, "Ten o'clock, Lord Kingston?"

"I will see you at ten."

Lifting Minta's hand, he pressed a kiss upon her fingers. "Good afternoon, Miss Nicholls."

Percy released her hand and hurried away.

Knowing the die had been cast.

Chapter Twenty-One

Bleary-eyed, Minta entered the breakfast room. She had barely slept. Nothing made sense to her about what Percy had done yesterday. He had deliberately dragged her to an area in which they would be seen and kissed her so they would be discovered and he would be forced to offer for her. And this was after he had told her that they would never suit.

Part of her understood it was his way of preventing that vicious gossip, Lady Vickers, from spreading tales about her. Even though the Season was young, Minta had already heard some of the rumors attributed to the countess. Her daughter, Lady Eve, was a plain young woman and despite the hefty dowry bestowed upon her, Minta believed it might take more than one Season for the girl to land a husband.

She supposed Percy would rather be attached to her than Lady Eve, which is why he had acted so irrationally. Still, he had saved her. Twice. Once, from the disaster of having been attacked by Lord Chatsworth, and then again to keep the gossip at bay and prevent Lady Vickers from shredding Minta's reputation.

Percy had done more than save her. Without knowing it, he had saved Sera, as well. If Minta had been ostracized from Polite Society, she knew the wagging tongues of the *ton* would have done the same to a blameless Seraphina Nicholls. She would make certain her betrothed would receive her gratitude for the both of them.

Uncle West greeted her as she took her seat and then went back to his newspaper. Aunt Phyllis did not meet her eyes. Her pinched mouth told Minta just how much she disapproved of the match that had been made. Or would be made once the marriage contracts had been signed.

They breakfasted in silence and she had a hard time getting anything down. Instead, she pushed the food around on her plate and took sips of tea.

Her aunt excused herself and her uncle waited until his wife left before dismissing the footmen, leaving them alone.

"I wanted to talk with you before Lord Kingston arrives with his solicitor, Minta." He paused. "Marriage is certainly a big step, one not to be taken lightly. I realize yesterday you were put in an impossible situation and that the marquess was responsible for it. Fortunately, he did the gentlemanly thing and offered for you. Still, I would not have you go to a man as his bride if you do not truly wish to do so."

It was sweet of him to believe she had a choice and she knew she would have his unconditional support. Polite Society was not so forgiving, however.

"Do you love him?" Uncle West asked, startling her.

"I am very confused by my feelings," she revealed. "I thought I might. And then Lord Kingston led me to believe that a future between us was impossible."

Minta was not about to go into telling her uncle about Viscount Chatsworth's behavior, much less what Lady Vickers had witnessed.

"I am not saying you have to love the man. I married your aunt without loving her. It is possible to make a good marriage and not be in love with your spouse." He studied her a moment. "What do you feel when he kisses you?"

She answered without thinking. "As if I am on top of the world."

He nodded. "The marquess would be a hard man to turn

down. I believe it will be a good match—if you agree to it."

Minta gazed steadily at her uncle. "I will do my utmost to see that my marriage is a success."

He placed a hand over hers. "You need to start thinking as two, Minta, my dear. There will be two of you in the marriage."

"*Our* marriage," she corrected. "I will do everything I can to make our marriage successful."

Uncle West squeezed her hand, smiling. "That's my girl."

She left the breakfast room, returning to her bedchamber, pacing it like a caged tiger and glancing out the window every few minutes, looking for Percy's arrival. When his coach pulled up, she hurried downstairs, wishing to meet him in the foyer so she could speak to him before he did so with her uncle.

When the butler admitted Percy and the solicitor that accompanied him, their gazes locked on one another. He looked as if he hadn't had a wink of sleep as he came toward her, taking her elbow and pulling her away so they would not be overheard.

They both spoke at the same time, Minta asking if he was certain about the betrothal and Percy asking if she had changed her mind. They paused—and then both laughed, breaking the tension.

"It would be difficult to change my mind because you have yet to ask me anything, Percy," she gently chided. "I would have had to respond affirmatively and then decide differently."

He glanced about and taking her hand, led her into the front parlor. Closing the door, he faced her.

Dropping to one knee, he clasped both her hands in his.

"I know we have not known one another long and that you have had a bevy of suitors, Minta, but would you do me the honor of becoming my marchioness?"

Tears brimmed in her eyes. "Yes," she said softly.

He rose, still serious. Though she longed to ask him why he had been so cruel in pushing her away, now wasn't the time. She wanted to relish this proposal and not ruin the moment between them.

But she wanted that answer before he placed a ring on her finger.

"Very well. I will meet with your uncle now."

He seemed reluctant to release her hands as he stood there, drinking her in. Minta tugged on his hands a bit. Percy knew what she wanted and he brushed his lips softly against hers. Just enough to reassure her.

It did. Love for this man swelled within her. She might not understand all of him yet but they would have years and years to learn about one another. She believed she was one of the few who could break through his shyness and get to know the man behind it.

"Come with me," he said, lacing his fingers through hers, causing her body to heat at the intimate touch.

Percy led her from the parlor back to the foyer, where the Westlake butler and now both solicitors waited.

"We are ready to see Lord Westlake now," he announced.

"If you will follow me, my lord," the butler said.

He moved, bringing her with him, and Minta said, "I don't understand."

"You will."

The butler knocked on the door to her uncle's study and they were admitted.

Immediately, Percy said, "Good morning, Lord Westlake. I have decided that Minta should be a part of these negotiations. They concern her. There is no reason she should be shut out of them, pacing outside as we decide her fate behind closed doors." He turned and smiled at her. "She should be an active participant in what is decided."

Uncle West beamed his approval at the suggestion. "A brilliant idea, Lord Kingston."

He invited them to sit. From the reaction of the two solicitors, Minta understood that what was unfolding was unheard of.

It made her love Percy all the more.

She was very aware of him beside her, mostly because he

continued to hold her hand and did so over the next hour of discussion. His touch brought a sense of peace to her. Whatever had driven him from her seemed to have vanished and along with it, her desire to press the issue.

As the negotiations went on, Percy was adamant about what he wished to be written into the settlements. Shock filled her at all he was awarding to her. He made provisions for her upon his death. Ones for if they had no children and a relative assumed the title. Dowries were established for any daughters they might have, as well as funds set aside for any sons beyond the hoped-for heir. She was given access to her entire dowry.

"All of it?" she asked. It was the first time she had spoken since the discussion began.

"It is yours. You should be able to do with it as you wish."

Minta bit her lip and thought a moment. "Might I simply return it to Uncle West then?" she asked. "If you are not going to use it, I believe he should have it since the large majority of it is his. He could even add it to what he has set aside for Sera."

Percy gazed at her and she saw tears mist his eyes. "You would do that for your twin?"

"I want to make certain that she makes a good match." She paused. "As I have."

He squeezed her fingers and warmth filled her.

"Then Lord Westlake may keep the portion of the dowry he was providing. I will bestow upon you the five thousand pounds instead."

"Percy!" she admonished and then flushed, realizing she had used his Christian name in front of the others.

"No," he said firmly. "I want you to have funds at your disposal now. To do with however you see fit. I should supply these to you."

"But you have already given me a generous monthly allowance for both my wardrobe and to run the household."

He gazed at her steadily. "I would give you the moon, Minta, if that would make you happy."

Now, tears sprang to her eyes. Her throat tightened with emotion and she merely nodded.

"I think everything is settled," Uncle West declared, instructing the solicitors to draw up the contracts and return at the same time tomorrow morning so they could be signed by all parties.

Once the two men left, her uncle said, "The two of you must have things to work out regarding the ceremony. I will leave you to do so."

She wanted to protest that they shouldn't be left alone but remembered how Aunt Phyllis had said that exceptions—up to a point—were made for an engaged couple.

After Uncle West departed, Percy didn't say anything. Neither did Minta, waiting him out. He still continued to hold her hand and she drew strength from that small gesture. She knew the bond between them was fragile and didn't want to sever it.

Finally, he said, "We should decide upon a wedding date."

"Well, it will have to be at least three weeks away. That is how long it will take for the banns to be called," she pointed out.

He frowned. "No, we cannot wait that long. There will already be talk as it is. We should wed as soon as possible. I will purchase a special license when I leave here."

"I have never heard of that," she admitted.

"It is a document I can obtain at Doctors' Commons," he explained. "It will allow us to marry anywhere and at any time within the month. It can be in a church. A home. A garden." He searched her face. "It is up to you, Minta. It is your wedding."

"It is yours, as well."

Her comment flustered him a moment and he blushed. "That is correct. But from what I gather, weddings are mostly about the bride."

She squeezed his hand. "Ours will be about us as a couple."

"Adalyn has offered to hold it at her and Ev's townhouse," he said. "If you don't have a preference, that might be a good venue for the ceremony. It would put a ducal seal of approval on things."

Minta nodded. "I would like that. Something small. Surrounded by friends and family." She touched her fingers to his face. "Are we doing the right thing, Percy?"

"Yes," he said brusquely. "It is the right thing for your reputation."

She gazed longingly into his eyes. "But is it right for you?"

He looked conflicted at her question but said, "We will make the best of things." Releasing her hand, he stood. "I shall head to Doctors' Commons. You need to get with your aunt and Adalyn regarding the ceremony." He swallowed. "I am only sorry your family cannot be here to witness it."

Minta wasn't satisfied with his answer. What had she expected, though? Words of love?

She watched him leave Uncle West's study, wishing she had spoken up and asked him about why he had intentionally hurt her before.

And what had changed his mind.

CHAPTER TWENTY-TWO

MINTA FASTENED THE diamond earring her uncle had presented her to her earlobe, thinking about how much had passed in such a short time since she had received his gift.

Today, she would speak her wedding vows. She would soon become the Marchioness of Kingston. Percy would be her husband.

She longed to unlock the secrets he seemed to carry close and wondered if he would give her a chance to do so. Or would they have a traditional *ton* marriage, where she would present him with an heir and hopefully a spare—then they would go their separate ways. At one time, that is exactly what Minta anticipated for her life.

Now, she longed for it to go in a different direction.

She hoped to grow close with her husband. Be a friend as well as a wife to him. She wanted to ask his advice and hoped that he might take some from her, too.

Most of all, she wanted to love him. Her heart told her she did but she had not uttered those words to him. She feared that if she did he might flee as a frightened doe. She decided she must take her time and not rush things with him. Show him the love she felt for him in her heart. Perhaps once he accepted that, she could say aloud the words she longed to tell him.

A knock sounded at her door and she answered it, finding her aunt standing there.

"This came for you," Aunt Phyllis said stiffly, handing her a box.

"Who is it from?"

"Him."

As her aunt turned away, Minta caught her arm. "Won't you come in, Aunt Phyllis? Together, we can see what Lord Kingston sent to me."

"Very well." Her aunt sniffed dramatically and stepped inside the bedchamber.

Minta followed and opened the velvet box, find a breathtaking diamond necklace within it, along with a note.

I hope this will match your earrings. P

She turned the box so that Aunt Phyllis could see what was inside and smiled at the gasp that came from her aunt.

"Why, this cost a fortune, Minta! As much as your dowry. Perhaps even more."

"I don't care what it cost," she said. "I care about the thoughtful gesture."

"You will be the envy of every woman in the *ton* when you wear this to the next ball. That should quiet the whispers."

Minta frowned. "Aunt Phyllis, I am not the only woman who was caught in a questionable situation. From what I gather, this is a regular occurrence at *ton* events during the Season. I am happy to be marrying Lord Kingston. He is a good man. I wish you would be happy for me."

Her aunt teared up, cradling Minta's cheeks in her hands. "Are you truly happy, my dearest? The marquess seems such an odd duck. You are so full of life and gaiety, while he is somber."

"We balance each other, Aunt. And he is not always so quiet and solemn. When he is with his friends, he can be most animated."

Concern filled Aunt Phyllis' face. "So, you do not regret this union?"

"No. I look forward to it."

Her aunt kissed Minta's cheek. "I am relieved. I would have been so disappointed if you were unhappy. As if I would have let both you and your mother down. She entrusted your care to me."

"You have done a fabulous job. I have enjoyed every minute I have stayed here with you and Uncle West."

Clearing her throat, Aunt Phyllis said, "Well, then, I suppose I should tell you of what is to come."

Puzzled, Minta said, "I know what is to come. Percy explained about the special license. How that is what allows us to wed at the Camdens' townhouse today."

An odd look crossed her aunt's face. "No, I mean after the ceremony."

"Why, there is the wedding breakfast. You know that. You helped me plan it with—"

"No, Minta," Aunt Phyllis said firmly. "I mean what passes in the . . . that is, when you go . . . when everyone leaves and you return to the marquess' townhouse."

She felt her face flame. "Oh."

Her aunt placed her hands on Minta's shoulders. "You will perform certain . . . acts . . . with the marquess. He will kiss you and touch you . . . in various places. *Many* different places. Just be prepared."

Embarrassment flooded her. "I understand."

"Good. I did not know if you had been prepared or not." Aunt Phyllis smiled brightly. "Well, it seems you have been. That is good to know. I will be leaving in our carriage now to go and check on things. Her Grace will send her carriage for you and Westlake."

Aunt Phyllis bustled from the room. Minta wondered why after all these years of marriage that her aunt still referred to Uncle West so formally. She had thought of Percy as Percy ever since she had learned of his Christian name. She knew it was not acceptable to refer to him as thus in company though she had noted the Three Cousins always called their husbands by name when in her presence. Adalyn even called her husband by his nickname, Ev, instead of Everett.

She moved to the dressing table and sat, lifting the sparkling necklace and placing it against her throat. Fastening the clasp, she studied herself in the mirror. It was hard to believe she would be a marchioness, married to a marquess, which ranked just under a duke. She had yearned for a husband who could provide material things for her.

And had discovered along the way that those things weren't as important as hoping she would one day claim Percy's love.

Bertha came in one more time to see if Minta needed anything, exclaiming over the necklace. The maid assured her that everything would be packed and transported during the wedding ceremony and breakfast to the Kingston townhouse so that it would be waiting for her by the time she arrived later today. Her uncle had been kind enough to allow Bertha to leave the household and accompany Minta, saying it would do her good to have a friendly face who would take care of her needs, large and small. She planned to share the maid with Sera once her twin arrived this summer.

"If there's nothing else, Miss Nicholls, then I will see you later today," Bertha promised. Smiling, she added, "Just think. From now on, I will address you as my lady."

"It is a little hard to take in," she admitted to the servant.

"You deserve all the good things in life, Miss Nicholls. And the marquess cuts a fine figure. So handsome, that one."

Minta grinned. "He is rather handsome."

And he will be all mine.

PERCY ALLOWED HUSTON to fuss over him since today was his wedding day. He wanted to look his absolute best for Minta.

Especially because she was marrying damaged goods.

Oh, he knew he was being selfish by taking her as his bride. It was what his heart had wanted all along and what he warred against, believing she deserved far more than he was capable of giving her. Two things had changed his mind, though. The incident with Chatsworth that he'd stumbled across when he had followed her brought a fierce protectiveness out in him. He would slay dragons for Minta Nicholls and lay their severed heads at her feet.

The other involved that witch of a woman, Lady Vickers. The woman had been actively hunting for a title for her drab daughter and had probably skulked through the gardens, hoping to come across a compromising scene and wield her threat of blackmail. Percy couldn't allow the woman to ruin Minta's reputation. He realized not only would the woman's gossip poison Polite Society against Minta—but it would also damage her twin, Sera, before she ever made her debut in London.

That was why he had decided to compromise Minta himself and make certain others saw it. It would give him the excuse to offer marriage to her.

And he could have her all to himself.

Yes, he was greedy. He was taking what should never have been his. Percy promised himself he would do the best he could to be a good husband to her. He doubted they would ever have the closeness the married Second Sons had with their wives but if he could share even a sliver of that with Minta, he would relish every minute of it.

"There, my lord," Huston said, stepping back and studying Percy with a satisfied smile. "You will not disappoint Miss Nicholls with your appearance."

He flushed, thinking how he would disappoint her in so many other ways. But he couldn't give in to that now, else he would not have the courage to go through with the ceremony. The only thing worse than the two of them being seen kissing at the garden party would be not to wed at all. As a man and high-ranking peer, it wouldn't do much to his reputation. But as a woman, Minta would be branded an outcast. Even if it was him breaking off their engagement, Polite Society always blamed the woman. That was another lesson Adalyn had taught him.

He would not do that to Minta. He loved her too much.

Wincing, he told himself he couldn't think of love. He certainly wouldn't be able to tell her he loved her. He was marrying her to protect her good name. They wouldn't be able to have the close relationship of the rare people who fell in love. He still had too many deficiencies that he must hide from her.

It made Percy wonder about what his valet had just said. That Minta would not be disappointed in his appearance. Yes, on the surface, he looked every inch the English lord, entitled, wealthy, and handsome. But Huston—and others in the household—knew there were things wrong with him that were beyond repair.

"Thank you, Huston," he said dismissively, watching the valet exit the room.

Alone now, he went and stood before the full-length mirror. He wore a white muslin shirt with a white, silk cravat. Over it was a black cutaway, tailed jacket, with the buttons left undone to show his dark waistcoat embroidered with silver threads. Tight, dark breeches hugged his form, as did the gleaming Hessians he wore.

Reaching for his top hat, he placed it on his head and left the bedchamber, heading downstairs to his carriage.

Tate and his wife awaited Percy in the foyer. "Everything will be ready for you and the marchioness when you return later today, my lord," the butler told him.

"I have prepared the marchioness' suite," Mrs. Tate added. "The first of her trunks arrived a few minutes ago and her maid is already upstairs unpacking things for her."

"Thank you," he told the couple. "We will see you later."

His nerves frayed on the short carriage ride to Ev's townhouse. As he got out of the carriage, Owen and Louisa's vehicle pulled up behind his and he waited for his friends to disembark.

Owen shook his hand and Louisa kissed Percy's cheek, saying, "You are marrying an exceptional woman. I know you will be very happy together."

He hoped he could make Minta happy. He would do his best to do so.

The trio entered the Camden townhouse and went upstairs to the drawing room. Spence and Tessa were already there with Ev and they spoke for a few minutes. As they did, much to his surprise, Win came strolling through the doors.

His cousin grabbed him in a bear hug and Percy's nerves now turned to elation.

"Why are you here?" he asked. "You have so much to do at Woodbridge."

"Not so much that I couldn't take the time to see my cousin wed. Owen sent word for me to come to town for the ceremony." Win grinned. "It seems this happened rather fast. What convinced you that Miss Nicholls was the one for you?"

Apparently, Owen had neglected to mention that Percy had been caught kissing Minta at a *ton* function and that a hasty wedding had been expected by Polite Society in order for Minta to maintain her good name.

"In all honesty, it isn't merely one thing," Percy told his cousin. "Yes, Minta's beauty is breathtaking but I have found she is as perfect on the inside as the outside. Perhaps even more so."

"She quickly became fast friends with the Three Cousins," Spence pointed out. "That alone speaks well of her. It will be great fun to have Percy wed and his wife so close to the rest of ours."

Win sighed. "Then I suppose I must give over and have Adalyn select a wife for me."

Ev chuckled. "Oh, she is already thick as thieves with Louisa, composing the guest list for the house party in late-August."

"Won't all the good choices for a wife be taken by Season's end?" Win asked.

"There are always hidden jewels among the *ton*," Owen said, slipping an arm about Louisa. "You will find your match, Win."

Then Adalyn and Lady Westlake appeared. Percy knew he needed to make an effort to win Minta's aunt over. He believed Lord Westlake had no problem with the marriage but Percy sensed Lady Westlake had quite a different opinion.

"We have been talking with Cook and making certain everything is ready for the wedding breakfast," Adalyn shared.

"Might I have a word, Lady Westlake?" Percy asked, drawing the countess away from the group.

"What do you wish to say to me, my lord?" she asked, suspicion in her eyes.

"I wanted you to know that I think the world of your niece, my lady. She is kindhearted and sweet and I will do my best to take care of her."

She regarded him a moment and then nodded. "I believe you will." Pausing, she added, "I have always wanted the best for Minta and Sera. Westlake and I were never blessed with children of our own and the twins have always been as surrogate children to us. I did not want Araminta forced into a marriage. From what she told me earlier, she is more than willing to enter a state of matrimony with you."

Lady Westlake placed a hand on his forearm. "Treat her well, Lord Kingston. If not, you will have not only Westlake but my brother-in-law to answer to once he and my sister return from Ontario."

Percy mustered a smile. "I look forward to meeting my in-laws."

They rejoined the others and soon the clergyman arrived. He was a jovial sort and had them take their places, saying he had seen the bride and her escort in the corridor and the ceremony needed to commence.

When the doors opened and Minta entered the drawing room on her uncle's arm, Percy's heart slammed against his ribs.

She was the most beautiful sight he had ever seen.

Her azure dress hugged her curves and brought out the blue in her eyes. Her copper hair shone as much as the diamond necklace he had sent that hung around her neck. Diamonds suited her. Bloody hell, everything suited her. Minta Nicholls would always take his breath away.

No, Minta Perry, the Marchioness of Kingston.

Lord Westlake guided his niece forward but Percy only had eyes for Minta. He held her gaze the entire way and as she reached him, she smiled, a sunny smile so radiant that warmth washed over him.

Percy leaned down and brushed his lips across her cheek, whispering, "You look ravishing."

She looked pleased at his compliment and he stood a bit taller, proud to be marrying her.

The entire ceremony passed in a blur. Percy managed to repeat his vows, his voice shaking slightly, but he noticed Minta's voice did the same. When he slipped the ring on her finger, he looked not at her hand but into her eyes, seeing down into her soul.

He wanted their first kiss to be chaste since others were present but the moment their lips touched, fire leaped through him and he kissed her for longer than was considered appropriate. Aware of a few chuckles, he broke the kiss and looked into her eyes.

"Thank you," he said quietly. "For agreeing to marry me."

Minta smiled. "Thank you for asking."

With that, he slipped an arm about her waist and they turned to speak to their family and friends as the vicar announced, "The Marquess and Marchioness of Kingston!"

CHAPTER TWENTY-THREE

PERCY AND MINTA thanked Ev and Adalyn for hosting their wedding breakfast.

"It is expected that you will miss tonight's musicale," Adalyn said, "but I hope the two of you will come to the Soames' ball tomorrow night. The *ton* will expect it since you are not taking a honeymoon at this point."

He had talked it over with the Second Sons and they agreed with him that since this was Minta's first Season, she should remain in London and enjoy the bulk of it. His friends usually left town after a couple of months, as the weather warmed up and the stench of the city grew more pronounced with the heat. He discussed with his fiancée if they should do the same or stay a bit longer and she had agreed to talk over things when the others left town to see what they might wish to do.

For his part, Percy didn't mind remaining behind when the others left. He thought it would be easier to hide from Minta in town. He could go to White's and wile away the day, keeping out of sight while she made calls on others and took care of household matters. He didn't want to grow too close to her or have her come to expect too much of him and their relationship. The sooner she realized he planned to keep her at arm's length, the better.

It would definitely be more convenient to wait and make a

decision once Sera arrived in England. Minta might want to take her sister on the rounds about town, calling on others and seeing to dressmaker appointments and other womanly endeavors. He assumed the twins would want to spend as much time together as possible and would not be opposed to Sera returning to Kingwood with them instead of remaining with Lord and Lady Westlake.

They made the rounds, speaking to everyone who had attended the wedding. Win walked them outside to their carriage, getting their promise to come visit him at Woodbridge as soon as they returned to the country.

Win kissed Minta's hand and said, "It is good to have you in the family. I cannot wait to meet your sister. Send word when she arrives and I will come to town for a day or two in order to do so."

The new Marchioness of Kingston smiled at Win and Percy felt as if he had been stabbed in the heart. She should have wed someone like his cousin, a charming, outgoing, carefree man.

Instead, she was stuck forever with him.

"Shall we?" he asked gruffly, helping her into the carriage and rapping on the ceiling, feeling the vehicle start up.

When they arrived at his London townhouse, Tate had the entire staffed lined up in the foyer so that Minta could meet everyone. Percy noted how kind she was to each servant, asking his or her name and what they did in the household or stables. She would repeat the name and he knew, in a matter of days, she would be familiar with everyone in the townhouse.

Once Tate dismissed the staff, he and Mrs. Tate remained behind.

The housekeeper said, "We can take a tour of the house tomorrow if you'd like, my lady. For now, I have a light repast for you in Lord Kingston's sitting room upstairs."

"Thank you, Mrs. Tate," Minta said graciously. "I look forward to seeing the house with you tomorrow."

Percy led her upstairs, pointed out her suite of rooms before they moved on to his. They entered the sitting room, which had a comfortable settee and several chairs, along with a small desk and bookshelf.

"My bedchamber is beyond that door," he informed her, knowing he would never have her in his bed. He planned to visit her in hers and then leave her there to return to his own.

And the nightmares.

She nibbled at a few things and he could sense she was as nervous as he was.

"Would you like to call for a bath?" he asked. "It has been a long day and that might relax you."

"Yes, that would be lovely," she told him.

"I will escort you to your suite."

Percy took her down the corridor and they entered a room similar to his.

"This is a parlor for your use alone. Your bedchamber is next to it. Our suites mirror one another, with each of us having a combination of dressing room and closet, followed by a bathing chamber. They are all connected for convenience."

He saw Minta swallow and wondered exactly what she had been told about what would occur between them tonight.

Bertha appeared in the bedchamber door. "I heard your voices," the maid said.

"Lady Kingston would like a bathe, Bertha," he informed the servant. "Then you might want to help her get ready for the night." To his new wife he said, "I will return in two hours' time."

Returning along the corridor, Percy rang for Huston and stripped off his wedding finery, donning his silk banyan before dismissing the valet. He sat in an oversized chair that overlooked the garden below. He let his thoughts drift, not wanting to place too much importance upon tonight.

Or his marriage.

Yet he wanted to please Minta. He would be the only husband she would have if his health remained good. He wanted to give her the world and every material item he could.

Just not himself.

Oh, he would physically give to her. He would strive to make love to her and give her as much pleasure as possible. He just couldn't let her into his heart. That was a lie. She was already entrenched there. But he could keep an invisible curtain between them. Insist that they have a typical *ton* marriage. He didn't sense that her aunt and uncle loved one another but they got on well enough and seemed to like one another. That is what he would hope their marriage could be like. That was the example Minta had.

If you didn't count her parents.

She had told him that the couple was a love match, her mother marrying down the social ladder because of the love she had for Minta's father. Percy had no idea when the pair might return to England. By the time they did, hopefully Minta would have already given birth to a child or two and that would be where she obtained her happiness from.

He looked at the clock and saw it was time to go to his wife.

His wife . . .

A year ago, he had been an officer in His Majesty's army, embarking on what he hoped was the final campaign that would defeat Bonaparte for good. Now, he was a ranking peer of the *ton* and had a wife and estates and so many responsibilities that, even now, they made him dizzy. How his life had changed in such a short amount of time.

This time, Percy cut through all the rooms that connected the marquess' suite to the marchioness' suite. As he passed through her bathing chamber, he stopped a moment and inhaled the vanilla that hung in the air. The scent would forever remind him of Minta. He reached the door to her bedchamber and paused, drawing on all the courage he had, and rapped lightly upon it.

She opened the door and he gawked at her, standing there in the filmy night rail, which was almost transparent. Her copper hair fell past her shoulders, almost to her waist. He restrained from touching it. For now. But he planned to plunge his fingers into the thick mass very soon.

Minta gestured for him to enter and closed the door once he had. Her eyes were bright but her movements jittery, giving away how nervous she was.

Taking her hands, he raised them to his lips and tenderly kissed them. That seemed to relax her a bit. He kept hold of one of her hands and led her to a chair. Seating himself, he pulled her onto his lap.

"Oh!"

"I thought we'd sit for a bit, if you don't mind."

She swallowed. "No. I don't mind."

Percy pulled her to him so that she lay against his chest, his arm about her. She snuggled close and his free hand stroked her unbound hair.

"What have you been told about what happens between a man and a woman?"

She stiffened slightly and he continued smoothing her hair. "That you know what to do and that I should follow your lead."

He chuckled. "That sounds rather like waltzing," he observed.

Minta gazed up at him. "I suppose it is. I trusted you in that. I trust you now, Percy."

He nudged her head back down. "Good. I will do my best in leading you in a new kind of dance."

Taking his time, he explained to her what to expect so that she wouldn't worry needlessly, not knowing what was to come next.

"It does hurt a bit when we come together for the first time because I must breach your maidenhood. After that, however, it should be pleasurable for you."

She nodded and he heard her yawn.

Enjoying the feel of her in his arms, he added with regret, "We can wait if you are overtired, though. I know the last few days have been a whirlwind for you. It might be better if we tried things another time."

He stood and slipped her from his arms into the chair. As he turned away, she called out to him.

"Stay. I want to be with you."

Facing her, a surge of desire rushed through him and he returned to her, pulling her to her feet and into his arms.

"Are you sure?"

Minta nodded.

"Then we start with kissing."

She smiled. "I like it when you kiss me."

Grinning, he said, "Oh, I have only kissed you in a few places. I plan to kiss you everywhere, Minta. And I do mean everywhere."

She frowned slightly and Percy knew she had no idea of where things would head. In a way, he felt proud to be the one to introduce her into the mysteries of love. The things they would do together would be only between them. She would not have shared them with anyone else.

"I plan to touch you everywhere, Wife. I want to find the places you enjoy being touched. I want to bring you exquisite pleasure. I want you to know you are cherished."

And loved.

Even if he never used those words.

He cupped her nape and kissed her at length, feeling his body heat and knowing hers did the same. Their kisses became deeper, longer, more intense. His hands roamed up and down her back as hers slipped inside his banyan, stroking his bare chest.

She broke the kiss. "You have . . . hair. On your chest."

Percy chuckled. "I do."

She pushed the material back and stroked him. "It's so soft. You are so warm. And hard."

He was hard but she wasn't talking about that. She meant the muscled wall of his chest.

"Yes, we are made differently from one another but we will fit together well," he promised.

She continued searching with her fingertips, studying him,

her look intense.

"Would you care to see more?"

"Yes," she whispered.

He captured her hands in his and kissed them, placing them at her sides and rising, setting her on her feet before untying the sash. Then parting the banyan, he shrugged out of it, letting it fall to the floor.

Immediately, Minta's blue eyes widened as they roamed up and down him. Then she smiled. "My gosh, Percy. You are . . . perfect."

Her gaze met his. "Not half as much as you."

She hesitated. "Would you like . . . to see me?" The last word came out as a squeak.

He placed his hands on her shoulders. "Very much so."

"I will need a little help," she confided.

He shrugged. "What are husbands for?"

He helped free her from the transparent night rail and could only stare for a moment.

"Minta, you are so lovely."

She was blushing but said, "I am glad you think so."

"I know so."

He caught her up in his arms, his mouth coming down hard on hers, kissing her until they both were breathless. He broke the kiss and swept her off her feet, carrying her to bed and placing her upon it gently.

Hovering over her, he said, "I will now make good on my promise and kiss you everywhere."

He began at her mouth again, kissing her tenderly, then moving to her brow. Her cheek. Her jaw. His lips slid to her ear as his fingers ran through her long locks. He softly bit into her lobe and she moaned, her hands moving on him restlessly. His tongue teased the shell of her ear and she sighed.

Then he began working his way down. Along her throat, where he nipped and licked, soothing the love bites with his tongue. He traced the curve of her breast with fingers and tongue as she wriggled. He played with her nipples, tweaking them playfully and grazing his thumbnail across them, seeing them pebble in need as she cried out.

He took her breast into his mouth, sucking and laving and feasting upon it as she made delicious noises that egged him on. He took both breasts into his hands as his lips trailed from the valley between her breasts, moving lower and lower, his tongue circling her bellybutton, causing her to laugh.

Returning to her mouth, he gave her drugging kisses as his hands caressed her thighs, moving higher and higher until his fingers reached her core. Parting her, he plunged a finger in and she gasped his name.

"Are you supposed to do this?" she asked.

His lips hovered over hers. "We can do anything we like, my sweet marchioness."

She smiled at his words and he kissed her again, his tongue mimicking his fingers now, causing her to writhe and gasp beneath his touch. He moved his mouth to her throat but continued to stroke her, adding another finger, bringing her to a violent orgasm.

As she cried out his name, satisfaction filled him.

"Ride the wave, Minta. Be daring and brave."

She bucked beneath him, gasping, panting, until finally she stilled.

But he wasn't giving her time to think.

As she lay limp, he rose from the bed and stood, moving her until her legs dangled from the feathered mattress. She looked up at him, her eyes glazed, a slight question in them. Then he rested her heels on the edge of the bed and pushed her thighs wide, plunging his tongue inside her.

"Percy!"

Minta pushed up, balancing herself with her palms. "What on earth are you doing?"

He lifted his head. "Making you mine."

He meant it. He wanted to possess this woman. Make her

want him as much as he wanted her. He wanted to be the only man who touched her like this. Made her come for him.

His hand nudged her back, resting on her belly, keeping her in place as he focused on her core. He used fingers and tongue to make love to her, sensing the orgasm building and feeling it explode within her as she cried out.

Quickly, he positioned his cock at her entrance and pushed inside her just as the throes of pleasure waned. She whimpered and he stopped, already seated to the hilt inside her.

"Get used to me," he urged.

"It did hurt," she said, pouting slightly.

"But never again." He kissed the tip of her nose. "Move a little and see what you think."

She did as he suggested, causing heat to wash over him.

"Mmm. I like that," she told him.

He pulled away slightly and pushed back into her.

"Oh! I like that even more."

Percy kissed her deeply. "Then let me make love to you, Minta."

Her eyes held trust in them and she nodded.

Slowly, he moved within her and, soon, she caught his rhythm. He increased the speed and found she met him, each of them flying high with dizzying passion. Finally, he released his seed deep within her, hoping it would be the beginning of their first child.

He withdrew and rose from the bed, finding cloths and a basin of water Bertha had thoughtfully left out for them. He quickly cleaned himself and then tended to Minta, who lay spent.

"I should be horribly embarrassed," she said, lazily gazing up at him. "But even this feels quite nice."

Percy finished his ministrations and returned to the bed, gathering her in his arms, kissing her hair.

"Sleep," he urged.

She did fall asleep and he held her close, breathing in her scent, his hand stroking the satin of her skin. He didn't know how long he did so, only knowing he could not leave her yet.

Eventually, she awoke and looked up at him, a smile curling about her lips.

"Can we do it again?" she asked, grinning.

"I cannot refuse you anything on your wedding day."

While their first coupling had been full of fire and passion, this one was slower. Gentler. Yet just as fulfilling.

When it ended, Minta fell into a heavy sleep.

This time, Percy left her bed and returned to his.

CHAPTER TWENTY-FOUR

MINTA AWOKE IN the night.

Percy was gone.

She sensed his absence before feeling it. His scent still lingered, both on the pillows and on her skin. Bereft, she curled into a ball, thinking on what had passed between them as she drifted off.

When she opened her eyes again, morning light streamed through the windows of the spacious bedchamber. She glanced about it, still amazed at how large it was, not to mention the huge closet and dressing room and separate bathing chamber.

She had no idea what she should do. Was she to breakfast with him? What was she supposed to do with her day? They had never talked about anything involving their day-to-day lives. In fact, everything from the past few days had occurred so fast, she didn't even know what day it was.

Ringing for Bertha, she allowed the maid to dress her. Usually, they bantered back and forth, but Minta was in no mood to do so today. She had much on her mind.

Last night, in particular.

Making love with Percy had been the stuff dreams were made of. She had felt womanly and treasured as he kissed and caressed her. And yes, he had touched places on her that Minta hadn't dared to touch herself. Being with a husband was mysterious and thrilling and exciting beyond measure.

Tonight, she wanted to explore him as thoroughly as he had explored her.

"Would you like a tray in your room, my lady?" asked Bertha.

"No, I shall go downstairs to breakfast." That is, if she could find where the breakfast room might be.

A footman directed her to it once she reached the foyer. Minta entered, finding her new husband already there, halfway through his meal, the morning paper resting beside his plate.

"Did you sleep well, my lady?" Percy inquired formally.

"Yes, thank you."

They only spoke a few times during the meal, all very stiff and proper. She did not know if it was because several footmen and the butler, Tate, were present or if this is how Percy always was unless with his friends. She still had so many things to learn about this man she would spend entire decades with.

She placed a hand against her belly, wondering if they might have made a baby last night. If they had, her focus should be on the child. Yet Adalyn was with child again and had already given birth to another and she behaved as a woman totally enamored with her husband. So did Louisa and Tessa, who also had children. Frowning, she wondered if Percy would allow them to become close as the Second Sons were with their wives. Surely, he would. At least she hoped so. Right now, they could be strangers having been placed at the same table for all the interaction between them.

Did Percy want a true *ton* marriage?

Minta hadn't thought so, especially not after their lovemaking last night. But she feared things behind closed doors might be different than when they emerged from them. She still was a bit put out that he hadn't stayed the entire night with her. Though her aunt and uncle kept separate bedchambers, her parents never had and from what she gathered, neither did the Three Cousins. Minta had merely assumed it would be the same with her and Percy.

Now she feared they wouldn't be.

He dabbed his beautiful mouth with a napkin and addressed her. "I will be gone all day. I have business to attend to. Have Mrs. Tate show you about the house and see if there is anything you wish to do to it."

"Do?"

He shrugged. "Redecorating. Or buying new furniture. Whatever you wish to do, my lady. You could even ask the Three Cousins to tea if you wish. The day is yours to do as you see fit."

Her heart sank. She had hoped they would spend the day together. After all, they had been wed less than twenty-four hours. Though they weren't embarking upon a formal honeymoon, she had supposed they would spend more time together.

Her husband stood and came to her, brushing a kiss against her temple. "Have a good day."

After he left, she brooded a bit, picking her toast apart as she sipped on her tea. Finally, she rose and asked where Mrs. Tate might be at this time of day. Tate took her to his wife.

It took a good two hours to tour the townhouse because it was so large. She lost count of the number of rooms it contained. The library was impressive, with shelves of books that reached the ceiling. The conservatory was warm and damp and full of beautiful blossoms. The ballroom was large and she wondered if they might host a ball this Season or wait until next year. She would have to ask Adalyn about that.

Returning to her suite, she sank into a plush chair. She didn't wish to invite her friends or aunt to tea. They would be full of questions that she would find too awkward. Besides, her mood was far too glum and would reveal just how unhappy she was.

She thought on that. If she had made the kind of marriage she had thought she would at Season's end, it would have been to a man she liked but did not love. She had expected them to lead fairly separate lives, only coming together for social events and in bed at night in order to make an heir.

Now, she found herself wed to a man she loved who apparently did not love her in return. He had given no indication of having those kinds of feelings and she had kept to the vow she had made to herself and not spoken of her true feelings for him. Minta promised herself to work hard tonight and show Percy just how much she truly cared for him. She would chip away at the armor he encased himself in, protecting himself from the world. She wondered if he was simply shy by nature or if something had occurred in his childhood to make him this way.

And she still questioned why he had tried to cut ties with her, only to kiss her publicly and marry her.

Confusion filled her as she mulled over their relationship for several hours. Then she pushed those thoughts aside and took out pen and parchment and created a list of things she wished to do around the townhouse. She would discuss everything with him first, of course, but she knew he hadn't been in London long and may not have bothered seeing the entire house as she had.

He returned for dinner and they dined together in a small dining room that only seated twelve. Sitting at opposite ends of the table, she practically had to shout at him to be heard. Minta asked about his day but he did not seem receptive to sharing much with her. She worried that she had done something wrong—and thought she saw regret in his eyes. Tears tightened her throat as she was afraid he had already decided the marriage wasn't to his liking.

"I need to dress for the ball," she told him, leaving most of her food on her plate as she returned to her suite.

Bertha prepared her for the evening and Minta made certain she wore one of her prettiest ballgowns, the shade of summer grass. She wore the diamond necklace he had gifted her, as well as the earrings from Uncle West.

He kept her waiting in the foyer and she thought they would be late to the ball. Finally, he appeared, looking far too handsome for his own good. In the carriage, they did not speak. Her dismay turned to anxiety, souring her belly.

They entered the Soames' townhouse and joined the receiving line, which had dwindled to only a few other guests. Lady Soames remarked upon their recent marriage and Minta pasted on a bright smile.

In the ballroom, they joined their friends and Percy asked if she would dance the supper dance with him. She wanted to dance every dance with her husband but knew that was not the done thing among members of the *ton*.

"Yes, of course," she told him.

A footman gave her a programme and though it filled as if she had not wed, she didn't care. She danced, merely going through the motions.

Then Percy arrived and her heart sped up, seeing as how he was the most handsome man present. They waltzed together and it was as before, pure magic as he twirled her about the slippery floor.

When it ended, he escorted her to a table where the Three Cousins already sat. They welcomed her as he excused himself and headed for the buffet.

"How are you?" Tessa asked.

"A little tired," she admitted.

Louisa beamed at her. "We know what from. I hope you find marriage with Percy suits you."

"It will," she guaranteed, not feeling that in the slightest.

Supper passed far too quickly, with plenty of good conversation. Percy remained rather quiet during it and, at one point, she took his hand under the table. From the look on his face, her action startled him—but he did not let go.

Once supper ended, she accompanied her friends to the retiring room and then returned to the ballroom, dancing with several gentlemen she had previously met, including Lord Boxling for the last dance of the night.

"You don't seem your usual sunny self, Lady Kingston," he said.

She smiled ruefully. "The strain and activity of the last few days have caught up to me. I'll admit I am very tired."

He studied her quietly and then the dance began, making further conversation impossible.

When it ended, the viscount returned her to Percy and bowed. "Thank you for partnering with me, my lady."

Percy took her arm and guided her out the ballroom doors and to their carriage. Again, they were silent on the entire ride home. Panic began to fill her and, again, she wondered if she had done something wrong.

They went up the staircase and he paused at the door to her suite.

"It has been a long day and night. You must be very tired." He kissed her cheek. "I will see you tomorrow."

Her husband walked away, leaving Minta to simply stare after him. She entered her rooms at the same time he did, finding Bertha waiting for her. The maid undressed her and quickly left, most likely assuming the master of the house would turn up soon.

Instead, Minta went to her lonely bed and cried herself to sleep.

CHAPTER TWENTY-FIVE

AFTER SEVERAL DAYS of this maddening routine, Minta thought she would be driven to drink. Every day seemed the same. Long. Boring. Lonely. At night, she and Percy would dine together and then attend whatever affair they had been invited to. She was tired of putting on a false smile and lying to her friends about how happy she was. Afterward, they returned—and went to their separate rooms.

Finally, she put her foot down.

"I think we should stay home from tonight's rout, my lord," Minta ventured as dinner came to a close.

"We have indicated we would attend, my lady."

She sniffed. "We are newlyweds and have attended a string of evening activities. Please? Our hosts will understand. I will even write an apology to them tomorrow if you wish me to do so."

Her husband shrugged. "Very well." He frowned. "I should have taken you on a honeymoon but I hated for you to miss your first Season. I am sorry I cut it short for you since you had so many suitors."

She heard something in his voice and realized it was vulnerability. "I did not mind at all, my lord. I am rather proud to have wed you and be on your arm as we attend events."

He gave her a shy smile, which made her heart sing with hope.

"Might we play a bit of backgammon tonight? I saw a game-board in your sitting room."

"If you'd like."

Percy rose and helped her to do the same, escorting her upstairs. Minta's heart beat furiously, happy that she would be spending time with him, away from all others.

They arrived at his suite and he seated her in one of two chairs that were next to a small, square table. It had a chessboard on it, which he took away, returning with the backgammon board.

"I do not know how to play chess. Perhaps you could teach me sometime?" she asked hopefully.

He chuckled. "You'll want Louisa to teach you that game. She is one of the best players around and soundly beats Owen and most other challengers on a regular basis."

"I adore spending time with Louisa. You know that. But I would rather you teach me how to play."

He stiffened. "We will see."

Minta knew what that meant. Every child did. It was a way of parents putting off a child. And now her husband used the same phrase on her. Anger simmered within her, which she tried to tamp down.

She helped Percy assemble the playing pieces and they spent a pleasant half-hour at play. He won the first game and so she demanded a rematch. When she took the second one, he said they must play a rubber match to determine the winner. Minta came close but, in the end, her husband won by the skin of his teeth.

He began sorting the pieces and took the board away. Instead of returning to the table, he said, "You must be tired. I will let you retire for the evening."

That was the last thing she wanted.

Minta reached and took his hand, threading her fingers through his, feeling his warmth and inhaling the spice of his cologne.

"Would you come to my bed?" she asked softly.

Percy gazed at her a long moment, looking as if he were wrestling with himself.

"Yes," he finally said.

Joy filled her. "Thank you."

Instead of leaving and going along the corridor, Minta led him through the maze of connecting rooms until they reached her bedchamber. Bertha sat waiting for her and quickly bounced to her feet.

"You may retire for the evening," she told the maid. "My husband will see to my needs."

"Yes, my lady," Bertha managed to say and quickly fled the room.

"She seemed a bit embarrassed," he quipped.

But Minta didn't want to talk. She wanted to kiss. To touch. To become one with this man. It had been almost a week since they had made love on their wedding night.

She latched on to his coat's lapels and pulled him toward her, their mouths melding and fusing. The passion sparked quickly between them as they lost themselves in the kiss, which continued on and on. Frantic not to lose him, Minta continued kissing him, unknotting his cravat and slipping the buttons of his waistcoat undone. He seemed as eager for her, almost tearing her clothes from her, stripping her of her layers of garments quickly, discarding them to the floor.

Soon, they were both naked and in each other's arms. Minta began kissing his neck, hearing the growl deep in his throat. She moved lower, knowing how much she had enjoyed his hands and mouth on her breasts. She tweaked his nipples and then circled her tongue about one, hearing him suck in a quick breath. She moved her hands, touching him everywhere.

Even his manhood.

It sprang to life in her hands and she stroked it lovingly. It was as strong as steel yet encased in velvet. She ran the pad of her thumb over the tip and found a bead of moisture there, spreading it. He groaned again and caught her wrist.

"Keep doing that and I will spend before I can get inside of you," he growled.

"I don't mind," she told him. "I want to please you as you did me."

Minta walked him to the bed, him backward and her nudging him on until he bumped into the mattress and fell onto it, taking her with him. Laughing, she walked her hands down his body until she grasped his cock in one and stroked it. Then bending, she kissed it.

Percy moaned.

She smiled.

Not knowing exactly what she should do but letting instinct guide her, she opened her mouth, taking him in, gliding her tongue along his long length.

"Yes," he hissed.

She continued experimenting on him, knowing what she did seemed to be working by the noises he made.

Then he grabbed her waist and lifted her, setting her down upon his shaft and lowering her upon it.

It was the most delicious feeling ever.

"Ride me," he commanded hoarsely.

Once again, she hadn't a clue what to do but between his hands on her waist and her moving, he seemed pleased. Minta realized she took him in more deeply in this position—and she could better control her own pleasure. Soon, their sweat-slicked bodies danced together in a timeless fashion and she felt the rising pressure grow and grow until it erupted. She cried out in pleasure and he did the same.

Collapsing atop him, she kept him inside her, her cheek nestled against his wildly beating heart. Gradually, it slowed.

He lifted her from him and nestled her against him, as two spoons might fit together. This was everything she had wanted. To love him. To be with him.

She struggled to stay awake, wanting to revel in the feel of his hard body against hers, his arms about her. It was impossible, though, and her eyelids slowly drooped and darkness engulfed her.

When Minta awoke, the bedclothes were tucked about her.

And she was alone. Again.

Why did he leave her? Why were they as close as two humans could possibly be and then he felt the need to desert her each time?

Determination filled her. Although it was almost light, Minta decided to go to her husband. Louisa had mentioned how wonderful making love was as sunlight poured into the room, bathing Owen's body. Minta wanted to see her husband's beautiful form in the light of day. She wanted to hold on to him as they made love and never let go.

Slipping from the bed, she pulled on her dressing gown and cut through the various rooms until she reached his door, hoping it would be unlocked. She felt a bit guilty entering his rooms uninvited but thought she was his wife. This was now her house as much as it was his. Nothing was going to stop her from climbing into her husband's bed and showing him how much she cared for him.

She turned the knob and pushed open the door, grateful he hadn't thrown the lock in order to keep her out. She moved across the bedchamber toward the bed, hearing how restless Percy was, moving all about the bed, mumbling in his sleep. A small bit of sunlight was starting to make its way inside the room and she gazed down upon her husband, love for this man filling her heart.

Her hand moved to smooth his hair when a bloodcurdling scream erupted.

For a moment, Minta froze, frightened by the suddenness and intensity of the noise. She watched as Percy's eyes flew open, filled with terror, and he wheeled, burying his face in the pillows and yanking the bedclothes over his head. The scream continued, though muffled, as he thrashed about, his body quivering violently. Then he raised up on all fours, a guttural groan sounded from him like some wounded animal.

She moved toward him instinctively and wrapped her arms about his torso, pressing her cheek against his back. He stiffened and grabbed her wrists, jerking them apart, freeing himself from her grasp.

He wheeled and she saw half a dozen emotions flicker across his face, one after the other. Fear seemed to dominant them but she also caught pain, regret, and then anger, which surged to the forefront.

"Get out!" he shouted, scrambling from the bed, coming to stand before her in all his glorious perfection. "I said get out," he reiterated. "Now."

Minta stood her ground, knowing he would not hurt her. "No."

Astonishment flickered across his face and, for a moment, he seemed vulnerable and unsure what he should do or say. Then resolve seemed to fill him and he coldly said, "You are not wanted here."

"I am not leaving, Percy."

Understanding built within her. Somehow, what had just occurred had everything to do with the vast gulf between them.

He stood, dumbfounded, then he said, "I am your husband, Woman. You vowed to obey me."

"I also vowed to love you," she said calmly, taking a step toward him.

He tried to back up but he was already against the bed and had nowhere to go.

Minta took another step forward and captured his hands in hers. "Is this what caused you to push me away, Percy?" she asked softly.

All at once, a sob broke from him. Instinctively, she wrapped her arms tightly about him, holding on as if her life—and his—depended upon the contact. Minta wanted to anchor him to give him strength.

She murmured encouraging words to him as he wept, not knowing if he even heard them. She had a good idea that whatever was wrong had to do with his experiences in the war. Finally, she stopped speaking and merely held him, willing her strength into him.

His sobs finally subsided and she lifted her cheek from his chest, gazing into the eyes of the man she would always love.

"I love you, Percy. Whatever is wrong, we can work on together. I love you. I think I have always loved you. And nothing will ever change that. So you might as well get it through that thick, male skull of yours that I am not going anywhere."

His eyes filled with tears at her words and his head bent, his lips grazing hers briefly. He broke the kiss and shook his head.

"I wanted you from the first moment I saw you, Minta, but I am damaged down to my very soul. The war did something to warp me and I will never be whole again."

He gazed at her with tenderness. "Yes, this is why I tried to force us apart," he revealed. "You deserved so much more than I could give you, and I wanted you to have a chance to have the kind of life you deserved with a husband who could give it to you."

She framed his beautiful face in her hands. "*You* are the one that I want, Percy. *You* are the one that I love. You may believe yourself broken and only half a man but are we not two halves destined to make a whole when together?"

Minta saw the turmoil in his eyes and knew that the storm within him was threatening to break loose, hoping her words had gotten through to him.

"I do love you, Minta, despite my brokenness. I have longed for the kind of love I see in the marriages of the Second Sons and the Three Cousins. I did not think I was worthy of this. Even when I forced your hand to marry me in order to protect your reputation from Lady Vickers' gossip, I did not believe we could have what my friends did. I wanted so much more for you."

Tears cascaded down her cheeks. "All I have ever wanted is

you, Percy. I did not understand even after we wed why you thrust me away. It is ironic because even though my parents are a love match, I thought I would be content with a typical *ton* marriage. One where I would remain polite and distant from my husband, providing him with his heir, even as we went about our separate lives."

Her thumbs stroked his cheeks. "But then I met you, Percy. You changed everything about what I thought I wanted. Now, I want a true marriage with you. One in which we love openly. Deeply. Richly. One in which we share everything, both the good and the bad. I want to be everything to you—wife, lover, friend."

"I want that, too, Minta, my sweet. But I may never be the man for you."

"You are all the man I will ever want, my love."

Minta kissed her husband. Breaking the kiss, she said, "I want to help you through whatever troubles you may have. They may never totally vanish but I believe if you share your burden with me, it will be a start to help dispel at least some of what troubles you." She paused and then added, "I plan to sleep with you every night—all night—whether in this bed or mine. And when the nightmares come, my darling, I want you to take comfort in my arms."

Percy wiped away her falling tears. "Then come to our bed, Minta. Now. Give me the solace that I seek."

They climbed into the large bed and he made slow, sweet love to her. She did her best to kiss and touch him everywhere, wanting to convey her deep love to him, both physically and emotionally.

They both reached a shattering climax together and lay spent in one another's arms, talking for hours. In that time, Percy shared atrocities he had witnessed, ones which chilled her soul. Minta listened, encouraging him to speak when his voice faltered, knowing he had never spoken of these events to anyone else. As the horrors of war unfolded, she prayed that Percy's soul would be restored and that any son of theirs might never have to go to war.

Her husband stroked her hair, a motion which soothed them both. He kissed her and said, "You are a balm to my soul, Minta. I love you with all my heart. I feared how my past bled into the present and would affect my future with you but you are giving me the courage to face my demons."

She caressed his cheek and said, "We will face these demons together—just as we will face anything else that comes our way. Together, we are stronger because the bonds of our love are unbreakable."

Gazing at her in wonder, Percy asked, "How did I ever deserve such a strong, brave, beautiful, caring woman?"

Her reply was to kiss him, showing him how much she truly loved him. Minta knew there would be challenges ahead and the days, weeks, months, and years to come—yet she did not fear these—because they would draw strength from one another.

"I love you, Percival Perry."

"And I love you, my incredibly fierce marchioness. I was wrong to think I could do this alone. I thank the stars in the heavens that fate brought us together because I know now that I can do anything, as long as I have you by my side."

He kissed her, long and deep, and Minta knew his kiss spoke of their love.

And their future.

Together.

EPILOGUE

London—Two months later

PERCY AWOKE, SHIVERING, the last vestiges of the nightmare receding. He felt the warmth of Minta next to him, her lips pressed against his temple, her fingers stroking his arm.

He sighed, knowing he was safe in the arms of the woman he had committed his heart, soul, body, and mind to. Though their marriage had a rocky beginning due to his keeping secrets from his wife, since he had opened up to her, they had grown incredibly close.

Kissing her, he murmured against her lips, "Have I told you how much I love you?"

He felt her smile. "Not today."

Breaking the kiss, he gazed down at his reason for living. "Then I will tell you. And how much you mean to me."

He kissed her deeply, his hands caressing her soft skin. "I love you, Minta, my marchioness. My life."

Percy meant to make love to her slowly but their passion erupted in heat and fire and he wound up taking her swiftly. She clung to him, calling out his name, like a song on her lips.

Afterward, they lay with limbs entangled, breathing heavily.

It was the best feeling in the world.

Minta lay sprawled atop him, toying with the hair on his

chest, smoothing it and then pulling it teasingly.

"Do you wish to go another round?" he asked. "It may take me more than a few minutes to recover from the last."

She kissed his chest and then stacked her hands under her chin, looking up at him with a smile.

"I have something to share with you."

He grinned. "I already know how much you love me."

She sighed. "I do, don't I?"

His wonderful wife gazed at him lovingly and Percy thought he could take on the whole world.

"But there is something else we should talk about." She tugged on his hair again.

"What?"

A secret smile made her lips twitch with amusement. He pushed his fingers into her silky hair and took hold of her head. "Tell me."

"We have something that we need to plan for. Something very important."

"What?" he asked, curious. "It isn't a house party. We will be attending one of those at the end of the Season. Do you wish for us to hold a ball before Season's end?"

"No, the social calendar is filled. We can do so next year. Hopefully, I will have regained my waistline by then."

It took a moment for him to comprehend and then he eagerly said, "You are with child?"

Minta nodded. "Yes. I think about eight weeks. That means the babe will come sometime in January."

Percy kissed her. Pride, joy, and excitement rippled through him.

"We will be parents," he said after the kiss ended. "Good parents."

"Yes. I cannot believe this will be our first. Hopefully, others will follow."

He held her, nestled in his arms, as they began making plans, talking of all the things they wanted to do with their child. What they would teach him or her.

Finally, she stretched lazily. "We should dress. Today might be the day Sera arrives."

They had sent a footman to the docks every day for the past week, checking to see when Minta's twin might arrive.

"When we greet her, it will be with this wonderful news," he said. "I cannot wait to meet Sera." He grinned. "And our babe."

Percy kissed Minta once more, knowing he had absolutely everything he had ever wanted—and believing even more good things would come their way in the years to come.

About the Author

Award-winning and internationally bestselling author Alexa Aston's historical romances use history as a backdrop to place her characters in extraordinary circumstances, where their intense desire for one another grows into the treasured gift of love.

She is the author of Regency and Medieval romance, including: Dukes of Distinction; Soldiers & Soulmates; The St. Clairs; The King's Cousins; and The Knights of Honor.

A native Texan, Alexa lives with her husband in a Dallas suburb, where she eats her fair share of dark chocolate and plots out stories while she walks every morning. She enjoys a good Netflix binge; travel; seafood; and can't get enough of *Survivor* or *The Crown*.

www.ingramcontent.com/pod-product-compliance
Lightning Source LLC
Chambersburg PA
CBHW061241210726

48293CB00003B/861